First published in 2016 by Crooked Cat Books

This paperback edition published in 2019 by Headline Accent
An imprint of HEADLINE PUBLISHING GROUP

1

Cataloguing in Publication Data is available from the British Library

ISBN 978 1 7861 5 7263

Typeset in Times New Roman

Printed and bound in Great Britain by Clays Ltd, Elcograf S.p.A.

HEADLINE PUBLISHING GROUP
An Hachette UK Company
Carmelite House
50 Victoria Embankment
London EC4Y 0DZ

www.headline.co.uk
www.hachette.co.uk

For James and Penny

Chapter One

Bethan Harley closed her eyes and savoured the caffeine buzz from her first swallow of strong, black coffee.

"Hi, Mum." Her seventeen-year-old daughter headed for the fridge. "You look much too chilled for a Tuesday morning." Poppy took out a carton of semi-skimmed. "Nothing to do with Dad, I suppose?"

Bethan felt a pang. Her daughter's tone was too hopeful. "Sorry, lovey, but I haven't spoken to your father since the weekend. I was just thinking about work."

Poppy nodded. "Yeah, right."

Bethan looked down at her coffee. "You know I enjoy my job, Poppy."

"Chill, Mum. You don't need to sound so defensive." Poppy placed her bowl of muesli on the breakfast counter and clambered onto the tall stool next to her mother's.

"I've taken on two or three gems lately. Most importantly, The Sugar House."

"Is that the one you said you could imagine living in?"

"Yep." Bethan knew better than to bang on. "I'm thrilled to have it on our books, but don't worry, I'm not thinking of buying it."

"That's a relief." Poppy bent over her mobile. "I'd hate to be stuck out there in the wilds."

"It's not that bad, lovey. Three Roads is a great place to live if you enjoy walking and – and, well, want to escape the real world."

Poppy smirked and looked down at her phone again.

Bethan knew her daughter mightn't care about peace and quiet, but many people were willing to pay top dollar for it. She also knew Eddie and Suzanne Deacon, vendors of this latest acquisition, had obtained valuations from two rival negotiators but Briggs, Caldwell and Balls was the agency watching the others eat their dust.

The Sugar House was a peach of a property. Some houses spoke to you the moment you stepped over the threshold. This residence welcomed you. Stole your breath. Yet it merged with the landscape like a 1950s Sunday school teacher unbuttoning her cardigan at a village fete. There was nothing flashy about the renovations and the vendors were proud of their house whisperer skills. To Bethan's experienced eye, they'd created a home possessing what many people called the wow factor.

A home. Not a house. Tucked away, up a track, in an almost forgotten community non-existent on any bus timetable, it demanded a buyer seeking a tranquil lifestyle, rather than a pleasant base for commuting to Cardiff.

Poppy looked up. "If Dad does ring, ask him when his next leave is."

"I won't forget." Bethan glanced at the clock. "Hey, time I got moving."

"It'd be cool to do something together when he's home again – the three of us, I mean."

2

Bethan slid off her stool. "Lots of teenagers wouldn't be seen dead with their parents."

"But I'm not like lots of teenagers, Mum. Funnily enough, family's important to me." Poppy switched on Radio 1.

Stung, Bethan went to get ready for work. One of her dark trouser suits plus silk shirt was already hanging outside the wardrobe.

She still brooded as she drove across the Llanbrenin Wells boundary and headed for the car park, ready to work at the former spa town's branch office.

Her usual base was the Knightly branch near her home. The home she and Tim had chosen with such joy. When Poppy had come along, Tim described his daughter's arrival as a shooting star showering them with fairy dust. Bethan smiled at this memory as she undid her seat belt. He'd soon toppled off Cloud Nine and they'd got on with life, dirty nappies, teething and all.

So how ironic was it when, at the point where Bethan and her husband could afford to live somewhere of The Sugar House's calibre, their relationship had wavered? She heaved a sigh. Checked her lipstick in the rear-view mirror. *Perfect Plum*. A shade her daughter had chosen.

When Bethan walked into her office, she filed away her personal life. She needed to check how this quarter's sales were going. One of her assistants had recently handed in her notice and Bethan must decide whether to advertise the job vacancy as part-time. Sales might dwindle now the summer hustle was fading. But what if her feeling about a golden autumn proved correct and the mid Wales property market didn't falter, despite these first damp September days?

With early browsers in mind, she turned the door sign around. Walked through the reception area and sat down at her desk. It would be fabulous if The Sugar House attracted a viewing today. Now that really would convince the vendors they'd chosen the right estate agent.

"Can you smell the rain, Dylan?" Ruth Morgan stepped inside her back door, inspected her fingernails and stooped over the old Belfast sink to scrub away soil.

The sleek black cat sprang onto the kitchen window seat, stared at his mistress and scrabbled his claws into the cushion's faded sunset fabric. Ruth barely had time to dry her hands before the telephone rang. She picked up the call, unsurprised at hearing the voice on the other end.

"It's Suzanne here, Ruth. How are you? I hope you don't think I've been avoiding you, my dear. It's just that Eddie and I have been rather busy of late."

Ruth opened her mouth to speak.

"I know it's a bit early but I – that is *we* – wondered whether you could pop down."

"I'm fine, thanks," said Ruth. "And no, I don't think you've been avoiding me. I've been busy too, you know. I've only come in from the garden because there's rain on the way."

"Ah."

Ruth listened to Suzanne's silence.

4

"But would you be free to come and see us? We do need to talk to you."

"Do you mean now?" Ruth eyed the slice of mountain range visible through her window, its distant peaks veiled in misty cobwebs.

"The sooner the better, to be honest. We have some important news, though I'm afraid it'll come as a shock." She didn't wait for an answer. "See you soon, then?"

"All right but I don't like shocks, Suzanne."

Her friend had cut the call. Ruth replaced the receiver, left wondering if either of the couple had been diagnosed with some life-threatening disease and, if so, which one was the victim. Expectation stirred within her, a mix of euphoria and apprehension. She grabbed her waxed jacket from the wobbly hook behind the door and put it on. Picking up her old black umbrella, she reminded herself, no matter what this was all about; she'd be ready with sympathy and advice.

Outside, the first fingers of dampness found her shiver spot. Eager to find out what was happening at The Sugar House, she quickened her pace. As the road straightened out, she noticed something so astounding, something so unforeseen, she halted, sucking in her breath as if thwacked in the chest by a cricket ball.

Planted upon the grass verge facing the road stood a sale board, displaying the red and white logo of Briggs, Caldwell and Balls, estate agents. Polite people knew them as BCB. Not so polite people referred to them as something far ruder. Ruth knew the bilingual reverse of the sale sign would read *Ar Werth* in tune with procedures. But whichever language it was, how could those words be true?

Rain fell now. Horizontal. Sneaking in from the right. Seeking her out. She put up her umbrella, tilting it sideways, as if shielding herself from something more sinister than a shower and hurried down the unmade road towards the house, thoughts buzzing like furious wasps.

Her hostess must have been watching for her. Before the tip of Ruth's finger touched the bell push, the elegant timber door swung open to reveal a petite figure. Why must Suzanne dress as though she still controlled the reception desk of the English seaside hotel she and Eddie once owned? Ruth eyed the knife-edge crease in her friend's navy gabardine trousers, her fine wool sweater in baby pink. A deeper pink silk scarf aimed to conceal the aging skin of Suzanne's throat. A wide, welcoming smile aimed to conceal guilt over hiding an important decision.

"I see you're using your Mary Poppins brolly! Very wise. Come in, Ruth, do."

Ruth wiped her feet on the coir doormat. How typical of the Deacons to have bought a mat embossed with the image of a big, friendly canine. The item doubtless cost twice as much as the ordinary sort.

"If I'd realised it was turning so nasty out there, I'd have asked Eddie to fetch you. I don't think I'll ever get used to the way the rain creeps across the landscape." Suzanne's expression changed into sucking lemons mode as she propped the dripping umbrella in the porch and shut the door in the weather's face.

She raised herself on tiptoe to kiss Ruth's cheek. Patted her friend's severe dark bob. "You're so lucky the damp doesn't frizz your hair. Come on through, dear. Eddie's been playing with that new coffee machine of his again. He might even have got it right this time."

The woman was twittering like a nervous fledgling. Ruth's lips twisted in a grim smile as she followed Suzanne towards the flight deck of the Starship Enterprise, her private name for the streamlined kitchen Suzanne and Eddie had installed. The aroma of gourmet ground coffee beans drifted into Ruth's nostrils.

"Do sit down, Ruth." Suzanne remained where she was.

Eddie stayed on his side of the central table. "Greetings, my dear. Coffee's on the way."

Suzanne still hovered. "We do appreciate your coming round so quickly."

"I imagine I'm here so you can tell me why you've put your house on the market?"

Ruth dragged out a chair, not missing the surprised glances the couple exchanged. Eddie hunched his shoulders. Shuffled his feet. Glanced at his wife a second time, his expression uneasy.

"How, er, how did you find out? Eddie and I decided to keep our decision secret from people until the sale was publicised."

"Really?" Ruth kept her voice calm, almost nonchalant. "Surely the clue is in the signboard?"

Suzanne groaned. "Oh, no. I didn't realise they'd stuck that up already."

"Someone must have done the job late yesterday afternoon." Eddie turned to tweak his shiny new toy.

"We haven't been beyond the back garden so far today." Suzanne folded her arms, heavy gold charm bracelet rattling. "What a shock that must have been for you. Oh, bless!"

Ruth fumed behind her calm façade. They'd kept their decision secret from people. *People*? Was that how they regarded her, after all those years of supposed familiarity? Did they really think of her as lumped together with other folk fortunate enough to share the same postal code as the golden couple of Three Roads?

"I suppose that means the jungle drums will be banging, eh?" Eddie swivelled round again. "What are they like? We'll explain all to you, dear girl. I've made a batch of that almond shortbread you're fond of."

"Once again he puts me to shame. But we all know he's a far better baker than I am." Suzanne's tinkling laugh didn't quite ring true.

Ruth eyed her friend. That annoyingly immaculate clothing couldn't disguise a neck made crepey by time. The gleaming platinum hair, helped by honey and toffee glimmers, revealed the frequency of trips to Abergavenny. How could anyone justify visiting the hairdresser so often? How could anyone enjoy spending hours roaming shops, scouring an upmarket store for exotic fruits flown from places where desperate workers braved scorching sunshine to pluck them?

Eddie broke the silence. "We'll do our utmost to find nice people to buy the old homestead, my love. Don't you fret now."

Ruth noticed how oblivious he was to the tension sparking between his wife and their visitor. Humming beneath his breath, he placed a porcelain mug of dark, aromatic coffee upon the scrubbed pine table before Ruth, and treated her to a playful wink.

"I must confess to feeling puzzled about your decision to sell. Isn't it a tad hasty?" Ruth focused on making her expression cheerful and inquisitive. Inwardly she fought a powerful urge to punch Eddie in the jaw and terminate his toothy smile.

"To be honest, it's really not." He fumbled with the strings of his navy and white apron but abandoned the struggle. "It's something that's been simmering for a while, actually. There's a combination of factors we've borne in mind."

Ruth pursed her lips as he took a seat opposite. How long had they been plotting without consulting her?

Suzanne leaned against the front rail of the Aga, beringed fingers wrapped round her coffee mug. Her expression remained wary. Ruth, knowing Suzanne shared certain knowledge with her, wondered why she didn't speak up. She must surely be anticipating a cloudburst of questions?

"Now, don't get me wrong, I haven't fallen out of love with this house and nor has my lady wife." Eddie gave a rueful grin. "The truth is, we're not getting any younger.

9

Breathtaking as the landscape is, each time another mid Wales winter rolls round, it's like one more nail being hammered in the coffin."

"Eddie, please!" Suzanne smiled at her friend. "What he means is, we're finding the months of bad weather drag terribly. Winter seems to affect us more than it used to."

"I didn't realise you both felt so strongly." Ruth made a point of looking around her, deliberately retaining a bewildered expression, taking in the spotless Aga radiating warmth, the strategically placed radiators, and triple-glazed windows. "This house must be the most inviting, environmentally viable and easily maintained property for miles around."

"Absolutely," Suzanne abandoned her default position in front of the dark green range and pulled out the chair beside Ruth. Her heady perfume sat down with her, like a companion mismatched by a dating agency. Her nails, enamelled shiny-turquoise, rivalled the Aga's gleaming façade.

"You've hit on one of the many prime selling factors, sweetie," she said.

"Sheesh, my dear wife's starting to sound like an estate agent." Eddie looked expectant, as though awaiting some sign of appreciation from Ruth. She didn't laugh.

"The worst thing is, we're finding it more difficult, driving to see Penny and the children," said Suzanne. "Apart from our creaking joints, eyesight's a big consideration, especially when we have to travel after dark."

"But I could drive—"

Suzanne cut her off. "It's all very tedious, sweetie, but it's true to say we've been pondering a while now." She waited a couple of beats. "And we think it best to make a move while we're still active enough to handle the hassle."

"You can be sure of smooth sailing if I have anything to do with it." Eddie pushed the plate of homemade biscuits closer to Ruth. "Dig in, girl!"

Ruth shook her head. She still waited for Suzanne to refer to the decision the two of them had made a while back. She must have talked to Eddie about it? Ruth longed to fling the china plate and shatter it along with his complacence but instead managed a tight smile.

"We're seriously considering Wiltshire, because of Penny and family, or maybe the Bournemouth area. Do you know that coastline? We both miss the sea, to be honest. Much more than we do the bright lights." She laughed but no one else joined in.

"Maybe you never should have moved to live inland then."

Suzanne's lips tightened, enhancing the fine lines between her nose and mouth.

"Your daughter's still living in Salisbury, isn't she?" Ruth kept her tone calm. Caring.

"Yes, she's very happy there but I know she'd love us to move closer. It's not easy for her, having to be a single mum when Declan's regiment is posted to some outlandish spot."

"With us around, she'd have free childcare for the ankle biters." Eddie guffawed. "Save herself a fortune."

11

"Don't listen to him, sweetie. He's soft as butter with the grandchildren. And with our son working in Dubai and heaven knows where after that, it'd be sensible for us to move closer to Penny."

Ruth watched Suzanne's face pucker. She heaved a sigh.

"But?" Ruth probed.

"We left so many close friends behind in Sussex. It was probably arrogant of me to think we'd ever make enough new ones to replace the old gang."

Ruth unclenched her fists beneath the table and forced herself to raise her mug to her lips. She took a sip of the hot brew. "Delicious coffee, Eddie."

"Good show. Plenty more where that came from." Eddie sat back and folded his arms across his chef's apron bib.

"Don't they say it's never advisable to return to a place, once you've made the break and left? I was just trying to recall how many of your old friends have come to see you since you moved here."

She watched Eddie's expression darken. Sensed his anger.

"And what about the friends you've made in Wales? Do they not count at all?" Ruth's bitterness burned too strongly for her to subdue a disapproving sniff.

Suzanne reached out an arm and hugged her round the shoulders. "Oh, sweetie, of course we'll miss all the lovely folk we know here. Especially you. You must realise that. We'll always keep in touch, have you to stay as soon as we're settled in the new abode."

Ruth's head swam. The stupid woman would be offering her a lollipop next. Maybe her friend needed a swift jog of the memory. "So, Suzanne." Ruth sat back in her chair and folded her arms, a mirror image of Eddie across the table. "Whatever happened to that plan we hatched?"

Chapter Two

"I'm sorry?"

"Come on, Suzanne. Surely you recall that afternoon we spent drinking the teapot dry in front of my log burner? It was only a couple of winters ago, after all."

Suzanne froze. She drew her arm back from Ruth's shoulders.

"All right, then how about the time we sat here in your kitchen talking practicalities, while Eddie was on the golf course? If only Sparkles could speak!" Ruth waved a hand at the golden Labrador snuggled in her basket beside the Aga.

"What's all this about a plan?" Eddie raised his eyebrows, dark and shrimp-like, in harsh contrast to his snowy cap of hair. He shot a puzzled look at his wife.

Suzanne shrank down in her chair, reminding Ruth of a floppy rag doll. She seemed to find gazing at the coffee machine easier than looking at either her husband or her friend. Ruth experienced a frisson of satisfaction. This was a woman who shied away from confrontation.

"I'm talking about the agreement we reached regarding the future. A way of life to suit all three of us." Ruth met Eddie's gaze. Beneath the table she tapped her left foot in a faint, percussive beat of disapproval.

Eddie's jaw slackened. "But you must be fifteen years younger than the two of us. You don't need to think about growing old yet, surely?" He flinched as Ruth banged her mug down on the table. "You know plenty of folk around these parts. Surely you understand it's that support system Suzanne and I are missing? The kind of network that takes years to build."

"Isn't he aware of what we decided?" Ignoring Eddie, Ruth placed her hand on Suzanne's arm. "Why don't you tell your husband what you said to me? What you insisted should happen a few years down the line. I can't believe you've forgotten. How could you possibly ignore something so important?"

Suzanne's mauve-tinted eyelids quivered like butterfly wings. "But we were conjecturing, surely? Wasn't it the kind of thing people muse about after a couple of glasses of vino? Throwing ideas around?"

She retreated a little further, the movement hardly discernible, but feeling Suzanne cringe from her touch, Ruth knew a physical blow couldn't have hurt more. She cleared her throat, stroking the fingers of her left hand down it in an instinctive gesture.

"So, my agreement to move in one day as your housekeeper and companion means nothing? I love this house. You know I do. I'd happily keep it in order."

She looked from one to the other. Neither responded. Neither met her gaze.

"You wouldn't need to worry about night driving becoming difficult because I'd do it! Do all the driving, shopping, most of the gardening. You know how much energy I have. More than enough for all three of us."

15

Eddie spoke first. "You're an angel, for sure you are. We've truly valued your friendship all the time we've lived here. Right from the start."

Ruth expected him to utter a comforting *there, there*, as though she'd fallen over in the playground and bloodied her knee.

"Naturally, I realised the plan wouldn't come to fruition for at least five years," she said. "But I've always assumed we had an understanding. Suzanne, are you honestly telling me we didn't?"

Eddie rapped on the tabletop like a chairman calling a rowdy committee meeting to order. He looked Ruth straight in the eye. "I know nothing about your so-called plan. It's the first I've heard of it but what I do know is it's time for Suzanne and me to face facts. The logical step is for us to downsize. After all, we do have family to consider."

Ruth frowned. Family. Did her friendship and support count for nothing at all?

"He's right, sweetie. I remember that kind offer of yours, but you must know, it surely wouldn't have worked?" Suzanne's laugh tinkled again. "You know what they say about two women in one kitchen?" She clawed at her coffee mug.

"My. Kind. Offer?"

Sparkles whined. Ruth stared through the window at the scudding clouds. The rain had at last stopped scouring the landscape. She heard Eddie crunch another piece of homemade shortbread. When she looked at him, she watched his tongue flicker like a lizard's as he licked a

16

crumb from his upper lip. Suzanne sought something fascinating among the fronds of the parlour palm in its plump terra cotta pot. A plant that fitted. Well-nourished. Like the couple currently shutting her out.

Ruth finished her coffee. She'd pushed enough. It was time for damage limitation. She knew what must come next. Knew the importance of regaining their confidence.

"Phew. I was on shaky ground for a while there. Completely taken by surprise." She turned to Suzanne. "You're absolutely right. Frankly, your decision comes as something of a relief. I didn't like to mention it before, but I was a little concerned over surrendering my independence."

"I should say so!" Eddie nodded. Smiled his approval.

"Far better you two downsize," said Ruth. "You need to find somewhere more convenient to your daughter's home. I have plenty of friends around these parts, as you quite correctly point out. Forgive me for being so thoughtless."

She patted Suzanne's hand. Watched the woman's petite frame relax.

Eddie sat back in his chair. "You had us going there, girl, for a while."

"Of course, we won't be off yet," said his wife. "It could take ages to find a buyer."

"Absolutely," said Eddie. "Though our estate agent's very confident."

"Obviously not everyone enjoys living somewhere as isolated as this village," said Suzanne. "It's a place that seems idyllic when you first discover it. Ten years down the

17

line, a house in the middle of nowhere can turn into a millstone."

"Indeed. Some might say why not wait until the daffodils are in bloom again, but if your move is meant to be, the right buyer will surely come along." Ruth smiled at the slumbering dog, silently complimenting herself upon converting her fury into reassurance. "So, I imagine you'll be looking for help sorting out and packing up? It's the perfect opportunity to throw out unwanted items."

Ruth sat hunched over her laptop, eyes widening in disbelief as she digested the obscene amount the agency website specified. She knew it must be realistic and that buying into the rural lifestyle was an important factor. Unless you craved roses round the door, timber beams and lime washed walls, the couple's house ticked all the boxes. They'd transformed the interior and turned it into a sought-after residence, according to Eddie, who would watch a TV programme featuring a multi-million-pound rabbit hutch if his wife permitted.

A click on the slide show allowed Ruth to move forward until she reached the beginning again. She went on watching the rooms materializing on the monitor like Tarot cards flipping over, each image revealing its own message. Creamy neutral walls bounced back light in all the right places. Eddie's north-facing study defied convention with its bitter chocolate paintwork and peacock blue wallpaper.

Ruth had slept in the house on several occasions, the first being when the couple booked a cruising holiday a year or so after they moved in. When she offered to house and dog sit, Suzanne jumped at the suggestion, admitting she dreaded leaving their beloved Labrador in untried kennels. By contrast, Eddie displayed a certain reticence. After Ruth took up temporary residence and began her observational tour of the property, it didn't surprise her to discover he'd locked his study, as well as the master bedroom.

She couldn't help feeling proprietorial. They'd been kind to her in many ways but their current level of insouciance probed a very raw nerve. Somehow, they must be made to pay. This was her future they were tossing out like a bundle of rags.

Ruth logged out of the BCB website and called up a national one, typing in her criteria to search on properties in the Bournemouth area. The ludicrous number of upmarket houses and bungalows for sale, in and around the seaside town, horrified her. Where on earth were all these people hoping to move? She called up Brighton properties, only to be dazzled by scores of secluded gardens and stunning sea views wrapped around houses whose sale prices read like telephone numbers.

So, Suzanne and Eddie would weigh up the benefits of proximity to their squeaky-clean daughter and over-indulged grandchildren against moving back amongst silver surfers who existed perfectly well without their erstwhile friends. Ruth felt sure her gibe had hit its target. To her certain knowledge there'd been no visitors to Three Roads from this magic circle of cronies for whom Suzanne professed to pine.

Ruth sat staring at other people's properties, wondering what to do. Wondering how best to make Eddie and Suzanne recognise the massive mistake they were making. She had much more need of them than did their daughter who already had child-minding facilities plus friends of her own age. What would happen when the military family was next uprooted and replanted miles away? Would Granddad and Grandma put their new house on the market and up sticks yet again? Had they even considered this possibility?

It was no use ranting and raving in an undignified manner. This could only result in the Deacons closing ranks, thereby preventing her from following their progress. They might remain in their current home for months yet, as Suzanne had intimated. Even if they found a purchaser, everyone knew how precarious the situation became if that buyer formed a link in a chain of people, nail-biting and counting the days until contracts were exchanged. Such uncertainty didn't bode well for Suzanne who detested inconvenience and insecurity. It could be a long autumn, leading to a winter of discontent.

A fledgling idea trembled in the dark recesses of Ruth's imagination. She sucked in her breath. Up went her hand to stroke her throat. It was an audacious notion. Some might say vicious. But surely it wouldn't hurt to put this flash of inspiration into practice? Discover whether she could make it work? It was a while since she'd needed to delve into her spare bedroom wardrobe, unless checking for moths or signs of damp. Why wait to find out? Heart bumping a little faster, she closed down her laptop and prepared to go to town.

Chapter Three

Ruth cherry-picked items and folded them into a rucksack. She left her cottage via the back door, checked the petrol gauge and set off, opting not to use the main road but following a woodland track through giant conifers, a route hardly ever used by villagers. Most people didn't relish being confronted by gigantic forestry vehicles. Ruth drove purely for convenience, not to satisfy any desire for speed, and she negotiated the winding trail in low gear until joining the main road leading to Llanbrenin Wells, a town once much favoured by Victorian ladies and gentlemen seeking to take the waters in congenial company.

As to what exactly she hoped to achieve once she transformed her appearance didn't particularly bother her. She might drop into the office of the freebie newspaper and make it known a certain house with a dubious history, in the village of Three Roads, was fresh on the market. Or she could visit the estate agency, pretending to be seeking a suitable home for her and the occasional visiting grown up children she didn't possess.

Of course, she daren't make an appointment to view The Sugar House and turn up in disguise, but she could drip feed snippets of information in the hope that an employee might wonder if such unsavoury details would deter prospective purchasers.

Thankfully the rain had stopped. She left her vehicle tucked behind a people carrier at the car park's far end, and headed for the public conveniences. Once inside a cubicle, Ruth shucked off trainers, sweatshirt and jeans and pulled on a lime green cotton top over a plunging padded bra. Casual cream linen trousers and long line oatmeal-colour cardigan came next. Bronze leather loafers completed the disguise, with the vital addition of an auburn brown curly wig, hiding her geometric coal-black bob.

At home she'd applied a layer of bronze nail varnish. Now she added a spray of perfume. Neither the metallic polish nor the sweet spicy fragrance would ever be worn by Ruth Morgan. She hadn't used scent or fussed over manicures since her residential job near Edinburgh, years before, when she worked as a housekeeper companion to an elderly couple, both retired doctors. They'd known her as Julia Hayes, a blonde softly spoken widow from Bristol. How shrewd she'd been to have adopted a new persona when applying for that position. No one in mid Wales could possibly suspect her of being anything but an upstanding citizen.

Ruth, with her everyday garments stuffed into the rucksack, waited to ensure no one who might have noticed her enter the ladies' toilets still lingered inside. When all she could hear was the drip-drip of a tap, she slipped out to leave the rucksack in her car and collect a hessian shopping bag which she thought suited her style.

She walked up the ramp to the main street in a different manner from her usual purposeful stride, hoping she portrayed a woman who suited casual clothing yet still looked stylish. Ruth had morphed into a person her imagination named Delyth.

She sauntered along the high street, gazing up at architectural triumphs and minor atrocities before pausing to examine the offerings of two different estate agents. Each time, Ruth took out a pretty floral notebook and jotted down a reference or two, taking care to appear engrossed in her task, and avoiding eye contact with passers by.

When she arrived at the offices of Briggs, Caldwell and Balls, she noticed a burly man checking out the window. He took no notice of her but concentrated upon two sets of particulars highlighted in the display. After a woman endowed with ample curves arrived, hooked her arm through his and snuggled into him, Ruth still kept herself to herself while she pretended to scrutinize a different set of details.

"I bought toothpaste," said the woman. "Silly me, forgetting to pack it! Can you see anything interesting, babes?"

"I quite like the look of one or two." Babes pointed to The Sugar House's photograph. "This here's property of the week. I reckon it's either just on the market or it's sat around so long, the owners are wetting themselves."

Ruth sidled closer. Cleared her throat. "Hello. I'm sorry to intrude but I couldn't help overhearing. I know this area well so if you have any questions and don't want answers wrapped in estate agency jargon, just say the word."

The couple chuckled. Visibly relaxed.

"Oh, that's so kind," said the woman. "My hubby has taken a fancy to that one." She poked a plump finger towards The Sugar House details. "I notice it's approached down a track. We're looking for somewhere nice and quiet but just how far from civilisation is this Three Roads place before we go in and get cross-examined?"

"Aw," said Ruth. "It's hard going, isn't it? Anything to do with property is always stressful."

"Are you house hunting, too?" The husband looked her up and down.

"Possibly," said Ruth, pulling a wry face. "I'm contemplating down-sizing now the children have left home." Her fictitious offspring would be Marc and Ffion if this pair bothered to ask. Delyth would choose such names. No husband around, and of course she still missed poor Geraint.

"But you asked about Three Roads. The name's deceptive in that it makes the place appear more impressive than it is. There's a narrow track leading from the village through forestry commission land, and there's the main road leading to Knightly."

"I don't think we came through there," said the husband.

"It's a small town between here and the village. The other road climbs up to the ranges and meanders down to the A40. You get lots of Outward-Bound activities happening in those parts, camping and orienteering – you know the kind of thing."

The husband nodded. "Action Man stuff."

"At times, the military have sole use of the ranges. That land is strictly monitored. They've even built themselves a mock village, for training purposes."

"But the soldiers aren't a nuisance?"

"I've never heard anyone complain. There are certain days when you can't use the road across MOD land, but everyone says you become accustomed to the sound of gunfire. Eventually." She saw the husband's eyes narrow.

"I'm Valerie, by the way," said the woman. "And this is Brad."

"It's lovely to meet you both. My name's Delyth."

"I knew you had to be Welsh as soon as I heard that pretty accent. Do you speak the language? We've not heard anything but English so far."

"The lady probably hasn't got time to stand nattering, Val."

"I'm truly in no hurry," said Ruth. "I can give you more of a run down on Three Roads if you wish." She smiled at Valerie. "In English, of course."

The woman tilted her head back and laughed, gaudy earrings glittering against a cloud of improbable magenta hair. "If you're sure you can spare the time, I'm gasping for a cuppa. What do you think, Bradders?"

He shrugged. "Fine by me. As long as you're sure we're not putting you out, Mrs...? Sorry, I didn't catch your name." His Adam's apple wobbled. Ruth thought how unattractive he was.

"My name's Delyth and you're not putting me out at all." Ruth cleared her throat again, stroking the fingers of

26

her left hand down it in one slow movement. Displaying a slender gold wedding band to establish her status.

The agency door flew open to reveal a tall, slender woman, smartly dressed in charcoal-grey trouser suit and heels. She wore her beige-blonde hair knotted high upon her head; the severe style softened by stray tendrils. Ruth stepped back, turning away as though switching her attention elsewhere. The woman gave the group a friendly greeting before hurrying off towards the car park.

"There's a lovely teashop just round the corner," said Ruth, when she was certain no one but the two house hunters could overhear.

Leading Delyth's new friends to the watering hole, Ruth fielded their irritating inquiries.

"So, do you work, Delyth?"

"Sometimes. I'm registered with an agency that provides temporary household staff, carer companions and that kind of thing."

"I can imagine you being brilliant at looking after people." Valerie tucked her arm into Ruth's. Somehow Delyth managed not to cringe.

"I've always tried to do my best," she said. "Now, I hope you'll like this place." She led the way around the corner and pushed open the first door along, holding it so the couple could walk inside.

"Oh, this is gorgeous. I'm a sucker for old beams and tapestry." Valerie looked around and settled her ample behind on a cushioned wicker chair. "Sit here beside me, Delyth. Teas all round?"

"Yes please. Earl Grey with no milk for me."

"Okay, hun. And Welsh cakes. We must order a plate of Welsh cakes." Valerie looked expectantly at their companion. "Unless you're fed up with them?"

"No indeed. I rarely make them now I'm on my own. Except when the children turn up, though that's not often these days." She gave a small, wry smile of resignation.

Valerie blinked and patted Ruth's hand. "I know, sweetheart. And I have to say I think you're so brave over your situation." She sat up straight. "Takes some getting used to – going it alone, I mean. With Brad and me, it's a case of second time around and making a fresh start."

"How wonderful for you both. So, do you mind if I'm totally frank with you? About The Sugar House, I mean."

"I think we'd prefer it, wouldn't we, Val?" Brad glanced up at the approaching waitress and placed their order.

Ruth waited until the girl hurried away although she'd never set eyes on her before. "In that case, I'd steer well clear of Three Roads if I were you." Privately she gloated at the ease in which her Welsh accent engaged and enriched when required. "The village has a certain charm but once you buy into it, should you change your mind and decide to move out, it's not that easy."

"Because of its location?" Brad shrugged. "I don't think that'd worry us. We're cheesed off with noise pollution and filthy pavements. Scum dossing in doorways."

"I can imagine," said Ruth. "I think, what I'm trying to say is, the village has a character all its own." She looked from one to the other to check she held their full attention. "I'm sorry but I find it rather hard to explain. There are some very pleasant people living there, but by its very remoteness, Three Roads tends to attract what you might call loners."

"I see." Brad shrugged his shoulders. "Sounds good to me. Can't abide nosy neighbours. So, are there any facilities at all? John Lewis? M & S?" Smirking, he righted his turned-over teacup and ripped open a sachet of white sugar.

Ruth chuckled. "Hmm, let me think. I haven't been over there for a while. Used to have friends in the village but they moved back to England. I got to know them through the arts centre here but they never really fitted village life." Ruth looked at Brad. "The expectation is sometimes overridden by the reality, I suppose."

"We're certainly not looking for somewhere like the area we live in at the moment."

"Understatement of the year, Bradders!" Valerie nudged Ruth's arm. "Poundland on Thames, we call it."

"I do know Three Roads has a derelict church but I'm afraid there's no local shop. There used to be a youth club." She hesitated, "I don't know whether that's still going."

"No problem. Neither of us has children living with us," said Valerie.

Ruth noted she expressed no disappointment over the derelict church. "The mobile library used to call every fortnight but these days, what with cuts, who knows?

Someone did once try to start a community shop but I heard it fell through in the end."

"Can you get a newspaper delivered?"

"I doubt it."

"Ooh, I'd be lost without my puzzles and celebrity gossip." Valerie grinned at her husband.

He rolled his eyes. "Come on! You could buy a bumper book of crosswords and we'd do a regular big shop. It's a matter of being organised, ladies. Keeping a list of essentials so you don't run out of toothpaste." He pulled a face at his wife. "And we're not ones for pubs and bowls clubs and the like."

"In that case, I'm sure you'd be fine." Ruth bent her head to check something in her handbag while the waitress placed tea paraphernalia on the table.

Brad thanked the girl. As he turned his attention to Ruth again, she dabbed her nose with a lace-edged handkerchief until the waitress was safely across the room.

"The good thing is, it's only fifteen minutes in the car to the nearest small town. That's Knightly, as I said. It has two medium-sized supermarkets and a small Friday market and an arts centre with a cinema."

"I'm inclined to ask for a viewing of The Sugar House as long as Broadband isn't a problem." Brad, perhaps remembering his manners, offered the sugar-scattered Welsh cakes to Ruth.

"Delyth, what exactly did you mean about Three Roads having – what was it that was hard to explain?" Valerie poured tea for everyone.

"I don't think for one minute it'll put you two off but it's only fair to mention it. There's a desolate feel about the place. Possibly – and you may laugh at me – possibly because a murder once took place there. It happened many years ago."

"I doubt there's anywhere in the world without bloodthirsty goings on in its murky past. Our part of London's not as safe as it used to be, believe me."

Valerie nodded.

"It's not about security." Ruth leaned forward and paused for effect. "It's more like something inexplicable lingering in the atmosphere."

"I'm not with you," said Brad, picking up his cup.

Ruth watched as he slurped his tea. Valerie put down her half-eaten Welsh cake and gazed at her. Waiting.

"It's just that the alleged murderer was not the most popular man around, even before the crime occurred. I should tell you, despite suspicion, there was no evidence to condemn him. The man didn't hang. He didn't go to jail. And he never, ever, went to church, which in those times was regarded as something of a sin."

"When you say many years ago, how far back are we talking?" Brad mumbled through a mouthful of cake.

"1930s or thereabouts."

"Goodness!" Valerie looked surprised.

Brad turned to his wife. "Bear in mind how attitudes in London and other big cities would've differed from those in isolated areas, Val."

31

"Exactly," said Ruth. "So, years later when this man died and it came to burying him, the villagers were up in arms at the thought of a murderer interred in their churchyard."

"Understandable, I'd say, but not much they could do about it, I guess," said Brad.

Ruth frowned. "Better brace yourselves, because apparently they took matters into their own hands. A couple of days after the burial took place, a group of them entered the churchyard in the small hours and dug up the coffin."

"Oh, my gawd," squealed Valerie. "That's too gruesome for words!"

"Remember it happened a very long time ago." Ruth patted Valerie's arm. "So long ago, the villagers used a pony and cart to take the coffin away from the churchyard and bury it on the nearest waste ground."

"Come to think of it, I have a certain amount of sympathy for those guys." Brad eyed the cake dish. "They probably didn't like the idea of their forebears lying next to a murder suspect's grave. I wonder if he really was the killer."

To Ruth's satisfaction, Valerie shuddered. "I don't want to know! But where was this waste ground, Delyth? Outside of Three Roads I hope?"

Ruth paused. "If you fall in love with the village, I very much doubt you'll give that old tale a second thought. But the story goes, The Sugar House was built upon the very parcel of land where the murderer was laid to rest."

"Are you serious?" Brad stopped lounging and sat up straight.

"I heard it from a very reliable source." Ruth waited a beat. "I'm not saying the area is haunted. Even if there have been reports of shadowy figures that disappear when you look at them."

She saw Brad's Adam's apple wobble as he swallowed hard.

"But it's what I meant when I referred to sensing something in the atmosphere." She paused again. "Something you can almost touch."

Chapter Four

As soon as she'd resumed her own persona, Ruth drove home, elated after the satisfying hour spent in Delyth's fantasy world. It had been pure serendipity to find the London couple just asking to be duped. That airhead, Valerie, made her views clear as an icicle to her tedious spouse, by stating she'd gone right off the idea of viewing a house whose every creaking stair tread or rattling window catch would give her the heebie jeebies as she described it.

Ruth told herself she mustn't attempt the same trick again. Not for at least a couple of weeks anyway. After she locked the back door of her cottage, she spent time sitting quietly with Dylan curled upon her lap, as the cat craved company for once. She also jotted down the date of her visit to Llanbrenin Wells, precise details of the outfit she'd worn, and the time of arrival at the teashop selected from five possible cafés for her cosy chat with the house hunters. The couple wouldn't fit into Three Roads anyway. Ruth felt certain of that. She'd done Brad and Valerie a favour, if they only knew it.

Next day, she planned to call upon the Deacons, taking with her a couple of pots of homemade produce. Eddie had a penchant for her beetroot chutney and Suzanne liked Ruth's piccalilli, even though her own cooking skills, with the exception of baking, were imaginative. Ruth had enjoyed many a scrumptious kitchen supper or Sunday lunch with the couple and didn't intend relinquishing this perk without a struggle.

In return she raided the jars jewelling her pantry shelves where blackberry jelly and gooseberry jam rubbed shoulders with tangy chutney and pickled shallots. On the run up to the festive season, she always produced sugar-free mincemeat and luscious lemon curd. This friendly bartering system worked perfectly, and Ruth didn't want it ruined. If the Deacons had any viewings lined up, she needed to discover details in order to plan the next stage of her operation.

Dylan jumped from her lap to answer a sudden call of the wild, leaving his mistress to wander over to the wine rack given to her by the couple a few years before. Eddie used a merchant's delivery service, choosing far superior vintages to the ubiquitous supermarket choices Ruth's budget allowed. This was another luxury she'd miss horribly in the event of The Sugar House changing hands.

Her lips twitched when she imagined Brad and Valerie going into the BCB office and giving their preferred criteria for a property. Probably the sales negotiator would pull up the Deacons' house, proudly presenting it like an old-time magician pulling a rabbit from a top hat. What would the employee think when Valerie blurted out the macabre tale besmirching the agency's property of the week? The Londoners would have accomplished a task Ruth daren't risk, even though it was tempting to contemplate wandering in, wearing her Delyth disguise, on some other occasion. She'd need to give that thought.

She selected a bottle of claret. Eddie had chosen a couple of mixed boxes last time he placed an order. Suzanne was drinking less, he said, before teasing Ruth about keeping him company on the rocky road to ruin. She'd always had a sneaking feeling he might be attracted to her.

Suzanne reminded Ruth of one of those cool, Alfred Hitchcock blondes, if a tad faded around the edges. It would never surprise her to discover Miss Goody Two Shoes had dismissed the habit of conjugal relations along with the curse. But Suzanne never went away, leaving Eddie to his own devices, though he had on occasions travelled on golfing jollies. Maybe it was something to address, though Ruth had no particular wish to seduce Eddie. Unless, of course, it proved advantageous.

No screw tops from this merchant. Ruth popped the cork, still pondering the next stage in her plan. Slowly she poured the velvety rich claret into a cut-glass goblet – also a gift from the Deacons – and walked across to her armchair. She'd bought a succulent fillet steak for her dinner, the perfect partner for garden vegetables straight from her freezer. She deserved a little treat.

"We really should invite Ruth round for dinner on the weekend." Suzanne peered at her husband over a pair of rainbow-framed designer spectacles.

"Feeling guilty, my darling? I mean over that garbage she spouted. Moving in with us one day, my arse!" Eddie looked up from his book and shifted against the pillows.

"When she was here this morning, I thought she looked decidedly green round the gills."

"Tell me about it! That was a very awkward moment."

"Bloody hellfire, what possessed you, Suze? You must've been well on the sauce to agree to something as daft as that."

"I'd more or less forgotten about it. Can't help thinking she's built it up in her mind."

"Hmm. I'm not dismissing all she's done for us since we moved here. Having her to house sit and look after Sparkles when we go away has been a godsend. But as for taking her in to live with us – over my dead body."

"Eddie, you know I hate that expression." Suzanne shivered and snuggled further into her lacy bed jacket. "But if we ever did need someone – you know, one day a long time from now – you'd have to consider her."

"If that day should arrive, we won't be living here. We need to look forward not back, girl."

"You must admit she's trustworthy. She's never let us down."

"That may be but we've done plenty for Ruth in return. Wined and dined the woman, taken her with us to the arts centre, dozens and dozens of times. Treated her to the ballet when that fantastic Russian company performed at the Millennium Theatre."

"I suppose I must confess to having a mad moment. I seem to recall you were away on that golfing weekend in Portugal at the time. Ruth and I were sharing a bottle of wine and I jokingly said something about you and me becoming decrepit long before she would. When I said maybe we'd be asking her to move in and look after us, she obviously took me seriously. I'm so sorry, Eddie."

"Just forget it. I think we made our intention to move on one hundred per cent crystal clear."

"Will you miss her?"

He shrugged. "She's not bad company. She's helped us out now and then when the laptop's played up." He paused. "She makes a mean chutney."

"Damned with faint praise. Poor Ruth. She's an excellent house sitter. Sparkles always seems happy to be left in her care."

"No question about that. And the woman's a genius in the garden. Lord knows I've tried with potatoes and so on, but no way would I risk frittering away good money, trying to grow soft fruits in this climate."

"Ruth's vegetable plot is sheltered, isn't it?"

"Yeah. We'd need a poly-tunnel and I've never got around to sorting all that. It certainly won't happen now."

"You're not what I'd call green-fingered. But I love you anyway." Suzanne leaned over and kissed her husband on the lips. "Night-night, darling. You go on reading if you want."

He pulled her close. Moved his hand down her cleavage. "You feel good." He nuzzled her neck.

"I'm really not in the mood, Eddie. Sorry, sweetheart."

He sighed. "Maybe in the morning?"

"We'll see." She sometimes wished her husband's libido didn't make its presence known quite as much as it did.

Maybe once the house viewings began, he'd have too much on his mind to think about sex.

She kept her eyes open and watched him sink into his crime novel again. Not for the first time, she wondered what Ruth did about her natural instincts. She was still an attractive woman, if somewhat scrawnier than Suzanne. Ruth had brought a male friend with her to a party at The Sugar House a few years back. Maybe she visited whatever his name was, now and then. He'd seemed a nice enough fellow from what she recalled but Ruth was a private sort of person, certainly not inclined to discuss sensitive matters of the heart or of any other part of her anatomy.

Suzanne closed her eyes. From nowhere came the swift and powerful image of Eddie and Ruth in an intimate situation. Had he ever strayed in that direction? The vision loomed with such clarity, Suzanne's eyes opened again as she wondered if she dared confront him. But Eddie was immersed in the latest book starring his favourite feisty woman detective and her laidback, always in the doghouse, male sidekick. Not Suzanne's cup of tea at all.

The telephone line at The Sugar House was down the next day. Eddie, exasperated, picked up his mobile phone and rang to report the fault. No sooner had he finished the call than his ringtone pinged.

"Mr Deacon? It's Briggs, Caldwell and Balls here. We couldn't reach you on the landline."

Eddie recognised the voice of the leggy blonde sales negotiator. "Hello, Bethan. It's a damn nuisance, but these things happen. One of the joys of living in the sticks… though I suppose I shouldn't say that, should I?"

"I'll pretend I didn't hear."

"So, any news for me?"

"Yes indeed. A couple from Worcester have expressed an interest in your property. Mr and Mrs Hunt are asking if they may view this afternoon, if possible."

"No problem. What time should we get the coffee on?"

"An old cliché but it can't do any harm, Mr Deacon. Is two o'clock all right?"

"We'll be ready."

"I'm sorry I can't bring the Hunts myself but we're short-staffed today. Fortunately, they seem quite happy to come under their own steam. The husband says they'll stop off in Knightly for lunch and a look around so that's a good sign, don't you think?"

"They sound a sensible pair. No good doing a whistle stop tour. House purchasing's far too serious a business."

"Indeed. Anyway, keep your eye open for a black Porsche. According to Mrs Hunt, it's her husband's pride and joy."

Eddie cleared the call and padded through to the conservatory where he found his wife watering her collection of plants. "Hey, we have our first prospective purchasers, my sweet, arriving this afternoon at two o'clock. And get this – they own a Porsche."

"Fabulous. They can't be short of a few bob, then." Suzanne beamed. "I'm glad we got the house spick and span for the valuation. I don't have to rush around tidying up, but I'll give both loos a going over."

Eddie threw up his hands. "The cleaner skinned the place alive yesterday, for heaven's sake. Everything's already beyond tidy and we need to have an early lunch, something like bread and cheese so the smell of food doesn't linger." He tilted his head to one side. "Is that someone at the back door?"

"It's probably Ruth. Shall I go?"

"Leave it to me. You do what you have to do and I'll get shot of her."

"Make sure she knows we have people coming later, Eddie. I don't want her turning up accidentally on purpose and putting her oar in."

"She wouldn't do that, would she? After all the fuss she made over our decision to sell, I got the impression she was ready to help when it came to packing up?"

Suzanne didn't answer.

Eddie hurried through to the kitchen and opened the door to find Ruth standing outside. She held out a wicker punnet containing two jars of glowing crimson chutney nestling in a bed of dark green tissue paper.

"Good morning, Eddie. I'm tidying my cupboards and wondered if you'd take these off my hands."

"Brilliant! My favourite." He hesitated. "I'd ask you in but we're a bit tied up. People coming to view after lunch, you know."

41

"Really? You must be pleased to have somebody biting so soon. Are you sure there's nothing I can do to help? Do you have plenty of fresh flowers around the place?"

"How kind you are, but we're pretty much organised. Before the valuation, I had to stop her indoors from buying half a ton of lilies. Talk about the Chelsea Flower Show."

"I can imagine. Please tell Suzanne I'll be thinking of you both." Ruth took a step backwards. "Well, I'll leave you to it, then."

"Why don't you come and have a cuppa around four o'clock? We can tell you how we got on. This couple sound promising – Suzanne likes the fact that they drive a Porsche, but it's early days, of course."

Ruth nodded. "Sorry, but I'm a bit busy today too. I should know better than to begin on cupboard tidying when I still have proof reading to finish."

"You know best. Well, the offer's there, my dear. If you change your mind, just turn up. The viewing is at two, just so you know. They're coming from Knightly, without the agent present, so I hope we make a good job of showing them round."

"Don't be silly. It's your home, you're proud of it, so who better than you two to show people around? See you soon, Eddie."

He watched their friend walk away. He hadn't wanted to seem churlish but, unless handled with the verbal equivalent of velvet gloves, his wife could become a little distraught. It was one of the reasons why, almost a decade before, he'd decided they should give up hotel keeping and seek a

42

quieter way of life. That and the valuation he received from the local estate agency. Now they'd made the decision to put this house on the market, he hoped Suzanne wouldn't rev herself up to High Doh each time the agents arranged a viewing. If that were to happen, maybe he'd tactfully suggest she go and stay for a week or two with their daughter in Salisbury. He had a feeling it wouldn't be long before someone fell in love with The Sugar House and made a realistic offer.

While returning to Rock Cottage, Ruth congratulated herself for calling round with the chutney, an action the Deacons would consider perfectly predictable but which had resulted in her learning about the afternoon viewing. Now, despite limited time at her disposal, from several options already considered, there was one she thought she could achieve without too much effort. Three Roads might be described as a village at the back of nowhere but its dearth of residents, plus the unlikely possibility of tourists venturing this way now that what passed for summer had ended, resulted in a factor more precious than platinum.

The idea slipped into her head like cream caressing a slice of apple pie. All she need do was prepare her missile and get herself in position on the bank above the last bend. Motorists had to negotiate this before the downward slope into the centre of the village, if you could describe it as such. She kept herself fit by walking and practising yoga and she knew this would help her carry out her plan. The spiteful prank mightn't be enough to deter keen buyers but it was the kind of thing that might play on the mind of someone looking to move into a small, rural community. Especially a female someone.

She let herself into her cottage. Too strung up to contemplate lunch, Ruth went upstairs and took out her exercise mat. An hour's stretching and meditating would calm her. After all, she was only trying to help her friends. They needed her more than they realised. Moving away from Three Roads was not the right decision and they must be prevented from achieving it. All she intended to do was nudge them towards changing their minds.

Afterwards, they could all return to their same, secure way of life. She'd be extra solicitous. She might even suggest they both took a relaxing cruise while she cared for their house and dog. They wouldn't be able to tap into that kind of trustworthiness once they moved away to live in Wiltshire.

By half-past one, Ruth, safely screened by foliage, crouched upon the bank adjoining the bad bend. The county highways department had long before placed appropriate warning signs and clearly only a reckless idiot would pretend to be a motor rally driver along that stretch. Ruth knew which village residents left for work each morning and what time they normally returned. People didn't travel home to lunch when their offices were situated twenty miles away. The scattering of forestry workers occupying the sturdy terraced houses on the far side of Three Roads made sure they took food with them each day. Meals on wheels weren't on the menu in Three Roads and none of the elderly residents as yet needed such a service anyway. A minibus whisked away the school age youngsters in the morning and returned them mid-afternoon.

Phil Sartin and his clapped-out tractor was the variable factor, but this morning he'd driven his land rover to a farm sale over Brecon way. Ruth, having passed the time of day with him on her way round to The Sugar House, resolved to take him a batch of scones and a pot of raspberry jam some time soon. The cussed old blighter possessed a tongue that'd slice carrots, but keeping in with Phil was the equivalent of insurance.

He still owned the swathe of land adjoining The Sugar House, including the ground fronting its driveway. The Deacons retained right of way across that area, a condition written into their deeds, though that wouldn't prevent Phil from making their lives difficult if Ruth tugged his strings. The farmer might be glad to see the Deacons go, given he didn't much approve of them, but equally, it might suit him to act awkward and give them a rough time over access, if it meant keeping in with Ruth, whose help Phil Sartin needed with paperwork and sundry other matters.

She shifted her weight, wedging one foot on a shelf of jutting-out rock, ensuring she could aim confidently with her right arm. Timing was crucial but fortunately she had sight of the brow of the hill leading to the steep bend. She'd played cricket at boarding school and didn't think she would misjudge the angle. Glancing at her watch she saw it was now a quarter to two. She sucked in her breath only

45

moments later, hearing the sound of an engine, but relaxed as she saw the familiar dark green of a forestry van tackling the slope down.

The Porsche must have been on the van's tail. Ruth saw its shiny black bonnet nose like a predator over the brow of the hill. She groaned in annoyance. It was a little too early, a little too close for comfort to the vehicle in front.

To her relief, the forestry van driver, having rounded the bend with caution, accelerated away along the straight piece of road through the village. She recognised the man's spiky blond hair. He used to carry out bob a job tasks for her late aunt. What would he think if he saw sensible Ruth Morgan, wearing grey jogging pants and baggy hooded top, waited, perched above the road ready to commit an act of vandalism?

But no one could have seen her slip through the undergrowth. As soon as she accomplished what she'd come to do, she planned on pushing her way back through the foliage into the wooded area behind. Once more on the footpath, she'd pull down her hood and walk for an hour, completing her usual circuit with the calm confidence people expected of her.

The Porsche progressed sedately down the hill. Ruth lifted her arm. Flexed her wrist. Hurled her ammunition. The nauseating bundle hit the windscreen with a satisfying squelch.

Chapter Five

Eddie paced up and down the Aubusson carpet in the drawing room, as Suzanne insisted on calling their sitting room. "I hope this pair won't keep us hanging around."

His wife looked up from her magazine. "You can hardly accuse them of being late. A few minutes or so when they don't know the area is perfectly understandable."

"For some reason, I've got the colly-wobbles."

"You're usually the calmer one." She smiled at him. "Don't forget how long it took to sell our hotel, Eddie. Maybe this decision is bringing back memories. The wrong kind of memories."

He ceased pacing. "I think I hear something. That engine sound might just belong to a Porsche."

Suzanne waited while he went to investigate. She frowned as she heard his surprised exclamation but following him, discovered he had already gone outside, leaving the front door gaping. He was standing beside a sleek black vehicle. Porsches always looked sinister to Suzanne but the iconic car wasn't responsible for the shiver down her spine.

Eddie was listening to something the driver was saying. Shaking his head. Something had to be wrong. Why weren't Mr and Mrs Hunt climbing out of their posh Porsche?

Combined aromas of lavender wax polish, Arum lilies and freshly brewed coffee drifting from her house had filled her with satisfaction but now Eddie was hurrying back across the gravelled forecourt and spoiling the moment.

"I need a bucket of soapy water, a sponge and a cloth. Can you go and talk soothingly to the Hunts?"

"Have they been in an accident?"

"Just go, Suze. You'll soon find out." He headed into the kitchen.

"Utility room, under the sink," she called after him before hurrying towards the Porsche.

"Oh, my word." Suzanne halted in front of the car to be confronted by a slimy mess. She wrinkled her nose. The gunk surely consisted of animal dung rippled with smashed eggshell fragments and it obscured most of the windscreen.

She went around to the passenger side and carefully opened the door. "Mrs Hunt? This must be very distressing for you. I can't think who'd do such a horrible thing." Wild thoughts raced through her head. Could this have something to do with animal rights protesters? Surely that made no sense?

Mrs Hunt unfastened her seat belt. Suzanne, while admiring her beautifully-styled silver-grey hair and caramel cashmere sweater, thought the woman's eyes sparkled with anger rather than shock.

"Mrs Deacon? The attack took us completely by surprise. Robert was driving very cautiously down the hill but if he'd been going any faster, who knows what might have happened."

Mr Hunt climbed out of the driving seat and came around to shake Suzanne's hand. She noted his grim expression.

"My husband will clean up your windscreen."

"The bonnet as well."

"Of course." Suzanne spoke soothingly. "There's coffee waiting to be poured. Why don't you both come inside and relax?"

"Relax! Tell me, is this the kind of thing you're forced to endure in these parts? Is this why you're moving? Trying to avoid some Welsh Mafia obsessed with keeping out we English?"

"Absolutely not." Suzanne appealed to Mrs Hunt. "I understand how traumatized you must both feel, but believe me, we are English and we've never known any incident like that happen before. Please come inside."

"You go, Marcia. I'll stay out here."

Suzanne made no attempt to protest. "My husband's on his way," she said. "Let's get you inside, Mrs Hunt." She waited to be invited to call the visitor by her first name but soon realised it wasn't going to happen.

"We'll go straight into the kitchen but that door on the left belongs to the cloakroom if you want to wash your hands."

"My hands aren't soiled. Robert put the screen wash and wipers on so he could see to drive the rest of the way. It wouldn't have been safe to stop on that hill, so we've absolutely no idea who threw that mess. Or, should I say, who attacked us."

"Please sit down. How do you like your coffee?"

"Black with a splash of milk, please. No sugar."

Suzanne saw Mrs Hunt glance around. Eddie always trumpeted how their kitchen fitted every woman's idea of country-dwelling heaven.

"I have to say the online photographs don't really do this kitchen justice." But Mrs Hunt spoke without enthusiasm.

"Thank you. The whole house needed massive renovation when we bought it and we've made even more alterations over the years we've lived here."

Mrs Hunt accepted her cup. "I'm sure. Do you mind if I ask why you've decided to move?"

"We want to live closer to our daughter." Suzanne didn't mention Penny was married to an army officer and might conceivably not remain in her current home for more than a couple of years.

"And where does your daughter live?"

"In Wiltshire," said Suzanne, her hopes plummeting. This woman probably couldn't wait to get out of The Sugar House, despite the allure of its culinary area.

"Tell me, have you enjoyed living in Wales?"

"Very much. I can honestly say these last eight or nine years have been among the happiest of our lives." She looked around, relieved, as the men joined them.

Eddie headed for the coffee machine. "Round the kitchen table, are we? Well, that's nice." He poured coffee into two mugs.

"Do sit down, Mr Hunt. Milk and sugar?"

Robert Hunt seated himself beside his wife. "Thank you. Glad to say the windscreen's pristine again. But what a welcome that was. Not."

Suzanne winced. "I was just telling your wife how happy we've been in this village. Believe me, I truly am flabbergasted. It's difficult to comprehend why such a horrible thing should happen when Three Roads is such a close-knit little community."

"Maybe a little too much so for us." Mr Hunt stared into his coffee. "And I doubt you can judge whether that was an act of random vandalism, or something more sinister. Whichever it was, the person or persons responsible have done your friendly community no favours."

"It's understandable you should feel like that." Suzanne sighed. "But we really wouldn't lie to you. To the best of my knowledge, nothing like this atrocity has ever happened here before."

"Seems a bit fishy to me." Mr Hunt glanced at his wife. "What do you think, Marcia? Are we being given some kind of message? Should we waste these good people's time any longer?"

Mrs Hunt looked apologetically at Suzanne. "To be honest, I don't think I could ever feel comfortable about coming back here. Although your house is just the sort of property we're looking for. But I do wonder if this village might be a little inward-looking for us."

Disappointment hit Suzanne like a stomach punch, making her gulp. "That seems such a shame. But I understand. And if you were to change your minds, I guarantee you could travel down that road and back ten times a day without any problem at all."

"Yes, well, good luck with your house sale. We should make a move, Marcia." Mr Hunt fidgeted with his key ring.

"Somewhere else lined up?" Suzanne forced a bright, enquiring look onto her face.

"Yes, we've an appointment to view River Cottage, just outside Knightly. We noticed the turning as we came through. We may as well get on our way, I suppose."

"I'm sorry you feel like this. All the best with your house hunting." Eddie rose as the couple got to their feet, Mr Hunt shaking his head.

Suzanne nodded to each of the couple in turn. "Goodbye, both," she said. "I really can't tell you how sorry I am."

Left alone, she surveyed the abandoned porcelain mugs. The couple hadn't even lingered long enough to finish their coffees.

"What kind of a sick bastard would do such a thing?" For Eddie's benefit, Ruth hoped her eyes glittered with anger. "I'm sorry to use that kind of language but those were your very first viewers and that despicable thing had to happen!"

"I'm glad you found time to call round, my dear. Suzanne's still lying down. I'll give her a shout in a minute."

"Eddie, please don't disturb her on my account. She must be devastated."

"To be honest, I'm glad she's resting. I don't want her getting worked up over this. It has to be a one off, surely? But why pick on Mr and Mrs Hunt? Talk about bad timing."

Ruth crossed one long leg over the other, remembering to wince before moving her leg back again. She sat, both feet neatly on the carpet, gazing out at the garden. Oh, but this was fun.

"Knee a problem? This dreary weather's enough of a pain as it is."

"It's just my arthritis playing up again." Ruth hesitated. "I was just thinking whoever did that to the Hunts couldn't possibly have known they had an appointment to view in the village. So, do you think it could simply have been Porsche envy? A couple of kids wandering around with nothing better to do?"

"Wandering from where? The village youngsters are all in school. And how many kids roam around with a bag of eggs and shit – sorry, dung – looking to find someone to sling it at." He shuddered. "The muck was stuffed into one of those fine mesh bags the supermarkets use. As soon as it hit the windscreen, the eggs smashed. And you know what? In my opinion, there's only one person I can think of cussed enough to do such a mindless bloody thing."

Ruth frowned. "Surely you don't suspect someone from the village?"

"How about Philip fecking Sartin?"

She stiffened, caught unawares but delighted by the supposition. "Really, Eddie? Surely Phil wouldn't do something like that? He's scruffy, yes, and a bit surly at

53

times but I wouldn't have put him down as spiteful and aggressive."

Eddie nibbled at a hangnail. "Now it's me should be minding my language. I'm sorry. But your trouble is, you see the best in everyone, Ruth. He's never liked us. The fellow finds it hard to pass the time of day if our paths cross. That indicates a certain mind set, given we bought the house in good faith without a clue Sartin had been trying for years to get his hands on the original parcel of land."

"I'd forgotten that old chestnut. But if that were so, you'd think he'd be cheering you on. Glad to see you go." She hesitated. "Though he'd probably be the only one in the village. Everyone I've spoken to thinks it's a shame you're leaving. I do think you should know that, Eddie."

Eddie's face softened. "That's good to hear. Thank you, Ruth. I like to think we've fitted in. Suzanne's always lent a hand with the kids' events. Brought shopping back for people if they haven't been able to get out. You know the kind of thing."

"Of course. Especially with poor old Mrs Frame. I suppose she'll rely on me for lifts and errands once you two leave." Ruth paused a few beats and sighed.

He spread his hands. "I don't know what else to say. We've made our decision. Anyway, someone at the agency rang to say we have another viewing tomorrow at ten o'clock. A bloke on his own this time."

"I'm sure it'll all go smoothly. Today's incident must have been an unfortunate coincidence. How could the vandal or vandals possibly have known prospective house purchasers were due at that exact moment?"

"But can you remember such a thing happening in the village before?"

"I honestly think it must have been a couple of lads from outside of Three Roads. Maybe they rode here on their bikes. A vehicle coming around that bend has to be moving very slowly and therefore provides a very satisfactory target for teenagers with time on their hands."

"Heaven help us all if that's the kind of idiot this country's producing nowadays. They must have brought the eggs with them, even if they collected the dung locally. Oh, what's the use! I expect you're right, my dear. Is it wine o'clock yet?"

Bethan Harley put down the telephone and frowned. She clicked on the page containing The Sugar House's particulars and scanned the main photograph before kick-starting the slide show. She'd been delighted to acquire the Deacons' house for her list but, so far, feedback from punters remained less than enthusiastic. And that was before anyone had even completed a proper viewing.

She pulled up the database and read the notes already logged by one of her colleagues. Bradley and Valerie Childs had come into the office but exchanged glances and rejected the suggestion that they view The Sugar House, even though it fitted their criteria like a surgical glove and they'd already visited somewhere similar, though much closer to Llanbrenin Wells. When coaxed to explain their apparent aversion to the property at Three Roads, they claimed they'd heard one or two disturbing things about the location. This had resulted in a mutual decision to give this particular house a miss.

When asked the nature of the information, Mr Childs repeated the story they'd heard from a charming lady called Delyth, who was also looking at properties for sale in the area. In fact, while they were browsing particulars in the BCB office window, she'd fallen into conversation with them and revealed some fascinating if gruesome facts about Three Roads, over a pot of tea and a plate of cracking Welsh cakes, to quote Mr Childs.

Bethan could do without negative input acquired so she made a mental note to make discreet inquiries, in case the woman lived locally and had an axe to grind. One never knew.

A second couple, Robert and Marcia Hunt, had reported a disturbing road-related incident while approaching the property with intent to view by appointment. Bethan's admin assistant had logged the occurrence as an unexplained and unprovoked attack by person or persons unknown. Mr and Mrs Hunt confirmed the Deacons couldn't have been more charming, and appeared devastated that such a thing could happen on their patch, but the experience had soured the Hunts' eagerness to view and they'd gone off to their next appointment, having ventured no further than the hallway and kitchen of The Sugar House.

There was no viewing booked for today but Bethan had a ten o'clock appointment for the following morning, with a Mr Kirby. She walked through to the outer office where an administrator sat typing up a new set of particulars.

"Chris, you know Three Roads pretty well, don't you? Am I right in thinking an aunt of yours lives there?"

Chris nodded and pulled out her earpiece. "My aunt lives just outside the village. Why?"

"Has she ever mentioned some rumour about a murderer being buried on the land where The Sugar House stands? It seems the villagers – bear in mind we're going back decades here – were furious over the fact that this criminal had been buried in the churchyard."

"I don't recollect her ever mentioning anything like that. Sorry."

"Don't be sorry. It may be your aunt knows nothing about it. Apparently, a little gang of locals took it upon themselves to exhume the body a couple of days after the burial."

Chris shuddered. "Ugh."

"Yes, well they apparently chose to rebury the coffin in a patch of unused land at the edge of the village. A long time afterwards, this land was bought by someone who obtained planning permission and built the original Sugar House."

"Would you like me to ring my aunt and make some discreet inquiries?"

Bethan hesitated. "Thanks, Chris but maybe it's best to leave things as they are for now. Put it down to bad luck the first potential viewers happened to get talking to someone who knows the village's history. To keep it in perspective, not everyone would be bothered about some long-gone incident like that."

"The couple who went to view yesterday seemed really shaken by that awful attack. I'd say they were more concerned about what might have happened rather than what actually did happen."

"Yeah. You can't do much about that kind of mind set but I think we can all understand how Mr and Mrs Hunt felt. It certainly hasn't been the best of starts for the Deacons with BCB."

"It's hardly our fault, Bethan."

"No, but Three Roads is the kind of place that will attract only a certain type of property buyer. Not only is the village five miles from the nearest town, it's on the edge of nowhere. So, we start at a disadvantage."

"Come on, it's not like you to sound so negative. On the plus side, the village sits in the midst of beautiful countryside, with stunning view and walks. That waterfall's straight out of Tolkien. The Sugar House ticks more than one very important box for any property buyer looking for a peaceful lifestyle."

"You're sounding like an estate agent." Bethan grinned. "I mustn't let myself brood. But tomorrow morning I'll make sure I drive over to Three Roads for ten o'clock so I can be there for our Mr Kirby. I can go straight on afterwards to my eleven o'clock valuation. It won't take me long from the village."

"I'll log it in the diary." Chris adjusted her earpiece. "Sure you don't want me to quiz my aunt about long ago dirty deeds?"

"Positive. Not yet, anyway."

Bethan headed back to her office. Something didn't seem right. And if someone out there had it in for the Deacons, what on earth could their motive be?

Chapter Six

"Now, let me get this straight. What you're saying, Ruth Morgan, is you want me to leave my tractor so it's blocking the entrance to your mates' driveway?"

"It's for their own good, Phil. Suzanne Deacon's health is delicate to say the least and moving house at her time of life is the last thing she needs. They've made a hasty, ill-conceived decision and someone has to help them see the error of their ways."

Phil Sartin scratched the nape of his neck where his greasy, grey hair straggled over the collar of his ancient waterproof jacket. "Husband's thick as pig shit if you ask me. I'm entitled to leave my own vehicles on my own land but it hadn't occurred to him to check out the small print when he bought that gin palace of his."

"We both know the Deacons have right of way to drive in and out of their gateway, Phil."

He shook his head. "Can't abide these legal shenanigans."

Ruth nodded. "I remember being asked to negotiate with you that time Suzanne was desperate to get out of the driveway for a hairdresser's appointment in Knightly."

"Hair-do? You'd have thought the woman was about to drop a calf, the bloomin' fuss she made."

Ruth noted the gleam of satisfaction in the farmer's eyes. "They hadn't been in the village very long and himself was doing his nut. I got a phone call asking me to sweet talk you into moving your old van from their gateway."

Phil Sartin smirked. "Now boot's on t'other foot. Those two hardly give me the time of day, not that I lose any sleep over it." He looked at her through narrowed eyes. "Right then, if that's what you want me to do, I'll drive the tractor over from my field nice and early tomorrow then nip back to my place and get off to market like I planned."

"That sounds perfect. I can assure you I'm acting in everyone's best interests. No one will come to any harm."

He leered at her. "And what's in it for me apart from those scones you brought? I've never forgot that nice shoulder massage you gave me a while back."

She hesitated. "I don't ask for a fee when I help you complete your tax return, do I?"

"No, I can't say as you does."

"And when you give me eggs or apples, you know you'll get fresh veggies or a jar of something nice in return?"

His rasping chuckle introduced a cough and a spit on the ground. "What if the husband rings the police? I don't want to get locked up, Missus. Don't you go forgettin' I've got stock to think about and no bugger to call on."

Ruth shook her head. "It's a civil matter, Phil. The police can't arrest you, and as you say, you own the land. The Deacons are entitled to drive to and fro to access the main road, so if you decide to prevent them from doing that, of course they'll kick up."

"I doubt I'll get back much before four, tomorrow afternoon."

"That's perfect. I'll make sure the Deacons don't stir things with the police. I can understand you don't want to waste time being lectured by a toddler with a clipboard." She wondered if she should have said iPad but decided Phil Sartin probably wouldn't understand.

"You fancy a cup of tea before you go back, Missus? I was just about to put the kettle on when you knocked."

Ruth's gaze took in the stained crockery stacked on the draining board. The stray teabags scattered on the tatty oilcloth covering the table. Phil Sartin's decrepit farmhouse kitchen differed from the one in The Sugar House as a homemade go-cart contrasted with a state-of-the-art sports car.

"No thanks, Phil. I have paperwork to finish so I must get back. I enjoy my little job, as you know."

"And you'll be around in the morning? Wouldn't mind betting your mates will be straight on to you to sort their problem out this time too." He wiped his nose on his sleeve.

"Oh yes. I'll be very much around. But you won't be. You have a good time at market. Thursday's sheep day, isn't it?"

"Aye. I'll need to be away early with the trailer."

"Perfect." Ruth stood up. "I'll see myself out."

Eddie opened one eye and peered at the alarm clock. It was only seven o'clock and he knew something had disturbed him. His wife still slumbered beside him as full consciousness arrived and he realised the sound he heard was the cough and splutter of a tractor engine firing up.

Sartin must be making an early start, driving his dilapidated bit of kit up the track and down the main road the short distance to his biggest field.

Eddie focused on what he was doing that day. They had someone coming to view the house at ten o'clock. That sexy sales negotiator had phoned from BCB to say she'd be turning up too. He was just trying to decide whether that would be a good thing or not when he realised the rasping engine noise had ceased. Abruptly. He wouldn't go back to sleep now, so he slid carefully from beneath the duvet and crept across the thick pile carpet to the window to check on the weather. Peering around pleated peach silk drapes, he saw an ancient Ford tractor parked slap bang in front of his gateway.

The silly old sod must have broken down. Eddie scratched his chest. Still, this next house hunter wasn't due to arrive for well over three hours. Everything would be fine. Suzanne had been jittery ever since that couple got their Porsche showered with crud, and couldn't wait to get away fast enough. Today, he'd awoken feeling things would be very different and he didn't want his wife agitated any more than she already was.

He grabbed his robe, pushed his feet into slippers and left Suzanne still sleeping. He'd known the time when he'd have slipped back into bed and begun making love to her. She'd have opened her eyes and protested but without really meaning it. Nowadays – best if he fired up the coffee machine. Eddie still missed having a morning paper shoved through his letterbox but it was a small price to pay for

63

living somewhere so tranquil. At least they had a halfway decent Broadband connection these days.

If he spotted the farmer returning to move his bag of tricks, Eddie decided he might put his head out of the door and call a friendly good morning. So, if a prospective buyer asked how he got on with his neighbours, he could quite legitimately give a positive response.

But when Suzanne arrived in the kitchen, showered, dressed, and immaculate as always, her face told her husband she was in no mood for pleasantries.

"Have you noticed what's blocking our gateway? I didn't realise until I drew our bedroom curtains." She slapped both hands palm down on the table so violently that Eddie's fingers slid on the laptop's keyboard and catapulted him on to the wrong page of the online newspaper he was browsing.

"Steady on, love. Yes, I know the score but it's not even eight o'clock yet. It's not as though we need to get off out in a hurry."

"Eddie. Watch my lips. We have someone coming to look at the house in two hours' time and currently they'll be unable to park anywhere but on the track. That means they have to reverse on to the main road afterwards. You're still in your dressing gown. Would you like me to go and enquire why there's a bloody great tractor sitting outside our property?"

Eddie jumped up. Suzanne rarely swore.

"Two minutes to get my kit on, then I'll give old Sartin a knock. You pour yourself a coffee and make us some toast.

I'll have a couple of boiled eggs as well, please." Eddie almost joked about not making them too runny but thought better of it, given his wife's present mood.

He got to his feet and plonked a kiss on her cheek before he headed upstairs. "I'll see what that old devil's playing at but I wouldn't be surprised to find someone turn up to sort things out. Sartin probably sloped off home to ring the agricultural engineers. He's probably sitting in his kitchen now, slurping tea and rolling one of those disgusting cigarettes of his."

"Let's hope you're right."

"See you in a bit. And keep your pecker up, love."

Left alone, Suzanne felt an unwelcome tummy lurch. A worrier by nature, she couldn't help wondering if they were jinxed when it came to selling this house. The woman from Briggs, Caldwell and Balls had prophesised there'd be no trouble shifting The Sugar House. But the property having been on the market a week, today was hopefully the first day when a proper viewing might be achieved. Mr Sartin normally left them well alone. They'd experienced only one incident, not too long after they moved in.

Ruth, their first new acquaintance in the village, had defused the situation. Clearly the farmer thought a lot of her. Ruth had informed them he'd known her since she was a teenager. Suzanne sent up a silent prayer, immediately feeling guilty about asking for help when she often went days and even weeks without giving a thought to the God in whom she'd been brought up to believe.

When Eddie reappeared in the kitchen with nothing to report, she smiled at him. "Eggs should be just as you like them. Eat your breakfast first, my love, and I'm sorry I got myself in a strop. You're right. There's still plenty of time for Mr Sartin to get things sorted."

"I'm not that surprised the tractor's kaput. He drives the thing like a madman. Clouds of smoke bellowing out of it and all!"

"So, will you ring Ruth, or shall I?"

"I'll give her a call shortly. But we need to play this down if the estate agent finds out, okay? If we have to tell a white lie or two in order to sell the house, how bad is that?"

Bethan Harley hadn't had the best of beginnings to her day. Unusually for her, she'd overslept, as had her daughter, and Bethan still struggled with that uncomfortable sensation of being caught on the back foot. Luckily, she'd left her desk reasonably clear and needed only a brief stop at the BCB office before setting off for Three Roads. Now, rounding the steep bend where the road descended into the village, she felt pleased she'd arrive in time to oil the machinery by giving these two clients a glowing report of the number of hits to the website page featuring their house. Certainly, her photographs enhanced a tempting slide show.

Bethan's antennae twitched as she turned off to drive down the short track leading to the house. With that tractor obstructing her clients' gateway, where was she supposed to park, now she couldn't access their spacious driveway? Worse still, what would her prospective purchaser think?

That galvanised her into action. She threw her arm across the back of the passenger seat and drove backwards to the point where the track met the road through the village. Here, turning her steering wheel as far as possible, she nosed sideways until she felt her tyres touch the verge. Two more turns and she could see any vehicle approaching to her right and drive with safety out from the track.

She parked in a lay-by she knew forestry workers often used for making phone calls if they couldn't obtain a signal in the depths of the woodland. Briefcase in hand, she zapped her keypad and hurried towards The Sugar House, checking her watch on the way. She'd give them a knock, leave her briefcase and walk back down the track, ready to alert Mr Kirby and offer a plausible reason as to why he couldn't park his car on the Deacons' driveway. Oh, great.

Bethan found Eddie Deacon standing in front of the tractor, his face taut. For the first time in their brief acquaintanceship, she noted the flirtatious sparkle in his eye didn't appear as he spotted her.

"Mr Deacon," she called. "Good Morning and please don't look so worried. If the farmer has a problem, I'm sure my client will understand. We are in the countryside, when all's said and done."

Eddie grunted. "Thanks for being so understanding, Bethan. I'm sure there must be a simple explanation. Unfortunately, I haven't been able to contact Mr Sartin. He's the farmer in question."

"These things happen. May I leave my briefcase with you while I go back to wait for Mr Kirby?"

He took the briefcase from her. "Come on, I'll walk with you. Suzanne's in the conservatory listening to one of her Pan Pipes CDs."

"Ah."

"No question about it, she's got the heebie-jeebies."

"I'm afraid selling a house is classed as one of the most stressful activities we poor humans put ourselves through. They say it's up there with divorce and bereavement."

"Understood. I wouldn't want your job, that's for sure."

They moved away from the looming bulk of the muddy old machine and walked along the track.

"Fortunately, I enjoy what I do."

"But you must agree, so far we're scoring two out of two on the annoyance scale when it comes to viewings. I bet your client feedback would make interesting reading."

Bethan winced at his bitter tone. "The Hunts may yet request another appointment so please don't be too downhearted. They were shocked at the time, but Mr Hunt admitted to me over the phone that they maybe overreacted."

"Is that right? They haven't actually asked for another viewing though?"

"I think we'll have to wait for their next visit to Wales. They went back to Worcester straight after their other appointment. So, you haven't been able to speak to the owner of the tractor yet? Does he live close by?"

"No and No. Phil Sartin owns this field to our left and, annoyingly, the patch of land in front of our gateway. Someone must've slipped up when defining the boundary but we definitely have right of way over his land written into our deeds."

"Of course. We've specifically mentioned the fact in our particulars."

"Sartin's house is across the village but there's a short cut so I used that this morning." He huffed a sigh. "Nowhere to be found, I'm afraid. After I found the bird had flown, I gave a friend of ours a ring on my mobile. She knows the fellow's routine pretty well but apparently his land rover and trailer are missing so Ruth thinks he's probably taken some cattle to market."

"Without explaining why he's blocking your gateway? Please be honest with me, Mr Deacon. Do you have issues with this person? I need to know so I don't give Mr Kirby the wrong impression. You must know there has to be absolute transparency when it comes to relationships with neighbours. Further down the line you'll have a solicitor's questionnaire to complete."

"I know. Boundaries, disputes, complaints and so on," said Eddie.

They stopped walking and stood on the corner.

"Sartin doesn't fit what I'd describe as a neighbour," he said. "Because his farmhouse is a few minutes' walk away, we don't see too much of each other."

"Are you quite sure you've had no problems in the past?" She watched Eddie's face, ready to read his reaction. "I don't recall you mentioning anything."

"Not long after we moved in, almost nine years ago now, there was an occasion when Mr Sartin blocked our gateway with his land rover. We hadn't long known Ruth Morgan but she called round with some homemade chutney as a welcome gift on our moving in day."

"That was a nice gesture."

"Yeah, she's been a good friend to us ever since. She was the only person I could think of to ring that first time too. She found Sartin at home and told him not to be such a bloody idiot. He moved the vehicle but I never received an apology. Since then, we've had no problems at all until today of all days." Again, he puffed air through his lips. "I'm sorry but I'd forgotten all about it until now. I honestly didn't mean to withhold information."

"I know you didn't. Sounds like Mr Sartin was marking his territory, like an animal. Do you think, now he's become used to you, he mightn't want you to leave? You've lived here – what did you say – almost a decade?"

"Yes, it did occur to me he might be the one who threw that gunge at the Porsche."

"I don't think the two things are necessarily connected, Mr Deacon. Best to put the first incident out of your mind. I'm sure there's a simple explanation for the tractor being abandoned."

Eddie grunted again. "We'll have to see. Ruth promised to get in touch, whether she found Sartin or not."

A vehicle appeared, nosing over the hilltop.

"I wonder if this is our man," said Bethan.

As the black Range Rover approached, she held out her hand, signalling its driver to slow down so she could direct him to the lay by.

"This is a great house you have here," said Ray Kirby as Bethan escorted him into the sitting room after showing him around.

"We think so." Suzanne smiled up at him from the window seat.

Bethan marvelled at Mr Kirby's melodious voice, considering he was such a great bear of a man.

"I hear you've decided to move nearer to your daughter." Kirby directed the remark at Eddie.

"That's right, tempus fugit and all that. It comes to everyone in the end, doesn't it?"

Kirby smiled politely. "I'll need to bring my partner so she can take a look before making any decision." He spread his hands. "I'm not bullshitting when I say I'm impressed. I like plenty of space. Even when I'm home alone."

"I can't apologise enough about this business with the tractor," said Eddie.

"That won't rattle my cage." Kirby stuck his hands in his jacket pockets. "Unless you're telling porkies, Mr Deacon?"

"Believe me, Mr Kirby, he's not." Suzanne got up from her chair. "Mr Sartin has parked a vehicle in front of our gateway twice in all the time we've been here. It's Murphy's Law that, on this occasion, it happens to be the very day we have a house viewing."

Kirby nodded. "Thank you for being so honest. As it happens, we wouldn't be forever backwards and forwards if we lived here. I work mostly from home and my partner's a singer, currently employed on cruises."

71

"How exciting! Would we have heard of her?"

He shook his head. "Nah, Mrs Deacon. I doubt you've heard of Claudia Kelsey."

"I don't think I have. Sorry."

"She has a fabulous voice. You can listen to her singing if you visit her website. Just type her name in your search engine."

"Is that Kelsey with an S E Y? I'll get my husband to look her up."

"That's it. She has a couple of albums under her belt, but in her off time all she wants is somewhere quiet with decent walks within reach. That's why neither of us is looking to be close to a big centre. If we do make an offer for your pad, I shall go and have a heart to heart with this farmer guy and see if we can establish what his problem is."

"I don't think there's any bad feeling involved." Bethan looked enquiringly at Suzanne.

"Definitely not. We hardly ever see the man but if he knocked at the door, we'd invite him in."

Kirby nodded. "Whatever the reason, trouble-shooting's on my CV, though I'm more into other stuff these days. By the way, do you get an online grocery delivery here?"

"Um, no. I'm afraid not yet," said Suzanne. "But there are good supermarkets within easy reach. And a few specialist shops in the high street of both our shopping towns."

"Okay. I don't foresee any problems with that. This must be fantastic country for walking?"

72

"Oh yes." Eddie gave a wry smile. "Although, nowadays, some of it's a bit arduous for us."

Kirby nodded again. "Well, I'll be on my way. Thank you. I hope all goes well for you."

"I must get on, too." Bethan turned to Suzanne and Eddie. "I'll be in touch soon, to touch base."

"I'll be straight with you." Mr Kirby's gaze moved between both the Deacons. "I intend viewing two more properties today. One's with Mrs Harley's outfit and the other with a different agent."

"We understand." Suzanne nodded her neat, blonde head.

"I'm afraid my partner's not due back for another few days. Unless either of the other properties succeeds in changing my mind, I'll email Claudia and suggest we make an appointment to come down a day or two after her return. The Sugar House definitely fits the criteria on our shopping list."

Eddie showed them out while Suzanne sank down into her chair again and gazed at the cut glass vase filled with green-stemmed, satin-smooth lilies.

"What do you think?" Eddie returned without delay.

"I think he's very attractive."

"Bloody hell, I didn't ask whether you fancied him, Suze!"

She grinned. "He's also rather scary. Did you notice the size of his hands?"

"You wouldn't want to tackle him in a hurry, that's for sure."

"Wouldn't it be great if a bruiser like him bought the place and saw off Phil Sartin?"

"Which reminds me. I need that tractor moved before this evening."

"Of course. It's your camera club tonight."

"And I don't propose walking the five miles to Knightly."

"If the worst comes to the worst, maybe Ruth would give you a lift. Doesn't one of the other members have to come through Three Roads on his way home?"

"Believe me, sweetie, if that tractor's not moved by half past six, I'm ringing for a taxi and sending the bill to that daft old bugger, Sartin."

"Oh dear. We don't want to antagonise him, do we? Not at this stage of the proceedings."

"Let's leave it to Ruth, like she's already said. We couldn't have anyone better than her looking out for us."

Chapter Seven

Ruth contacted as many of the farmer's neighbours as she could. Not that the number overwhelmed her. A couple of the female residents taught at Knightly Primary School and their husbands worked for the Forestry Commission so were out all day.

A divorcee called Charlotte lived in a cramped little cottage tucked behind Sartin's farmhouse. This woman, in her forties and who, according to local gossip, had given up on men, knitted sumptuous woollen garments to sell at country fairs and also supplied two or three boutiques in larger mid Wales towns. She and Ruth ventured to the cinema together occasionally but Charlotte was no great fan of Sartin.

"All I can tell you is, he got away very early because the sound of the tractor woke me. I must have been listening to Radio Four when he came back and loaded his sheep for market. Do you want pen and paper to write him a message?"

"Thanks, but after Eddie called me, I tried Phil's number before I dropped everything to go and look for him. I've left a message on his answer phone so there's a good chance he'll check that, in case there's anything to do with business on there."

"He laughs in my face when I tell him he should buy a mobile phone," said Charlotte. "If I hear him come back,

I'll pop round to the yard and ask if he's lost anything." She pulled at a strand of hair, a bright purple flair amongst black. "I see The Sugar House is up for sale. I imagine you'll miss the Deacons."

"Of course I shall. But they haven't gone yet," said Ruth, turning on her heel.

Charlotte didn't respond. But Ruth realised her expression might have been a little contemptuous. She turned around again. "What I meant to say was, these things often take longer than one anticipates. I'll let you know how they get on."

"Speak soon." Charlotte called.

Ruth left her friend and continued with her charade of a search. It was only when she reached the rundown little community hall where there was a red mailbox in the surrounding brick wall, that she realised she'd mentioned rushing straight out of her house as soon as she left Phil Sartin an answer-phone message. Charlotte might have wondered, why, in that case, Ruth was carrying a rucksack. Bad mistake.

While waiting for the postman to turn up, she decided it would appear suspicious to hurry back and explain herself. Charlotte, who could be amazingly scatty sometimes, probably hadn't even noticed. The mailman, nicknamed Knocker, pulled up moments later and said he hadn't clapped eyes upon the farmer that morning.

Ruth made her way back down the main road and walked to The Sugar House where she rang the front doorbell rather than go around to the kitchen entrance as she often did.

"Any luck?" Eddie stood on the eco friendly doormat, arms folded across his chest like the nightclub bouncers Ruth had seen, although only in films.

"Sadly, no news yet. Do you need to go anywhere? If so, I can soon take you in my car."

His face softened. "We're going to miss having you in our lives, Ruthie. I shall need to go out later because of my camera club meeting but surely the old devil will be back well before then?"

"I'm a little concerned about Phil Sartin, you know, Eddie. In fact, I'm seriously concerned he might be suffering from some kind of mental aberration. If he is, that could be the reason why he's acting irresponsibly."

"It's beggars belief he could do such a thing on purpose. If the tractor's kaput, why hasn't someone arrived to repair it? And why didn't he give us a knock earlier to let us know? If he'd had the grace to apologise, I wouldn't be feeling so angry."

"Eddie? Are you keeping Ruth on the doorstep?" Suzanne walked across the hallway.

"I'm not thinking straight. Sorry, my dear. Come and sit down. I think we all deserve a glass of something."

He led the way through to the conservatory. "You ladies make yourselves comfortable and I'll bring the drinks through."

Ruth settled in one of the luxurious cushioned wicker chairs facing the garden. "That sounds good. How are you coping with it all, Suzanne? I hope you don't mind my saying, but you don't have much colour in your cheeks, dear."

"I'm fine, thank you. Just a bit stressed by the last few days."

"Well, if there's anything I can do, you know you only have to shout. I feel so sorry for you both. You must be wondering if you've made the right decision?"

Suzanne shrugged. "Not really. These things happen."

"But you have such a delicate constitution, Suzanne." She leaned forward. Lowered her voice. "Just between the two of us, I'm surprised Eddie has put your house on the market at this time of year. Everyone knows the run up to Christmas is not the best of times to shift a property. You can do without extra pressure like that."

"Christmas is still a long way off. Anyway, Eddie says we only need one buyer."

"What does your estate agent think of these, um, mishaps?"

Suzanne sat bolt upright. "Oh, Bethan is very positive. And the man who came to view this morning didn't strike me as being at all bothered. He took an instant liking to the place, didn't he Eddie?"

Eddie, carrying a bottle and three sherry schooners, crossed the room and began pouring the pale gold liquid. "He certainly seemed to. Apparently his partner's a singer, working on cruise liners. He didn't say what age she was but neither of them hankers after the bright lights."

"Just as well, if he's contemplating moving here," said Ruth. "So he'll want to bring this partner of his to view the house, I imagine? What did you say the man's name was?" She accepted her glass and sipped. "Mmm. Dry but with a lovely nutty undertone."

"Are we talking about Mr Sartin?" Suzanne giggled.

Eddie looked puzzled. "I don't think I mentioned his name, did I? Not Sartin. The man who viewed the house."

"Oh, sorry. I don't mean to be nosey."

"Of course you don't," said Suzanne. "He's called Mr Kirby. Do we know his first name, Eddie?"

"Roy? Ray? I feel much happier now the guy's been and gone. You know, in a funny way, I rather hope old Sartin really has had some kind of senior moment. That'd be much more forgivable than knowing he dumped his tractor on us out of spite."

"If you don't mind, I'd like to offer my services as a mediator," said Ruth. "If I tell him I wanted to drive down and pick you up, Suzanne, for a trip to Knightly, he won't feel so threatened."

"I'd bloody threaten him, given half a chance!"

Ruth waited for Suzanne to scold her husband. And wasn't disappointed.

"Now, Eddie, Ruth has a good point. Mr Sartin must be well into his seventies. We should have a little compassion. I shouldn't have joked about him being nutty." Suzanne sipped her sherry.

Eddie looked from one to the other. "I suppose you're right, both of you. Okay. I'll back off but it better not happen again is all I have to say."

"Any more viewings arranged? Again, I don't mean to seem nosey, but if you tell me when the next one is, I can make absolutely sure Phil behaves himself. The main objective is to get your house sold, though I can't believe I'm hearing myself say that." Ruth bit her lip and turned her head away, as if wishing to hide her emotions.

"Dear Ruth, we'll be forever in your debt."

"Thank you, Eddie, but there's no need to feel like that. We're friends and I hope we always will be, even if you are deserting me."

"You know we both hope you'll come and stay with us once we've settled into the new abode, wherever that may be."

Sparkles the golden Labrador padded into the room and headed straight for Ruth.

She bent and stroked the dog's head. Fondled her ears. "How sweet. I think this old lady's agreeing with you."

Eddie rose to top up their glasses. "The dog's the reason why we have a big favour to ask."

"If you need help, you know I'm always here for you." Ruth waited for confirmation of what she suspected was coming.

The couple exchanged glances. "We feel we should continue with our plan to move, even though we've got off to a rocky start."

"It's your decision," said Ruth. "At least you have one definite prospect and that's very positive."

"Whatever. Recent events have taken a bit of a toll on us, especially Suze, despite what she says. So, we thought we'd take a couple of days away and view two or three properties I found on the internet. They're in the Bournemouth area."

"And you'd like me to look after this one?" Ruth patted the dog's head.

"If it's not too short notice. We can take her and park her with Penny and the kids but we all know Sparkles isn't the best of travellers these days."

"You mustn't even think about it. It'll be a pleasure. When do you plan to set off?"

She watched his eyelids flicker with embarrassment. "I'd like to leave the day after tomorrow, by eight, if you're okay about it."

"No problem."

"If anyone wants to see the house, the agent has a key but I can tell them you'll be around as well. Just in case Sparkles takes a dislike to strangers coming in without us being here."

"Very wise. That would be all you needed. Imagine coming home and me having to give you awful news!" She paused. "I won't arrive until after you've left, though. I don't want to get in your way. Sparkles and I can take a nice walk and be back home by nine. Make sure you leave your answer phone on, in case the estate agent rings and I don't reach the phone in time."

"Oh, how stupid of me!" Suzanne sat up straight. "How is your poor knee, Ruth? I forgot to ask you."

"Gracious, I'm not surprised, with all you've had on your mind. It's not too bad, thank you but I'm afraid it's arthritis setting in."

"Join the club!" Eddie grimaced.

"It doesn't stop me going for walks but I can't kneel down properly these days. Nor move very quickly at all."

"Everyone's so used to seeing you striding along," said Suzanne. "Have you thought of trying Pilates? A lot of people swear by it. You could ring the leisure centre and see if there's a course."

"I can probably find out about sessions if I check online." She smiled at Suzanne. "You still don't feel comfortable using a computer, do you?"

"No, and I don't mind admitting it. As for your leg, are you quite certain you feel well enough to move in here for a few days?"

"Absolutely. It's only a stiff knee, after all. You mustn't worry about a thing."

"Well, we're very grateful. Help yourself to whatever food you want but don't feel obliged to stay all day if you've things to do at home. You still have Dylan to think about."

"I think that cat hardly misses me, as long as his food turns up on time. I'll definitely sleep here though, if that's all right. I wouldn't feel comfortable leaving Sparkles alone in the house. Dylan comes and goes like a ghost during the hours of darkness."

82

"Both guest rooms are ready so you can take your pick."

"It's like the Ritz up there," Eddie chimed in. "I daren't leave anything hanging around for fear it's thrown in the laundry basket. Wherever that may be lurking at the moment."

Ruth chuckled. "I'll use the room at the back and I'll take the bedding home with me to wash once you let me know which day you're returning." She held up her hand. "It's no use protesting, Suzanne. We must make sure you don't become exhausted, mustn't we?" She got up. "So that's settled. If I could just visit your bathroom before I set off?"

"Feel free, my dear."

"I'll be kind to my knee and use the downstairs cloakroom. If I take my rucksack with me, I can let myself out. You'll be wanting to get on with lunch."

"Why don't you stay and have a bite with us?"

"You're such a kind man, Eddie. But I'll get back and sort myself out, if you don't mind. Thank you for the sherry."

"Hey, what have you got in there, the kitchen sink?" Eddie laughed at his own weak joke as Ruth picked up the rucksack.

"I packed a first aid kit and a brandy miniature, in case I found Mr Sartin collapsed under a hedge." Ruth looped the rucksack over her shoulder and walked to the door. "I'll be in touch as soon as I've got the delightful farmer on the move. Don't forget to keep out of the way, you two."

"We won't. You might as well pick up the spare key from the drawer in the hall table now. Or shall I fetch it for you?"

"No!" said Ruth. At once she changed her expression to one of puzzlement. "Sorry, Eddie. I honestly didn't mean to sound so bossy. I'll pick it up on my way out. You sit there and enjoy your drink."

She was still within earshot when Eddie made a comment to his wife.

"The woman's bloody marvellous most of the time. It's a shame she's on her own. I bet she'd make a wonderful wife."

In the downstairs cloakroom, Ruth bolted the door behind her and dropped easily on all fours. The wonky knee excuse could well come in handy, given any alter ego she assumed during her campaign would show no signs of such a disability.

She opened her rucksack. Took out a small plastic box. Slipped on a pair of disposable gloves. Prised off the box lid and extracted a dead field mouse. How helpful of Susanne to have embellished even the smallest room in the house with elaborate fixtures, fittings and ornaments. Even better, the couple – or rather, Eddie – had made this snap decision to go house-hunting, leaving Ruth in charge for the next few days. Things looked promising. With the couple out of the way, when the atmosphere in here deteriorated, she would leave well alone. And reap the benefit when the stench was unleashed.

In one corner of the cloakroom stood a large conch shell, which Suzanne had brought back as a souvenir of Barbados or somewhere equally exotic. Ruth felt it should have been left in its natural surroundings, but for this purpose it would prove ideal. She slipped the tiny corpse inside the cavity; ramming the body deep down so not even the tip of its tail gave away the creature's existence. She replaced the shell in the corner, removed her gloves and stuffed them back in the plastic box before stuffing it back in her rucksack.

Ruth flushed the toilet, washed her hands, dried them on the cream-coloured hand towel and unbolted the door. She helped herself to the spare key, picked up her rucksack and crossed the hallway to the front door where she let herself out into the crisp, early autumn morning, with a feeling of intense satisfaction.

Chapter Eight

"I'm so looking forward to seeing Penny and the children. It seems ages since our last trip." Suzanne gazed through the windscreen as the car cruised smoothly.

"It was during Wimbledon fortnight, wasn't it?"

"It was. Declan hadn't long bought that monster television set for their tenth wedding anniversary."

"It was almost the size of Centre Court." Eddie chuckled. "And we toasted the happy couple and the British champion. Seriously though, the distance between Penny's house and ours is the main reason why I suggested selling up. Fair play, you don't go on about it, but I can tell how much you miss them all."

"It was different when she and Dec were moving round. But when I rang yesterday and Penny told me they intend staying in the Wiltshire area after he leaves the Army, I felt very relieved."

"I like the idea of Declan and a fellow medic planning to establish a practice together."

"Absolutely. Otherwise, we might be thinking of hanging on here a while longer until they settled for good and all."

"It also means, with us in the equation, Penny can make use of her Open University qualification. At the very least she'll be able to look after reception and admin while the guys get going. We can help out with childcare. Perfect."

"We haven't sold our house yet, Eddie. I'm still nervous about these incidents."

"Well, I'm sure they're all done with now. Life plays silly tricks sometimes. It's brilliant having Ruth to sort out Sartin and make sure he behaves himself but, frankly, I don't care if he sets up camp with fourteen vestal virgins as long as we're safely sold up and away."

"I know you're making fun but you can't really mean that? I'd hate to think of territorial disputes spoiling life for the new owners, whoever they may be. It's such a lovely house and it deserves owners who'll cherish it."

"You're such a softie! But you're right, of course. By the way, I forgot to tell you I didn't have a problem with Sartin when I was outside before I left for my meeting. You were on the phone to Penny. He seemed pretty vague about it all. Wouldn't meet my eye. I wonder if he really is losing his marbles."

"I meant to ask you what his explanation was but there's been so much on my mind."

"Tell me about it! It appears there was some muddle over the engineer turning up to look at the tractor. Our friendly farmer moved it on to the track and left the key in, ready for when the man arrived. Someone got the day wrong, either the agricultural engineer or Sartin himself."

"I still think it's a bit fishy. Mr Sartin must have known it wasn't functioning properly as soon as he started it up. Why didn't he leave it in his field, on his own ground?"

Eddie kept silent as another vehicle overtook them. "Technically he did leave it on his own ground but let's not worry about that now. If he's going a bit doolally, our move is perfectly timed."

"Poor man."

Eddie snorted. "Tell you what – it's great being on the way to England for a change. We've been stuck in a rut long enough and now, with a bit of luck, we're climbing out of it." He pointed ahead. "Look at that view. I'm glad I chose to drive through the Forest of Dean. Further down the road we'll find a decent pub and stop for an early lunch. We've plenty of time. So, let's forget Sartin and forget the village and concentrate on our future. I'm sure we've made the right decision."

"Wouldn't it be amazing if Ruth showed someone round while we were away and they fell in love with the place?"

"Suze, what will be will be. Maybe it'll be that Kirby bloke or maybe someone we haven't yet met. Who knows? Who cares as long as they come up with the readies? Once we were sure Ruth could keep an eye on the place, I made three appointments for this weekend. It'll be our turn to be the ones turning up to view."

"That was fast work. You didn't say."

"I wanted to surprise you. We'll set off tomorrow morning and see if we strike gold." He reached across and stroked her thigh. "A little rest on the bed wouldn't come amiss, once we get to our hotel room."

"Only if you're a very good boy."

He chuckled, letting his hand linger. "That's more like it. I knew the break would do you a power of good."

Noticing a warning sign for deer on the road, Eddie replaced his hand on the steering wheel and slowed the car. It had been a brilliant idea to whisk his wife away from The Sugar House and spark her interest in relocating. Everything seemed to be coming together now. Except for the faint but odd smell he'd noticed in the downstairs cloakroom last night.

He should at least have left the window slightly open. It would be embarrassing if their faithful house sitter found herself having to contend with a blocked drain. But she'd just have to ignore it and use the guest bathroom upstairs. Knowing her, she'd find something to spray around or light one of those perfumed candles. Nothing seemed to faze that woman. She could probably sell The Sugar House single-handed if she put her mind to it. Watch out Bethan Harley!

Ruth drove up the track and through the open gates, parking her old blue Nissan so it faced the driveway. It gave her a kick to use the space where Eddie left his BMW. She revelled in being mistress of the house and this time with even more reason to rejoice. Having assured Eddie she could hold the fort for as long as he wished, she wouldn't mind betting he took her up on the offer. A couple of nights might well stretch to four or more.

She took her suitcase and rucksack from the back seat and left the car unlocked. Inside the hallway she stood still and looked around. Sparkles must be shut in the utility room as usual. She'd leave her there while she sorted herself out before taking the dog for a walk as she promised Suzanne she would. There'd be no need to feign a troublesome arthritic knee once alone on the forest trail.

Ruth walked towards the downstairs cloakroom and paused outside the door. She sniffed and didn't detect a thing. Good. She'd leave sleeping rodents lie and check how things were later. With any luck, Eddie hadn't noticed anything amiss and she knew Suzanne rarely used the downstairs facilities, preferring to walk upstairs for that little extra bit of exercise to help her stay mobile as long as possible, a little foible of hers, but sensible of course.

Suddenly Ruth remembered the cleaning lady who came in once a week to give the place a thorough going over. She thought Monday was the usual day. Unless Suzanne had booked for an extra few hours, so intent was she on keeping the house a candidate for a glossy magazine centre spread. She'd surely have warned Ruth if the cleaner was booked to arrive during the Deacons' absence. It would be a pity to have a devious plan fall flat before she could capitalise on it.

"Ah…" She remembered the woman didn't have a key because one of the Deacons made sure always to be in on the cleaner's day. Eddie didn't trust too many people. It was a measure of his reliance upon Ruth that she was the only person left with the run of The Sugar House. As soon as the couple were home again, he'd have his hand out for that spare key, though – unless she took steps to rectify that situation.

She made her way upstairs and along the landing to the guest room where she planned to sleep. Swiftly she unpacked her case and laid her folded nightdress in the centre of the cream linen pillow. She preferred the décor in this room to that of the other. These walls were hung with pale apricot wallpaper, engraved with swirls. Cream paintwork harmonized with the rust and cream carpet. The room contained a television set and had a connecting door to the guest bathroom, with a bolt either side. Suzanne and Eddie hadn't stinted on décor and furnishings. They'd told her their hotel sold just at the right time, leaving them well able to buy a suitable house in a part of the country where prices were never going to soar as fast as they did in the London area or the more affluent of the shires.

She smiled at her reflection in the dressing table mirror, admitting to herself how much she didn't want to lose the various advantages that came her way. Correction. She'd no intention of waving goodbye to a lifestyle carved out with more than a little co-operation from Eddie and Suzanne Deacon. All her efforts were in their own interests. After all, they'd find childcare very restricting after years of pleasing themselves. And did they really possess the energy to cope with high-spirited grandchildren?

Suzanne could become quite tetchy sometimes. In fact, she'd been more than a little offhand with Ruth on the odd occasion. That would be down to tension. Possibly Eddie had talked his wife into agreeing to his plan and she didn't feel one hundred per cent happy about it and didn't dare speak up. Suzanne had confided in Ruth about her strict upbringing and how fortunate the couple were that she possessed the guile and strength of character to address this problem on their behalf.

How strange that by instigating the situations she already had, Ruth felt she'd jumped right back into the couple's good books. The sensation of control gave her a physical jolt. She opened the lid of the silver biscuit barrel on the dressing table to discover Suzanne had stocked it with her favourite shortbread. Tea making equipment stood ready. All she needed do was remember to bring a jug of milk upstairs.

On a whim, she left the room and tried turning the doorknob of the master bedroom. Sure enough, Eddie hadn't locked it though he must have gritted his teeth at the thought of his house sitter roaming where she wished. She walked over to the big dressing table in front of the window and opened the drawer where she knew Suzanne kept her less precious pieces of jewellery.

Ruth picked up a gemstone necklace, held the string of amethyst and turquoise chunks against her dark blue blouse and nodded with satisfaction. She deserved the pleasure of pretty trifles like this. Fastening the necklace around her neck, she admired her reflection in the mirror before crossing to the door accessing the small balcony. She turned the key and stepped outside; again enjoying the feeling of empowerment this action afforded her.

The distant hills formed a purple brown backdrop to a swathe of conifers so dark she longed to drape a string of glittering fairy lights over it. This frivolous thought failed to bring another smile to her face, since her solitary childhood hadn't included many festive moments. On becoming an orphan at age fourteen, she'd been brought up by the austere aunt who'd bequeathed Rock Cottage to her only niece. Until she reached school leaving age, she was a boarding-school pupil who couldn't wait to be allowed to make her own decisions.

Ruth's gaze switched to the nearby river, which, always in a hurry to join up with its big sister further down the valley, produced a comforting whooshing sound. She watched a red kite swoop then plummet into Phil Sartin's field before flying off again in the direction of the military ranges. A faint rattle of artillery peppered the breeze.

She turned back into the bedroom and closed the balcony door. She was downstairs and heading for the utility room when the phone rang. She hurried to pick up the kitchen extension.

"Ruth Morgan speaking."

"This is Bethan Harley, Mrs Morgan."

"It's Ms, actually. I thought your office didn't open until nine."

"I'm so sorry if I've disturbed you. The thing is, Ms Morgan, I have a couple with me who'd very much like to view The Sugar House. I know Mr and Mrs Deacon have gone away and I just wanted to advise you I'd like to bring these people over now."

"You mean immediately?"

"Well, yes. I'm at Llanbrenin Wells this morning so we'll take about forty minutes to get to you."

"It's extremely short notice," Ruth calculated how many more hours might be necessary before the dead field mouse reached maximum putrefaction point.

"Mr Deacon assured me any time would be all right but as his dog was in the house, it was best to check you were around in case Sparkles became uneasy with strangers walking in."

"Yes, of course. Look, may I call you back, Ms Harley?"

"It's Mrs. Actually." Bethan's tone was pleasant.

Ruth waited a few beats. Why not keep the bitch on the hook? All she cared about was her commission.

"You'll appreciate I have potential clients to think of," said Bethan. "We don't want to frighten them away, do we?"

Ruth's heart skipped a beat. Surely this irritating woman couldn't possibly suspect something? She gathered her wits.

"I'll have to check with the person I'm planning to visit and ring you back in a very few minutes. I have your number here."

"Excellent. Thank you, Ms Morgan."

Ruth put down the phone and crossed the kitchen to the hallway. Outside the door to the downstairs facilities she stooped and sniffed. A faint yet musty odour met her nostrils. She pushed on the handle to open the door a crack and almost gagged. Hastily she closed it again and returned to the kitchen, hardly able to contain her glee. She counted to fifty. Slowly. Picked up the receiver and punched in the number on the business card left by Eddie.

A cheerful receptionist answered. "Briggs, Caldwell and Balls. May I help you?"

"This is Ruth Morgan ringing from The Sugar House. Would you be kind enough to tell Mrs Harley I've been able to change my plans and that she may drive over with her clients whenever she wishes?"

Ruth replaced the receiver and debated whether to brew coffee or not, despite feeling disdain for so called house whisperers who recommended grinding coffee beans and creating tantalising aromas of newly baked cookies and such nonsense. Yet, the idea contained a certain irresistible irony, in view of what Ruth knew was about to happen. She moved across to the fancy machine and decided, given Eddie had never shown her how to unleash the monster, to leave well alone.

But might the brewing of coffee send a potent message regarding Ruth's good nature and desire to help her friends sell their house? She reached for the big cafetière. The Deacons favoured a particularly muscular type of coffee. Ruth took the *Fortnum and Mason*'s container from the fridge, shovelled beans into the grinder and blitzed them while she counted to the requisite number before tipping the dense powder into the cafetière. It was a little early to make this brew, but if her plan worked as she hoped, the trio of visitors was hardly likely to sit around making polite conversation.

Chapter Nine

Bethan Harley drove out of her parking space with Mr Salani in the passenger seat and his delightful wife seated in the rear. The pair chatted almost incessantly but she'd taken to them as soon as they pushed open the door at twenty minutes to nine, each of them looking as if they really wanted to get on with life. Now, Bethan listened as she joined the trickle of traffic driving through the town.

"We're on a touring holiday for a week, with no particular itinerary. We love the lack of rush and bustle you enjoy in these parts," said Mr Salani. "At home, it's nothing but roaring engines and emergency sirens blaring down the main street."

"You'll find total tranquillity once we get closer to Three Roads."

"That's what we're hoping," said his wife. "To discover a haven for this next stage of our lives now our children are all over the world."

"In case you're wondering, that actually means only three of them out there!" Mr Salani chuckled.

"I'm trying to explain to Bethan how we feel the time has come for us to do our own thing. Your art – my music."

"We're both doctors," said Mr Salani. "Consultants with retirement just around the corner."

"You obviously live busy lives," said Bethan.

"Yes, we've become disenchanted with commuting," said Mrs Sarani. "But if we can find the right property, when we both have a free weekend, we'll be able to escape to our safe haven until we finish work next year for good."

"I hope I can help make your dream come true," said Bethan. "The Sugar House is gorgeous. You'll love the way the village nestles in a little valley although it's high above sea level. There aren't many houses, but the nearest town, which we'll drive through on the way, is only five miles from Three Roads."

"We checked out your website last night and both of us liked the look of this property. It was a spur of the moment decision but sometimes these things are meant to be."

"I'm delighted you called at the office. These vendors are away, in fact, but they've asked a friend to house and dog sit. I hope you don't mind dogs? This one's a very placid old Labrador but I'm sure she can be put outside if you prefer."

"We have no problem with dogs. In fact, we might consider having one of our own later on when work isn't an issue."

"Provided there are decent kennels not too far away," his wife suggested.

"I know for a fact there are," said Bethan. "But the Deacons prefer to use this friend of theirs, because the animal is so used to her. She's also keeping an eye on the house of course. Not that there's a high crime rate in this area."

"Horse theft and turnip swiping maybe?"

"Perhaps once in a decade, Mr Sarani, if I'm pressed to answer that." Bethan glanced sideways at him. "You'll find Powys a very different county from Leicestershire. Three Roads has a character of its own which doesn't suit some people but from what you've told me, it offers everything you're looking for."

"We realise incomers sometimes find it difficult to be accepted."

"I'm pleased to say Mr and Mrs Deacon would tell you otherwise, Mr Sarani."

"That's good. We wondered about The Sugar House's name? We think it sounds rather intriguing."

"It's quite a quirky story." Bethan halted at the traffic lights on the edge of Knightly. "During the second world war, the owner of the house was operating a nice little business in black market goods. I don't know the whys and wherefores but sugar was obviously one of the main attractions. Goodness knows how this person got hold of an item in such short supply, but they must have had a contact and, according to the vendors, the locals christened the house and the name stuck."

"Fascinating," said Mrs Salani. "We both prefer to live in a house that comes with its own personality."

After Bethan rang the bell, Ruth deliberately took so much time to limp from the kitchen that the estate agent, clutching the spare key Eddie had provided, was left aiming it at the house sitter's throat when the door finally opened.

"Oh dear, I'm so sorry to keep you all waiting." Ruth made her voice drip honey as her gaze took in the elegant Asian couple. "I was just putting the dog outside in her play area and I daren't hurry, with my leg playing up as it is."

"Oh, poor you. But we must go and visit the dog, if that's all right?" Mrs Sarani held out her hand. "It's so kind of you to house sit for your friends."

"I couldn't stand by and let them put Sparkles into kennels." Ruth stood back to allow the visitors entry. At once her mouth dried. The third person in the party was unmistakeably the trouser-suited woman leaving the estate agency while Ruth stood outside with Brad and Valerie, the couple who'd treated her to tea in exchange for local information. Despite the fact that Ruth had adopted a disguise, she realised how shrewd she'd been to avoid locking gazes with the sales negotiator now once again close by.

She held her nerve. "Good Morning. I hope you enjoy looking around The Sugar House." She gestured towards the half-open door at the end of the hallway. "I'll be in the kitchen if you need to know anything. You're very welcome to a cup of coffee if you wish."

"Most kind," murmured Mr Sarani, extending his hand to shake hers. "I'm afraid I've already exceeded my caffeine allowance this morning. The Queensbridge serves such a particularly excellent breakfast; I'm looking forward to tonight's dinner menu already. But how about you two ladies?"

His wife shook her head.

"Many thanks, Ms Morgan," said Bethan. "The coffee smells delicious but I think we'll start with the ground floor, make our way upstairs then explore the garden."

"As you wish. I'll leave you to it." Ruth stepped away.

"The conservatory leads off the drawing room," said Bethan, leading her clients from the hallway. "It faces south and the view of the garden is stunning. Mrs Deacon has taken care to plant the right kind of shrubs for the local soil and weather conditions."

"Should we be concerned about those conditions?"

"Not at all, Mr Salani. There can be early frosts in these parts so what I meant was, there's nothing planted in the garden that can't cope with the elements. Mr Deacon told me his wife's rhododendron hedge attracts photographers and artists when it's in full bloom."

"There you are my love, an opportunity to offer cream teas on the front lawn."

Ruth heard the sales patter as she sat at the kitchen table, leafing through one of Suzanne's many glossy-jacketed cookery books. She listened for every movement as the sales negotiator took the couple through the rooms. Heard the murmur of voices and the laugh out loud moment following what had to be some stupid quip of the Harley woman.

When Bethan led the couple into the kitchen, she found Ruth on her feet, smiling a welcome. "I'm so jealous of Mr and Mrs Deacon's domestic domain. I make vast quantities of chutney and jam when my soft fruit's in season and I'd kill for all this workspace."

"How talented you are." Mrs Sarani turned to her husband. "You see, Jalil? If we buy this house, we can be customers of Ms Morgan... if she will allow us."

"It would be my pleasure." Ruth sat down again. "There's a walk-in pantry next door to the utility room. Another thing I admire."

"Yes. Thank you," said Bethan. She turned to the couple. "Do feel free to open doors."

"I don't like peering into people's cupboards. I can tell everything's pristine but I will take a look at the utility room, if I may."

"Take all the time you need, Mrs Sarani."

Mr Sarani beamed and followed his wife.

Bethan stood in silence.

"I do apologise, Mrs Harley," said Ruth. "In my haste to tidy my bedroom and get the coffee on, I forgot to check the downstairs cloakroom. Should I slip across now and check there's a clean towel and so on?"

"Please don't concern yourself, Ms Morgan. From what I've seen, Mrs Deacon will have thought of everything. I can't remember ever before arriving to carry out a valuation and finding a house so spotless and so beautifully appointed."

Ruth beamed. "What a wonderful thing to say. I shall make a point of telling Suzanne when we speak later. I've promised to ring each evening and tell her how Sparkles and I are doing."

This didn't feel right. Bethan shook her head. "Ms Morgan, I think I should warn you Mr Deacon has asked me not to give any feedback about the house until he and his wife return. He's concerned that she shouldn't be bothered with what's happening back here. In my experience, sometimes prospective purchasers enthuse about a property when they're viewing it, but contrary to the vendors' hopes, turn around afterwards and find a reason not to make an offer."

Ruth sighed. "I think, as her friend, I'm the best judge of what Mrs Deacon may or may not wish to hear."

"Fine. I'll wait in the hallway." Bethan turned on her heel and stepped out of the kitchen.

How she wished she could dispose of Ruth Morgan as easily as Ms Morgan had dealt with that dear old dog who'd been absolutely fine on first acquaintance and endeared herself by escorting Bethan back to her car and resting her sleek head on her knee, anticipating a pat, when Bethan sat in the driving seat.

But this awful woman who called herself the Deacons' friend, came over as a cold, controlling piece of work. Worst of all was the way she acted as though she owned the house. Her expression had turned positively hostile when she lectured Bethan. What was her problem? She shouldn't let the woman get to her, yet... Inwardly seething, Bethan puffed air through her lips and did her best to think charitable thoughts.

Mrs Sarani reappeared, her husband in her wake. "Sorry to hold you up. We were peering through the window at the dog."

"Sparkles is a sweetie and you can meet her shortly. Shall we take a look at the downstairs cloakroom before going upstairs?"

Bethan crossed the hallway, ready to grasp the cloakroom door handle. She pulled open the door only to recoil, gasping, as the sickening stench of decay hit her nostrils. She slammed the door shut again and whirled around, horrified.

"What is it?" Mr Sarani stepped forward.

Bethan swallowed hard, having to call up every ounce of her professionalism, in an effort not to gag. "I don't know, sir, but whatever it is, I'm sure it can be dealt with. Why don't you and your wife go on upstairs and I'll ask the house sitter to investigate. It might be the cloakroom window's open and the farmer's been spreading slurry in the field or something like that."

Mr Sarani laughed. "The joys of country living! Yes, I caught a whiff but such pungent smells are far preferable to exhaust fumes, believe me. I'm sure the cloakroom facilities are absolutely fine. Like everything else we've seen so far."

The moment Bethan walked back inside the kitchen, she knew Ruth was up to something. She looked for some physical indication of mischief-making but the woman's face appeared expressionless. Too much so. She'd poured herself a coffee and sat facing the door.

"Is everything all right?" She looked expectantly at Bethan.

"I'm afraid it's everything but all right. You mentioned not having checked the cloakroom. It seems odd I should open the door to be met by such a disgusting smell."

"I have no idea what you're talking about." Ruth remained seated. She frowned. "As I've already told you, I didn't even open the cloakroom door when I arrived earlier."

"I heard exactly what you said." Bethan locked gazes with Ruth. "And I can't imagine how you can remain so calm, when that lovely couple are upstairs looking around, and will come down wondering why they're not being shown the facilities. I doubt they'll bother viewing the garden once they're knocked off their feet by that unbelievable stench! Once you've experienced it, I think you'll agree."

Bethan watched the other woman raise her left hand. Watched her long fingers travel to the base of her neck. She heard the nervous sound of Ruth Morgan clearing her throat. At once something stirred in her memory. She still retained a vague picture of Brad and Valerie Childs in her mind's eye. She remembered giving the couple a swift glance that morning she'd flown out the agency door to fetch the mobile phone left in her car. They'd returned her cheerful greeting. But there'd been a third person standing there. A woman who turned away, averting her gaze, when Bethan tried to include her in the greeting.

A while after her return, the same couple called at the agency and Bethan had immediately recognised Mrs Childs's fuchsia pink jacket and heavy turquoise eye shadow. The pair of them had trotted out that creepy tale of the murderer's burial as an excuse for not wanting to view The Sugar House.

But, this woman before her now, surely couldn't be the same woman who'd stood beside the couple looking in the agency's window the other morning. That one's hair was longer, a different colour, and styled differently from Ms Morgan's. The other woman's clothing spoke of casual yet chic boutiques, in sharp contrast to the house sitter's practical attire. Yet, Bethan couldn't get that gesture and – something else – yes, that nervous tic out of her mind. How odd was this?

"I expect you're exaggerating," said Ruth. "But I suppose that's what people like you do for a living."

Bethan didn't bite back. "Would you please go and see what I mean? Humour me. See if I'm exaggerating or not while I go upstairs. We need to come up with a plausible explanation for that revolting smell."

She left Ruth taking her time about getting up from her chair. The woman must be playing some sort of game. There was something about the way Ms Morgan conducted herself that fired red exclamation marks. Maybe it would be safer to hold off further viewings until the Deacons returned and Ms Morgan was safely off the premises. Yet how the heck could she explain her misgivings to the vendors when it was their trusted friend under suspicion?

She sprinted upstairs, banishing all such thoughts, telling herself she had two potential buyers to think about. "How are you doing?"

"We're doing fine," called Mrs Sarani from the master bedroom. "I love this balcony, overlooking the forest. You can get two chairs and a little table on here. I could sit reading and gazing at the trees, with Jalil beside me, dreaming over his sketchpad."

"Yes, it's a beautiful feature. You'll have a grandstand view of red kites and buzzards if you're interested." Bethan hesitated. "I may as well be frank with you both. That dreadful smell in the downstairs cloakroom definitely isn't coming from outside and I can't for the life of me think why the Deacons would go away without warning me about it."

"Didn't they mention it to the house sitter?"

"Apparently not. I've asked Ms Morgan to check it out but I'm not sure what she can do without calling in a drains expert."

Mr Sarani raised his eyebrows. "I'm accustomed to smells. Would you like me to investigate?"

"I don't want you to be put off the house."

"That's not going to happen," said Mrs Sarani. "As long as there's some logical explanation, which I imagine there must be, we won't allow it to influence our decision."

"Thank you." Bethan was touched by Mrs Sarani's calming bedside manner. "But be warned," she said. "It's stomach-turning, even for a medic."

Ruth called to them from the hallway as the three descended. "It's highly unpleasant. I can't understand how my friends haven't said anything. I fear it must be something to do with the plumbing."

"Mr Sarani has kindly volunteered to take a look."

"If it's something deep-seated, needing a tradesman's attention, surely it's not worth him bothering?"

Bethan clenched her fists behind her back. "Let's allow him to be the judge of that, shall we?"

"Of course. I didn't mean to seem ungrateful." Ruth composed her features to show concern.

Mr Sarani walked across and flung open the door to the downstairs cloakroom.

"Ah," he said, disappearing inside. "It smells very much as though something's died in here."

"Ugh, that's nasty," said Bethan, unable to resist shooting Ruth a triumphant look. "Can you see anything?" She stopped herself from blurting out anything connected with a possible infestation.

"I'm sure Mr and Mrs Deacon would have warned me about anything I needed to investigate." Ruth hovered behind the two women.

Mrs Sarani turned away. "It could be that everything was fine when they went away. Why don't I open the front door?" She glided across the hallway.

Her husband, now on all fours in the cloakroom, whooped with triumph. "Here's our culprit." He got to his feet and lifted the opalescent conch shell from the corner. "One decomposing field mouse in situ."

"What an odd thing to happen," said Mrs Sarani.

Ruth spread her hands in a gesture of disbelief. "It must have come into the house some time when the front door was open. Or, maybe the dog brought it? Yes, that's quite likely, don't you think?"

"I'd opt for your first suggestion, considering how well-concealed this poor little chap was." Still holding the conch, Mr Sarani walked towards the front door. "I'll deposit the victim on the track and let Mother Nature do the rest."

Bethan turned to Ruth. "Well, isn't that a relief, Ms Morgan? I'm sure you'll find a way of eliminating the smell once we've gone."

Ruth nodded. "Of course. I'll go and see what I can find in the utility room."

"Most importantly, some disinfectant please, for Mr Sarani." She turned to Mrs Sarani. "Your husband might like to wash his hands in the utility room before we make a tour of the garden."

Bethan had now made three visits to The Sugar House. On each occasion, the door to the smallest room, plus its window, had been shut. How very unfortunate that both front door and cloakroom door must have been open at the same time in order to allow the dog to carry the field mouse to its last resting place.

Dr Sarani obviously thought the small rodent must have wriggled inside the conch shell rather than have been placed there by the dog. Or, should someone other than poor old Sparkles or the field mouse be the one to shoulder the blame?

Chapter Ten

"I'll ensure I call personally when Mr and Mrs Deacon return. I know how devastated they'll be to hear about this." Bethan drove up the slope leading back to the main road.

"Whatever you think best," said Mr Sarani, who'd opted for the rear seat this time.

"We certainly won't let a dead rodent cloud our judgement," said his wife.

"No. Both of us like the house though I think we need to view two or three more, before making a decision. I can't help thinking the possibility of being marooned once winter sets in is rather an important factor."

"None of us can escape extreme weather conditions, Jalil."

"No, of course not. What do you think, Bethan?" Mr Sarani leaned forward. "Make believe you don't have your estate agent's hat in place, why don't you?"

She chuckled, wishing more house viewers were as amiable as these two. "I won't try to pretend Three Roads doesn't become cut off for an odd day or two during hard winters. But the local farmers as well as the forestry workers soon sort things out, even if the council can't get there too quickly."

"In the scheme of things, not a problem, I'd say. We wouldn't be trying to get to work." Mrs Sarani turned to look at her husband but he kept silent.

"So, did you notice anything else on our books that appeals? I can think of one or two possible properties."

"We may as well see what you can come up with," said Mrs Sarani. "Preferably one without a rodent sarcophagus in its downstairs facilities."

"I doubt we'd find a repetition of this morning's fun and games," said her husband. "As for winter in the village, I can well imagine the peace and beauty but I can't disregard the annoyance of having three ways out and every one of them uphill."

"It's poor Mrs Deacon I feel sorry for." Bethan negotiated a stretch of zigzag bends, willing Mr Sarani to stop dwelling on something no estate agent could control. "She'll be mortified when she hears what's happened."

"Well, our feedback won't include the field mouse," said Mr Sarani. "If the vendors had been at home, they'd have noticed something was wrong before the creature decayed any further."

"At least they have their friend staying. She's sure to put matters right before anyone else happens along."

"Yes, indeed, Mrs Sarani, and thank you again for being so understanding." Bethan's lips set in a tight line as she accelerated on the straight road into Knightly. She could feel this potential sale slipping away.

Bethan let herself into what she privately regarded as her jewel of a house, dumped her briefcase on the carpet and kicked off her high heels with a sense of relief.

"Poppy? I'm home."

"In the kitchen, Mum."

Bethan padded across the hall carpet and through the wide-open door. "Good day?"

Her daughter shook back a waterfall of chestnut hair. "Not bad. It's cool, being in the sixth form. And it's great having Miss Price for French."

"Doing four A levels will be a challenge, but you already know that."

"Watch my lips. I. Can. Handle. It."

Bethan opened the fridge and took out a bottle of wine. "I know you can, sweetie. I can't help going into mother hen mode now and then."

"Especially without Dad around."

Bethan watched her daughter eye her as though she was the disobedient child and Poppy the watchful parent. "I had a difficult day," she said defensively. "I need to sit quietly and chill, as you'd doubtless say."

"Poor Mum, you're forgiven. I turned the slow cooker up, by the way. The chicken thing smells yummy."

"Thank you. And you're a star." Bethan took a swallow of Chenin Blanc. "Mmm, that's very welcome." She pulled out a stool and joined her daughter at the breakfast bar.

"Want to talk about it? I bet you'd bend Dad's ear if he was here." Poppy picked up her glass of orange juice and sipped.

"Yeah, too true. We may be estranged but we're still on amicable terms."

"Is that because of me?"

Bethan blinked hard. "You know how much we both love you, Poppy. You also know your father and I tend to clash when he comes back. Maybe we need a bigger house. I don't know."

She knew she sounded defensive. And Poppy didn't take prisoners.

"You're the estate agent. Find us a bigger house if that means you and Dad can hack it under the same roof!"

"If only it were that easy. Anyway, I don't intend on sharing my work problems while your father's far away on an oil rig."

"I bet he wouldn't mind if you did."

"Probably not."

"So, Skype him."

"I'm sure he's got enough on his plate already. I can sort this. I have to sort it."

"Sounds heavy."

Bethan gave her daughter a quick hug. "Actually, if you don't mind, I would like to run something past you, Poppy. Of course, it might just be me being paranoid."

"So, what's new, Mum?" Poppy twirled a long strand of hair around one finger.

Bethan ignored the jibe and began from the beginning.

Poppy listened without interrupting until her mother finished her story.

"So, what do you make of it, lovey? Am I being paranoid, do you think?"

"Dunno. She does sound pretty creepy, this Morgan person."

"She is, though you wouldn't think so from the way she looks."

"How old is she?"

Bethan turned her wine glass slowly around on the breakfast counter top. "Difficult to say. Probably knocking on fifty but she's very elegant in an ageing model girl kind of way."

"Like Twiggy?"

"I'm impressed you've even heard of Twiggy. Yes, a little younger but nowhere near as lovely. The awful thing is, today I could've sworn Ruth Morgan was wearing a necklace I saw on Mrs Deacon the day I carried out the valuation."

"You're joking! Are you sure you're not mistaken?"

"Positive. I told Mrs Deacon how much I admired the gorgeous combination of gemstones. I hate to say it, but somehow I can't help having bad vibes about this woman."

"Maybe Mrs Deacon gave her the jewellery as a gift for looking after her house?"

Bethan shrugged. "Maybe. But my hunch about the house sitter makes me question some of her actions. Why would she dress so differently and put on a wig unless she was up to something?"

"That's like, too bizarre for words, Mum."

"Well, I think so. And the other thing niggling me is, when I left our office the day Brad and Valerie Childs were in the town, I caught a drift of expensive perfume from either Valerie or the other woman – the woman who

113

wouldn't catch my eye when I called Good Morning on my way to the car park."

"So?"

"I adore scent, don't I? Always notice it on other people. But the woman who came in to see us told me she and her husband had just been to a teashop with a nice lady who offered to tell them about Three Roads. Valerie was wearing such a very different scent from the one I noticed earlier. I'd have recognised that other, much more subtle and probably expensive fragrance, which tells me the unnamed woman was the one using it."

"You're not making sense, Mum. Unless you could smell that same subtle scent on the house sitting person."

"My point is, Poppy, Ruth Morgan's more carbolic than Chanel in her choice of perfume. I told you it was just a minor niggle."

Poppy took a gulp of her drink. "If, and it's a big If, your suspicions are right, why shouldn't this Ruth person use scent as part of her disguise?"

Her mother stared at her. "Clever…"

"But what you're saying is this Ruth person's trustworthy enough to be invited to house sit but you're afraid she's doing weird shit – weird *stuff* – so The Sugar House won't sell and she can keep things as they are?"

"Something along those lines."

"I can't understand why she'd do such a thing. It's so not her business."

"I believe Ruth Morgan thinks it's very much her business and it's probably all about feeling needed. It appears she befriended Mr and Mrs Deacon soon after they moved in. She gave them some homemade produce and provided contact numbers of reliable tradesmen. Did all the kind of stuff that's so useful for anyone moving into a new area."

"So, couldn't she do the same for the new owners, whoever they may be? Those two doctors sound great. The Morgan person would soon make friends with them, surely?"

"Mr and Mrs Sarani are charming. And by the way, he's drop dead gorgeous. Reminds me of Omar Shariff." She paused. "Except you don't have a clue who I mean. Your gran would, though."

"Enough, Mum."

"Okay. I'd love them to buy The Sugar House and not just for the commission. But there has to be something bugging that house sitter. Something important enough to make her determined to keep the Deacons from moving out of Three Roads."

"You seriously think she'd do stuff like dress up and spread rumours to put people off buying the place?

"Not only put them off buying, Poppy. Put them off even viewing it. I have never, ever before, experienced a situation like this one. Too many odd happenings are hindering proceedings."

"I'd hate to live out there in any case. Being snowed in and missing school's one thing but having no public transport is totally pants."

"There is a train station only a few miles away."

"I rest my case." Poppy's smile was triumphant. "Anyway, Mum, I think you must be mistaken about the woman you noticed outside the office. It sounds too much like one of those rubbish TV detective things you like watching."

"I wish I could agree but the more I think about the mystery woman, the more I can see the shape of Ruth Morgan."

"Maybe she has a sister?"

Bethan frowned. "Good point, but remember, taking note of people's body language is an important part of my job. I can still hear that same throat clearing noise, like a nervous scrape. I can clearly picture those long fingers stroking her throat."

Poppy shuddered. "So, when are the Deacons due back?"

"Not for a few days. My only hope is that I can delay any further inquiries until then. No way do I want any more prospective purchasers being hassled by Ruthless Ruth."

"Nice one." Poppy sat up straight and stopped playing with her hair. "Guess what."

"Um, judging by your expression, you can't wait to tell me."

"It's something very important. Callum's asked me out."

"Callum as in he whom you've had a crush on for, like forever?"

"Very droll, Mother. He told me he's been trying to get rid of his girlfriend and now it's happened. Sweet!"

116

Bethan twiddled the stem of her half-empty wine glass round and round in her fingers. "Don't you feel a little bit sorry for this poor girl?"

"Nooooo! She's done him a favour. Found someone else and dumped him. Cow."

Bethan winced. "Where exactly does Callum want to take you?"

"Cardiff. He's got tickets for a concert in the Millennium Stadium. I so have to go, Mum!"

"Well, there's a surprise. How will you get there?"

"Chill, Mum. Callum's folks are driving us. They'll go and get dinner and walk around and whatever while we're watching *Faithless*."

"*Faithless*?"

"Not relevant, Mum."

"OK." Bethan drained her glass and slid off her stool. "One of those groups is the same as the others and, before you say it, yes, I'm showing my age, lovey. As long as Callum's parents are doing the driving, I'm happy for you to go. I'll ring to thank them later. Now I need to get changed before I dish up."

She pretended not to notice her daughter's extreme eye rolling skills.

Before closing the front door and dropping the safety chain into place, Ruth watched Bethan Harley's sleek silver car disappear down the track to reappear as it climbed the slope then vanished around the bend. She wasn't sure how well her plan had gone. The two doctors hadn't seemed all that fazed by the dead field mouse and now she was left to deal with the sickening stink. She daren't ignore the problem, in case the irritating sales negotiator brought more people to view and kicked up about it. Mrs Up Her Own Arse Harley would be sure to ring Ruth and check if the cloakroom was returned to its former pristine state.

Ruth sighed. Maybe it was time for a change of tactics. This last couple had mentioned wanting to view other properties but she didn't think they suspected anything odd about the incident. They'd made all the right noises and might well come back for another viewing. Unless...

She took her mobile phone from her pocket and walked through to the kitchen where she knew the satellite signal was strongest. She kept the call brief. By asking an old friend to join her for an early evening drink, she could turn up at the Queensbridge Hotel as if it was the most natural thing in the world. There wasn't too much choice when it came to good places to eat in the area and, if Mr and Mrs Sarani had been out and about, viewing properties, she wouldn't mind betting they'd choose a relaxing evening without needing to step from their hotel. Hadn't the husband mentioned anticipating sampling the dinner menu?

Chapter Eleven

Ruth drove into the car park behind the stately stone building and found a parking space without trouble. The clock on the dashboard showed her it was five minutes to six. She cut the engine. Huw Blayney was a widower whom she met years ago in her tennis playing days when they'd partnered one another in mixed doubles. Their friendship had remained platonic and therefore amicable. They hadn't seen one another for some months and Huw had sounded delighted when she rang to ask if he was free that evening. In fact, he'd offered to buy her dinner.

She couldn't believe her luck. She needed to be perceived as a friendly, outgoing woman who thought the world of her friends, Suzanne and Eddie, wanting only the best for them. She considered it vital to allay any suspicions of devious practices while, at the same time, endeavouring to get the Sarani couple on her side.

Ruth had showered and washed her hair, using the upmarket products Suzanne provided in the guest bathroom. Every bottle and jar proclaimed its contents as satiny or sumptuous, creamy or velvety, though Ruth wondered whether the experience really did differ from her usual shower procedure using the slightly antiseptic-smelling soap, a brand she'd favoured for years.

She hesitated when choosing what to wear. She could change when she called at her own place to feed Dylan. Or, she could borrow a slinky jersey frock in silver-grey she'd already tried on when Suzanne first brought it back from one of her shopping fests. Ruth had condemned the garment as a little too clingy for a woman of Suzanne's age but knew better than to comment.

"It's amazing how well it fits you," her friend had exclaimed after urging Ruth to try it on. "Considering I'm several inches shorter than you. I guess my extra rolls of fat must be the reason why we can both wear it."

We can both wear it. The words rang in Ruth's head. Suzanne had meant the comment as an invitation. And her friend must have known the string of turquoises and amethysts would look stunning on the pale skin exposed by the scoop neckline of the simple yet stylish dress. Her reflection in the full-length wardrobe mirror in Suzanne's bedroom confirmed how right she'd been.

Ruth locked her car and walked to the hotel's rear entrance and down the long, carpeted corridor leading to the foyer, ignoring the many framed photographs and watercolour paintings showing glorious local landscapes. Huw, a grey-haired, slightly crumpled man of around sixty, was waiting for her outside the entrance to the bar. He spotted her and beamed.

"How lovely to see you, Ruth." They exchanged hugs. "I thought I'd turn up a bit early and save you walking in on your own."

"Always so thoughtful, Huw. Am I allowed to buy you a drink?"

"I wouldn't hear of it. I'm very pleased you got in touch, my dear. I don't see you often enough."

"Ah, well there's a reason for that."

"Let me order some drinks and you can tell me all about it. Is white wine still your tipple?"

"A spritzer, please. I have to drive home, remember."

"You're welcome to stay the night at my place. Spare room's always made up, you know."

"That's very sweet of you, Huw, but I have animals to care for and I really can't stay away from The Sugar House. I'd be betraying a trust."

"Why don't you sit down? You look as if you could do with a bit of relaxation."

He moved towards the bar and Ruth took a look around and saw only two middle-aged couples plus a sprinkling of businessmen peering at tablets or tapping at laptop keyboards. She deliberately chose a table by the wall, allowing a view of the whole room. If Mr and Mrs Sarani were, as the husband had indicated, dining at their hotel, there was only one entrance into the restaurant and that was through the lounge bar.

"The barman will bring our drinks over." Huw took the seat opposite her. "Now what's all this about?"

Ruth launched into an account of how, over the last few months, her days had become spent at her friends' beck and call. She spoke of driving Suzanne Deacon to hair appointments and helping her with shopping excursions. She said even Eddie wasn't particularly computer literate, so she often helped them research the occasional short trips they took, to stay in luxury hotels in Europe. She explained how their daughter lived miles away and in any case was the mother of two young children with a husband currently deployed overseas. Of course, the family rarely came to stay with Suzanne and Eddie and none of their erstwhile friends from Sussex ever took the trouble to visit. What else could Ruth do but offer her services?

Huw shook his head in wonderment. "I didn't realise how much your friends relied on you. You've never complained to me before. I can't help thinking they're amazingly lucky to have you close at hand," he said.

Ruth waited while their drinks arrived.

"I'm pleased to help. It's not as if I don't love their house and their gentle old dog."

Huw raised his glass and waited for Ruth to chink hers against his. "Let's drink a toast to the future."

"Oh, Huw, I wish I could join in on that one but I'm desperately worried about the years to come. Suzanne and Eddie's as well as mine."

"I can see you're upset. On a lighter note, you do scrub up well, my dear. You look extremely elegant tonight – makes me wish I'd got my hair cut when I was last in town!"

"You're fine, Huw. I wanted to make an effort, having not seen you for ages." She paused. "I'm sorry about this. Can't help feeling I'm not much of a jolly dinner companion, am I?"

"Don't be silly. What are friends for?"

"You're a sweetie."

He cleared his throat. "So, how long are Suzanne and Eddie away for?"

"A few nights. Apparently, it's open-ended."

Huw frowned. "That doesn't seem very fair, given you have your own life to lead. Though I guess you can spend time at your cottage during the day?"

"I'm afraid there's more to tell yet. The Sugar House went on the market recently. I knew nothing about it until Suzanne rang to invite me round, saying what they had to tell me would come as a big surprise." Ruth gulped. "It was more of a bombshell, to be honest!"

"They didn't talk it through with you then?"

Ruth shook her head. "But it's pointless holding a grudge. I offered to house sit for them, which of course means I have to be very much around, in case someone wants to view it. I'm on call during office hours. Understandably, Eddie was worried in case the dog became agitated when strangers arrived. The agents have a key of course but with me there, Sparkles is fine. It's a good job my cat is such a loner."

Huw whistled. "It sounds as though your friends trespass far too much on your good nature. I hope you don't mind my saying this, but wouldn't it be a blessing if they upped and went? Left you to live your life as you wish?" He reached out and patted her arm. "I might see more of you then. I'd like that very much."

"I'd forgotten how you cheer me up, Huw. And I don't mean to make the Deacons seem nasty people."

"You see the best in everyone, my dear. Though, that time you took me along to their drinks party, they seemed very friendly. Well, on the surface anyway."

"Huw, over the years, the three of us have got on very well. So well, that a few years back, Suzanne made it clear that with me being so much younger than the two of them, it'd be a sensible idea for me to sell my cottage some time in the future and move into The Sugar House as their companion housekeeper."

"Are you saying they'd want you to sell up and go and live with them in this new house, wherever it may be? Wouldn't that be a terrible wrench? I remember how thrilled you were when your aunt left her cottage to you. That was just before I first met you, wasn't it?"

"That's right, but it's not going to happen. My moving in with them, I mean. They've reneged on our agreement, if you can describe it as such." Ruth kept her tone flat. She gave a half sob and sipped a little of her drink.

"I don't like the sound of all this, my dear."

"To be brutally honest, financially it'd be a good proposition for me. But this isn't all about money. As regards the important things – as in friendship and companionship – I'm sad to say Suzanne fudged around the issue when I had the temerity to remind her."

"That's appalling. Even if you decided not to take up the offer, they should have informed you of their decision to move, instead of leaving you to find out in such a crass manner." He leaned over and patted her hand. "Dear girl, you do have a predicament, don't you? What next? I still can't help feeling you'd be well rid of this pair."

"You're thinking in practical terms, Huw. I can't help my emotions."

"I know you can't." He smiled at her. "Don't I always see the practical side? I'm also thinking of your welfare. You know I'm fond of you. Call me selfish, but I hope you'll never leave the area."

She reached across and patted his hand. "You're such a comfort. I should have confided in you sooner."

"Yes, you're naughty to have gone on bottling all this up. Why don't you tell me what you'd really like to happen?"

"I'm hoping they'll see sense and take the house off the market. It's no good pulling a face. I'm very fond of Suzanne and it's quite plain that, well, to put it mildly, her health isn't robust at the best of times. How on earth Eddie can contemplate letting her go ahead and offer her services as a child minder after they move, is beyond me. He can be extremely pigheaded sometimes."

"It certainly sounds as thought he hasn't thought things through properly."

Ruth didn't respond. Instead, she drew her escort's attention to a smartly dressed man and woman approaching the bar. "My goodness. That couple who just came in are the people I met this morning when the estate agent brought them to the house."

Huw craned his neck. "They make an attractive pair. And look at those colours in her sari." He turned back to Ruth. "So, did they seem interested?"

"Very. In spite of a rather unfortunate incident."

Ruth related the field mouse saga, skilfully turning it into something that might have happened in a TV sitcom. She watched Huw's jaw tighten when she told him how Bethan Harley had been quick to allocate blame on the house sitter. Out of the corner of her eye she saw Mr and Mrs Sarani turn away from the bar and walk in their direction.

Ruth waved as they approached. "Hello there. I didn't think our paths would cross again so soon. Are you meeting someone, or would you care to join us?"

Mr Sarani hesitated. Huw scrambled to his feet and held out his hand. Ruth handled the introductions.

Mrs Sarani spoke swiftly. "We'd love to join you, if you're sure we're not intruding."

"Not at all." Huw pulled out a chair.

"We're going in to dinner at seven." Mr Sarani took the seat next to Ruth. "But yes, this is very civil of you. It's quite a coincidence, seeing you again like this, don't you think?"

Ruth had already decided that, if asked, she'd deny any prior knowledge of where the Saranis were staying. After all, she'd had plenty on her mind at the time it cropped up in conversation. She chose her words with care. "Around these parts, I'm afraid there isn't the same choice of eating places as you're accustomed to. This is definitely the best hotel for

126

miles. Otherwise, it's a choice of fish and chips, a curry or a Chinese meal, though all very nice, I hasten to add."

"Don't forget the local Kebab house," said Huw. "Ruth's spot on, of course. Like-minded folk in this area often bump into one another at the same places when they want a night out. You either embrace it or it drives you crackers."

"Your drinks are coming," said Ruth. "Huw, don't try and put Mr and Mrs Sarani off the area. That'd never do, especially after the less than fragrant incident this morning."

"Ruth's told me about that," said Huw. "She'd no idea what was lurking inside the conch shell. She's afraid you might both have been put off any thoughts of making an offer."

"You couldn't possibly put us off this beautiful part of Wales." Mrs Sarani locked gazes with Ruth. "Who knows, we might yet end up being near neighbours."

Ruth cleared her throat. Stroked her fingers from beneath her chin to where the gemstones gleamed above the pearly sheen of Suzanne's frock. "Oh dear. I really don't know which way to turn. I've just been telling Huw what a difficult position I'm in. I'd so much like to confide in you but I don't want to seem disloyal."

Huw turned to Mr Sarani. "In my humble opinion, Ruth isn't exaggerating and frankly I hate to see her so worried. She's extremely conscientious over her house sitting duties and very torn over her responsibilities as a close friend of the Deacons. I apologise if I'm putting my Number Elevens right in it, Mrs Sarani, but if you're seriously interested in

The Sugar House, maybe you should allow my friend here to give you some back story."

Ruth watched Mr Sarani's eyes narrow. He'd opened his mouth to speak when his wife leaned forward.

"I take it we're not talking structural problems. Tell me, are you concerned about us not fitting into the neighbourhood?"

"Absolutely not," said Ruth, allowing her gaze to focus upon the other woman's sari, a silken swirl of blues and greens, shot with gold. "As in any small community, there's the odd person living in Three Roads who doesn't hold with incomers, as they're known. Strictly speaking, I'm an incomer; the Deacons even more so, of course. But there are probably more of us there now, than there are people born in the area."

"So..." Mr Sarani splashed more tonic water into his glass.

Ruth had practised her agonised expression earlier. "I feel more justified in saying something, simply because you're both doctors."

"Really? Despite not knowing our specialities?"

Ruth noted Mr Sarani's gaze wasn't as friendly as his wife's. She felt a swift flash of satisfaction as the other woman placed her hand upon her husband's sleeve.

"Please, Jalil. Let Ruth say what she needs to say. She's hardly going to jeopardise her good friends' house sale, now is she?"

"Thank you, Mrs Sarani." Ruth allowed herself a rueful smile.

"Please call me Zoyah." Mrs Sarani smiled back at her.

"What a beautiful name. As Huw says, I find this situation extremely difficult, Zoyah. My friendship with the Deacons goes back to when they first moved to Three Roads. It's because we have become so close over the years, that I feel I should speak my mind. You two are the ideal purchasers for The Sugar House and I know we could become friends, if you were to move in."

Ruth didn't miss the way Mr Sarani's body language contrasted with his wife's.

"I'm sorry," she said. "But to be blunt, you should know that Suzanne is what you might call highly-strung."

"I've no idea. As you know, we haven't met the vendors," said Zoyah.

"I realise that. Frankly, I find it worrying how Suzanne couldn't wait to get away for this short break. It's as if she's already finding the process of house hunting rather challenging. Unless of course, Eddie has railroaded her into it. That wouldn't surprise me."

"What are you saying?" Mr Sarani folded his arms.

"I'm saying I don't think Suzanne's fit to move. I'm convinced her condition is unstable enough for her to suffer some kind of breakdown. Eddie will be devastated if that happens, especially as he's the one who decided to set this whole business in motion." Ruth reached for her bag, pulled out a handkerchief, and blew her nose. "I'm sorry. My gut feeling is he'll have to take the house off the market until Suzanne's better placed to cope with such a life-changing situation. It really was a snap decision, you know. I couldn't believe my ears when the Deacons invited me round and I saw the sale board for the first time."

"Your friends didn't say anything about their plans?"

Ruth felt she had an ally in Mrs Sarani. She held back a sob. Shook her dark head. "They didn't even drop a hint about wanting to leave the village. I'm sure you'll understand how hurt I felt, being asked to call, only to clap eyes on a house for sale sign."

"I agree this must have been a shock," said Mr Sarani. "But your friends could have been contemplating this move for a while. The decision to sell up is often an emotional one, despite the practicalities prompting it. Perhaps they feared you might try to dissuade them?"

Ruth didn't need to feign a flash of anger. "Mr Sarani, you don't understand! Suzanne confides in me. We've been close for years now and I don't think she'd be capable of withholding such an important decision from me, regardless of the time element. Eddie must have arranged for a valuation to be done in secret. Suzanne's often out of the house with me when I'm driving her around for shopping trips and so on. It's perfectly possible for him to have engineered the appointment to coincide with his wife being away from the house for several hours."

"I have no doubt he has her ultimate well-being in mind. A lot of folk prefer to spend their latter years living closer to family," said Mr Sarani.

"Do you think Bethan Harley is aware of Mrs Deacon's health issues?" Zoyah took the leather-bound menu her husband passed her but didn't open it.

"I very much doubt it," said Ruth. "Mrs Harley's pulling out all the stops so as to get as many viewings as possible. Hasn't she mentioned the other people who've already been to view the house?"

The couple exchanged glances.

"No," said Mr Sarani. "I enquired whether anyone had made an offer yet. Apparently, no one has."

Huw nodded. "Speaking as a mere observer, I imagine the husband wouldn't wish to give any impression that his wife's delicate condition might lead to his withdrawal of the house from the market."

"There are one or two more properties we're viewing tomorrow. I must admit we're both very taken with your friends' place though." Mrs Sarani looked pensive.

"Well, don't fall any further in love with The Sugar House, my dear," said her husband. "Not until we've seen these other properties and considered our options."

Ruth squared her shoulders. "I hope you agree I've done the right thing in sharing my concerns. To be honest, I'd dance for joy if having to lose the Deacons meant welcoming you two into Three Roads." Again, she noted the couple's quick glance at each other.

"But I'd hate you to begin negotiations and spend money on a survey only to… but let's not look on the black side. I'm sure you have lots to discuss over dinner. Huw and I will be dining a little later on."

Mr Sarani got to his feet. "We appreciate your honesty, Ruth." He turned to his wife. "Let's go through and make our choices at the table. We've taken enough of these good people's time already."

The Queensville Hotel website stated its dining room provided a relaxing ambience. The couple were shown to a table for two, upon which pink candles shed a soft glow in the dimly lit corner of the room.

"This is more like it," said Jalil. "Why do I feel as though I've come through a wind tunnel?"

"That's a little harsh, darling. We mightn't have wished to hear what Ruth had to say but I'd prefer to be aware of the situation than be kept in the dark, don't you agree?"

"In any event, I'm sure we'll enjoy a better meal than the egg sandwiches we ate in our room last night."

"We packed a lot in yesterday. I'm not sure I'd have appreciated sitting down to a big meal so late." Zoyah gave her husband a stern look. "Nor am I sure how seriously you've taken that explanation we just heard. Care to illuminate?"

"I think our starters are on their way, darling. Ah, yes, here comes the wine as well. Things could be far, far, worse."

"But do we cross off The Sugar House or do we still keep our options open?" Zoyah whispered as the wine waiter arrived, carrying the ubiquitous silver bucket.

Jalil took a sip of Chablis and nodded to the waiter to pour for them both. "If that woman's telling the truth, it sounds to me, if we make an offer, we could be in for a stressful and ultimately disappointing few weeks or even months."

"We can both do without that, but why on earth would she lie to us?"

"Because, Zoyah, I think Ruth Morgan's up to no good. Didn't you notice her eyes?"

"Jalil, that's so unfair. She's obviously distressed over the whole thing."

"Or she's deserving of an Oscar for her performance."

His wife stared at him. "I still don't understand what's in it for her, if she puts us off. Why pick on us?" She sipped at her wine. "You surely don't think she's trying to prevent The Sugar House from being sold to anyone at all? Not just you and me because of our origins?"

"As I said, if she's lying, she must have a reason. I don't for one single moment think she's concentrating solely upon us. Ms Morgan, in my humble opinion, has a very big axe to grind. And if she has, Bethan Harley should be made aware of the situation so she can meet with the vendors on their return and make clear her justifiable concerns."

Zoyah shook her head. "Jalil, I really don't think it's our place to interfere. Maybe that house is not for us after all?"

Chapter Twelve

Ruth drove back to Three Roads with the satisfaction of not only having enjoyed a delicious meal with an old friend, but also from having injected doubt into the minds of the two consultants.

Huw, unaware how much help he was providing, had manufactured several gold bullets for her to shoot. He insisted he and she should see each other more often and she'd promised not to leave it too long before arranging another meeting. She didn't plan on inviting him to visit her at Rock Cottage too soon though. When the Deacons returned, she intended on dropping a few choice crumbs of information designed to play upon Suzanne's conscience. Her friend must be made aware how Ruth, as a close and trusted friend, should not and must not be treated in such an offhand way.

She let herself into The Sugar House and discovered a flashing red light on the answer phone. Eddie had rung not long after her departure for her evening date and Ruth listened to what he had to say, her lips setting in a tight line of disapproval. She picked up a pencil from the hall table and, hearing the upbeat tone to Eddie's voice, snapped the pencil into two pieces, almost without noticing.

He sounded, she thought, like a crowing cock, as he reported how Suzanne had perked up and shown no signs of tiredness. Their daughter and grandchildren were thrilled to see them and he confessed to having a lump in his throat at the sight of Suze down on her knees, happily playing with the kids and their toys. Having already viewed two properties in the area they had in mind, Eddie considered both as strong possibilities. He hoped all was well back home but emphasized his wish for Ruth not to contact them regarding viewings.

That comment pleased her. Hopefully the Harley woman would be putting her foot in it sooner or later.

Eddie went on to remind her there was no one more suitable to house sit, and promised to ring again when they knew which day they'd be driving back. He didn't even mention the dog, so caught up was he with his rose-tinted perception of his and Suzanne's new life.

Ruth replayed the message one more time and went through to the utility room to see Sparkles. She let the dog into the garden and stood, staring up at the sky while the Labrador snuffled and squatted her way around. This was the kind of night no city dweller could hope to enjoy. Big sky. Stars blazing against dark velvet. A perfect full-beam moon lighting the countryside.

She called to the dog to come back and, followed by an adoring Sparkles, locked the back door and headed for the sitting room. She switched on a couple of lamps and helped herself to a generous measure of vintage brandy from Eddie's drinks cabinet. Settled into a corner of the settee, Labrador nestled at her feet, she sipped the rich, powerful liquid, feeling its tingling warmth spread through her. She slipped off her shoes, burrowing her feet into the thick carpet pile.

Becoming indispensable. Luxury. Security. Control. All these things were seductive. Addictive. Why couldn't this foolish couple, while appearing to have everything, appreciate how much they needed her to help run their lives? Ruth vowed, having begun her campaign, she would not now give up, even if Eddie and Suzanne floated on a cloud of optimism while planning a future that didn't include someone who had every intention of destroying it.

In the kitchen next morning, Ruth rummaged through Eddie's bits and pieces drawer until she found the coffee machine instructions. She experienced a ridiculous surge of triumph as the rich whiff seeped into the atmosphere. The two croissants she found in the bread bin felt dry beneath her fingers but she gave them a light toasting under the grill and ate them with a dollop of her own blackcurrant conserve, sucking the sweet, tart jam from her long fingers afterwards.

A glance through the window confirmed the capricious nature of the weather. The evening before, she'd driven back beneath a starry canopy and stood gazing up at the moon afterwards. This morning, a sullen sky oozed rain blown around like crinoline frills by an equally truculent wind. Ruth smiled as Sparkles appeared in the utility room doorway and lumbered forward. She fondled the dog's head.

"How about a walk, old girl?" With an odd jolt of satisfaction, she realised she'd used Eddie's favourite term of endearment for the family pet. "Your mistress doesn't like taking you out on wet days, does she, Sparkles? Never mind, old lady. You've got me and I like walking in the rain. Isn't that lucky? Let's stretch our legs, shall we?"

Still chatting to the animal, Ruth went to the utility room where she'd hung her wet weather suit. She stepped into the trousers, pulled the jacket over her head and drew the hood toggles together beneath her chin.

Woman and dog left the house via the back door. Ruth narrowed her eyes as a powerfully built man got out of a black range rover and buttoned himself into his waterproof jacket. Who could this be? Surely it wasn't a curious time-waster who'd noticed the sale board and hoped to look around the property? If so, whoever it was could turn around and go away again. She put her head down, shortened the dog's lead and marched purposefully onward, ignoring the stranger.

But the man turned towards her and waved. "Good Morning," he called. "Could you tell me if this is the best place to park, if I want to walk to the waterfall?"

Ruth hesitated.

The stranger took a couple of steps towards her. "I should apologise for accosting you," he said. "Rotten weather. Stranger in the camp and all that! My name's Ray Kirby and I viewed the house down the track the other day. I've come to check out the local terrain before heading back to London." He kept his eyes on her face. Something pinged

137

in the part of the brain that hoarded useless information, but he ignored it. "I can ring the estate agents if you'd like to check me out."

Ruth forced a smile. She cleared her throat, the fingers of one hand automatically moving to the neckline of her waterproof jacket. "That won't be necessary, Mr Kirby. As it happens, Mr and Mrs Deacon mentioned your name to me."

"You're a friend of theirs?"

"Friend. Helpmate. Chauffeur. House sitter."

This read like a CV. Why did he feel as though he knew her? Ray bent down to pat the Labrador. "Of course. Dog walker, too. Hello again, Sparkles, old girl."

Ruth watched the animal wag her tail. "You haven't chosen a very good day for sightseeing. I have to go out in the rain, whereas you don't."

He raised his eyebrows. "Rain doesn't bother me. If you take a liking to a place when you see it in foul weather, you'll be even more enthusiastic when the sun shines."

"I suppose so."

"I thought I should check out the area so I can describe it to my partner. Having good walks within easy reach is important to both of us."

"Some of the countryside around here is rather challenging," said Ruth. "You need to take care."

"I wouldn't let Claudia go for walks alone. You obviously know the area well?"

"I know the places to avoid, yes."

"If you don't mind my saying, you sound a tad negative, Mrs...?"

She didn't pick up on his unspoken query. "I'm being realistic. Three Roads is not a place for the vulnerable."

His laughter rumbled like thunder. "This gets better. Sounds like I should pack a crucifix and string of garlic next time I visit. So, are you planning to walk up the hill?"

"That depends upon whether you'd like company or not."

His eyes narrowed. "I'd appreciate it if you pointed me in the direction of this Pwll-y-Diafol place, ma'am."

"You need to practise the correct pronunciation but I've heard worse.'

"I stand corrected. How about you tell me the English translation?"

"It's known as The Devil's Pool."

"Is it now? Okay. As it happens, I'd appreciate your company."

"I'll walk up the hill with you and part of the way down the track you'll need to take. Sparkles isn't as young as she used to be but I'll make sure you know the route before I turn back."

"Aren't you afraid I might slip and tumble into the water?"

He was a great lighthouse of a man. Stirred something within her that didn't fit with how she should feel about someone who posed a threat to her future. She didn't know why she'd agreed to join him on his walk. She didn't know if he intended to interrogate her about the house and surrounding countryside. He might question her motives if she badmouthed the half-pint village in an effort to put him off purchasing the house he so admired. He might say something to the Harley woman. That could make life difficult, should Suzanne and Eddie get wind of it, which, with what she'd gleaned about Bethan Harley, was a given.

Ruth wiped a raindrop from the tip of her nose. "I'm afraid all I can say is, on your own head be it."

"Cheer me up, why don't you?" He shot her a quizzical look. "As it happens, I have a military background. I shan't get myself lost and I'm certainly not scared of getting my toes wet. But I'd like to take some photographs before I set off home. Chocolate box landscapes never appeal to me."

Ruth, having temporarily forgotten to keep up the pretence of a stiff knee when others were around, slowed her pace for effect. "It's no good." She screwed up her face in exasperation and tapped her right leg. "I tried but this knee of mine won't allow me to keep up." She paused. "Our climate probably doesn't help. I do hope neither you nor your partner suffers from arthritis."

He shortened his stride. Offered his arm. "Hang on to me. I promise not to go too fast. Arthritis isn't a problem for either of us. What intrigues me is why an intelligent woman chooses to live in a dead end like Three Roads. Are you wearing any significant rings beneath those leather gloves, I wonder? Or are you an artist who needs inspiration in order to create? An author maybe?"

Again, Ruth felt both annoyed and intrigued by this man who'd interrupted her day.

"I'm sorry," he said. "I know I shouldn't be curious but I have the oddest feeling that I know you from somewhere."

Ruth froze. Surely this big Englishman who so strangely attracted and repelled her couldn't possibly have read those odious conclusions reached by reporters with no better story than a possible love triangle? There'd been a photograph and fleeting television coverage on the Scottish news. Surely, after a decade, her former alter ego, Julia Hayes wasn't going to haunt her?

She'd resented Kirby's curiosity. Now she feared it. When he first mentioned visiting the waterfall, she'd experienced a sudden mind's eye flash of the shawl-shaped falls plunging into a subterranean, rock-infested pool. A circle of nothingness surrounded by steep, almost vertical cliffs. Phil Sartin once told her that years before she took over her cottage, a middle-aged couple, touring the area, had drowned in the deep, rushing waters.

This persistent stranger, probably accustomed to getting his own way, and who, from what she'd heard, was a self-declared trouble-shooter to boot, suddenly loomed too large in her cloistered world. He could prove a much greater threat than the couple she'd manipulated the night before. Now fate had thrown her into Ray Kirby's path and she needed time to reconcile her tumbling whirlpool of thoughts. The cunning option must surely be to answer his questions and also learn whatever she could about his personality.

"I'm single," said Ruth. "My elderly aunt died some years ago leaving me as her only beneficiary. I found a tenant for my flat in Llanbrenin Wells and moved into the small cottage I inherited in Three Roads. I live on the other side of the village from The Sugar House."

"Have you ever worked in or near Edinburgh?"

"Never." The lie slipped from her lips but her heartbeat tripped.

He shot her a quizzical look. "I spent a couple of years living in Church Hill. Sometimes go back to visit one company I still deal with. It's just that you remind me of someone. Someone I didn't know but whose picture was in the papers. I didn't have much of a life outside work in those days and the case intrigued me."

Ruth's chest hurt. Safer not to comment. Let him stew.

"Quite obviously you know nothing about this. I apologise. So, do you work locally?"

She kept her cool. "Not in the sense you mean, apart from proof-reading assignments now and then."

"If I buy The Sugar House, I'll be needing someone to help keep my records in order, maybe type up some reports. Someone trustworthy."

Ruth didn't respond. Ray Kirby maintained a steady, slower pace and she hadn't taken up his offer of a helping arm.

"I should say, Claudia is springtime to my autumn and we both lead busy lives." He looked sideways at Ruth as if expecting a reaction. "What, no sarcastic comment about age differences?"

"It's none of my business. Equally, I can never understand what makes people ask why I never married."

"I can imagine. I've had my share of snide remarks but who cares what others think? And if we settle into what we consider the perfect home, when the time comes to hang up my driving gloves, I'll have to adjust to Claudia chauffeuring me, I guess. If she's still around by then, of course."

"I gather she's often away. Wouldn't being based here prove inconvenient for her? Each time she returned to the UK, she'd face a long drive to mid Wales."

"We've talked about that. Claudia has a sister living near Southampton and she leaves her car there and spends the night if necessary. Anyway, she doesn't take on too many cruises nowadays. Claudia has song-writing ambitions and other interests she can't wait to pursue. Hence the desire to live somewhere off the beaten track."

"I see."

"But in view of the village's situation, and the Deacons being on the mature side, I can imagine why they feel the time's right to move somewhere offering more amenities."

"You have absolutely no comprehension of the situation, Mr Kirby!"

"Hey, I'm sorry if I touched on a raw nerve."

At once Ruth changed her tone to one of slight puzzlement. "I'm sorry too. I don't wish to seem impertinent, but you sound quite ambivalent about this future of yours. I can't imagine remaining in a relationship unless I felt certain the other person felt equally committed. None of my business, really."

Again, he let rip his growl of a laugh. "Yeah, right. That sounds to me like the triumph of hope over experience. I enjoy life while it's happening. If Claudia returns from her latest trip and announces she's fallen madly in love with a passenger, I reckon I'll have to take it on the chin."

She saw him shoot a sly glance but kept her eyes focused on the road ahead. "Is that right? I consider myself lucky to be single."

"Don't tell me you haven't had offers."

This was going too far, even though she realised he was teasing. "Let's say, that'd be telling."

"Touché. Hey, is this the track?" He gestured to the left.

"It is."

They walked on level ground but Ruth didn't increase her walking speed.

"How much further?"

"Less than half a mile along, you'll find the track divides. You need to take the left-hand fork then keep straight on. You'll hear the waterfall before you see it. I think Sparkles and I will turn back now we've seen you on your way."

"Of course. Thank you." He held out his hand. "I've enjoyed our chat. Maybe you'll tell me your name before we part company?"

"It's Ruth Morgan with a Ms."

He nodded. "I hope we'll meet again soon, Ruth Morgan with a Ms."

Deliberately she looked up at the leaden sky before making her way back. She knew she shouldn't let him go to the waterfall alone. Not in such treacherous weather. Clearly, he saw himself as tough. But Pwll-y-Diafol possessed a history as deep and dark as the underwater cavern beneath its surging cascade.

As she walked, in her mind's eye Ruth pictured the craggy rock wall over which the falls tumbled. Only the most experienced climbers and abseiling experts dared scale its unforgiving cliffs. Health and Safety officials would need to lie down in a darkened room if they paid a visit and realised the death trap lurking in the woodland depths. Without doubt, safety rails and warning signs should be installed.

Ray Kirby had opted to visit the waterfall and the rest was up to Fate. Or was it? She knew an alternative route, an old walkway through the woodland and one only forestry workers used. Without having to feign a limp, she could navigate the undergrowth in minutes. A small grassy plateau on the bank near her access point would be the obvious place for a photographer to stand. On saturated ground, Kirby would need to tread carefully or risk losing his foothold.

If some invisible force propelled him forward, there would be only one way to fall. The perpetrator could melt into the forest. Who would know? And if he should survive, surely such a shock would unhinge him? Convince him to reject Three Roads as his love nest?

All she need do was tether the dog somewhere nearby. Maybe the wooden bench tucked into a clearing overlooking Pwll-y-Diafol Falls. The seat was dedicated to a former village resident and wildlife lover. Sparkles would wait patiently, she felt sure. After all, who in their right mind would be wandering the forest tracks on a miserable day designed to host a funeral? Or a drowning? Ruth felt in her pocket for a doggy chew. Like a harbinger of doom, a buzzard circled overhead, its plaintive mew echoing in her ears.

Kirby posed dual danger now she knew she'd triggered something in his memory. She'd concealed her past notoriety so well. Until now.

In her office Bethan punched in a number, allowed it to ring, and heard the answer phone respond. "Good morning," she said, opening the file before her. "It's Bethan Harley. If you pick this up, Ms Morgan, I have another couple wishing to view The Sugar House. We'll arrive at eleven o'clock but please don't worry if you can't be there. I'm sure Sparkles will present no problem."

She cut the call and replaced the phone. It would be bliss if the house sitter happened not to be in residence even though Bethan wasn't sure this couple were good prospects. They were, in her opinion, somewhat too young to be mummified in a place like Three Roads, but they were keen, possessed savings and longed to live somewhere offering the tranquillity they craved.

The husband, a mathematician, tutored for the Open University, and the wife wrote articles on lifestyles and health issues. They'd exchanged contracts on their property in the Midlands, so if Mr and Mrs Barnard fell in love with her clients' house, there was in theory a good chance of them making a sensible offer, something which no doubt would please the Deacons and possibly give Ray Kirby something to tell his partner when he next contacted her.

Bethan checked her watch. She'd missed breakfast but she could spare time for a quick sandwich before driving to Three Roads. The prospective purchasers wanted to meet her at the property and Bethan threw a quick prayer into the ether, visualising the farmer's dilapidated tractor blocking the Deacons' gateway. Or Ruth Morgan constructing a magic pentacle.

She told herself not to be so negative. Bethan reached for her raincoat, checked she had all she needed in her briefcase, swung her bag over one shoulder and collected the house key from the safe.

The small delicatessen attached to the town's best coffee shop attracted a steady trickle of customers all year round. She breathed in the aroma of ripe cheeses and garlic sausage while selecting a hummus and tomato wrap, paid up and headed for the car park. She'd be early for her appointment but better that than have the Barnards arrive without her being around. If her suspicions about Ruth Morgan had substance, would this warning phone call energise the woman into mischief making? But what, given such short notice, could she possibly do without blowing her cover?

The windscreen wipers clunked like a noisy metronome. Bethan drove out of the car park, the sound reminding her of the backing to a song her daughter currently rated as cool. She switched on the sidelights, waited to join the main

147

road traffic and changed to dipped beam in tune with the other motorists. She'd learnt not to fret about having to show off a house on a day best spent beneath the duvet, and in this particular case, a downpour meant nothing compared with the curious incident of the field mouse in the daytime.

Mentally, she ticked off the list of possible purchasers. The Hunts, despite a half-hearted attempt to assure her they hadn't let the windscreen attack put them off, still hadn't been in touch regarding a second viewing. The two consultants had originally asked to be informed if someone made an offer on The Sugar House. But Bethan's assistant reported Mrs Sarani had rung that morning to check whether the Deacons still planned to keep the house on the market. What was that all about?

When questioned by the receptionist, Mrs Sarani had apparently sounded vague about her reason for asking but mentioned her concern about Mrs Deacon's fragile health status. The consultant posed the possibility of the vendors taking their house off the market, albeit temporarily. Bethan felt a rush of impatience as she tried to stifle her suspicions about the Deacons' house sitter. Tried to recall whether Ruth Morgan could have been alone with the couple long enough to give them food for the wrong kind of thought. Surely not?

Ray Kirby was, without a doubt, the most likely person to make an offer. But he wouldn't do so until after his partner viewed and approved his choice. That was fair enough. At least, by the time his lady returned from her cruising gig, the vendors would be back in residence and the sinister Ms Morgan in her own home, hunched over her cauldron. Bethan couldn't help grinning as she enjoyed that image. Poppy would scold her if she could read her mum's thoughts.

Yet, she still couldn't zap the memory of the woman with long dark auburn hair, a woman whose tapering fingers, nervous tic, and erect posture chimed with Ruth Morgan's appearance. But wasn't that ludicrous? Perhaps Poppy was right in suggesting these odd but explainable mishaps had undermined Bethan's usual confidence. Had she merely got off on the wrong foot with the Deacons' friend? To be fair, if Bethan had to leave her own home in the hands of a trusted house sitter, wouldn't she be pleased if that person guarded the place like a Rottweiler salivating to show off its sharp teeth?

Still she couldn't dismiss her doubts. How odd was it that yobs just happened to target a car belonging to people coming to view a house? The Deacons swore they'd never heard of such an incident occurring before. Word got around swiftly in small communities like theirs and Bethan had no reason to doubt them. But how about the tractor left blocking the gateway? Again, the annoyance was timed to interfere with another house viewing. The farmer owned the land over which the Deacons had right of way. Was that issue destined to cause trouble, despite what the deeds pronounced?

More importantly, wasn't the presence of that field mouse in the downstairs cloakroom like seeing a vagrant taking tea at Claridges? Time needed to elapse before vermin began to stink the place out. Bethan recalled the foul smell in her father's shed when she'd been a curious twelve-year-old and poked around his neat workspace, holding her nose, until she pulled out a plastic bin and found a dead hedgehog hidden behind. Her father had given her extra pocket money that weekend. Had the house sitter revelled in asking Bethan if she should check the downstairs facility, knowing full well the nasty consequence of entering it?

Bethan slowed down for the 40 mph zone and indicated left for Three Roads. A cloak of mature conifers sheltered the road either side. Further on, she drove past what she knew were young trees, planted to replace ones felled on that land. A sign pointed her to one of the many forest trails traversing the area but she ignored it and drove on, changing gear as the incline grew steeper, reminding her to take the bend with care.

Bethan cursed softly. She'd turned on to the track only to find Ruth Morgan's car parked neatly upon the gravelled turning space. The gates were closed. Bethan got out of the driving seat and opened them, propping them wide with the bolts provided. Back in her car, and with a flash of malice, which gave her an equally swift flash of guilt, Bethan parked so close to the house sitter's vehicle that no way would the woman succeed in driving off without Bethan moving her own car. Why she did this, she was at a loss to explain.

The car clock showed she'd arrived five minutes early. She left her car locked. Walked slowly away from the house and along the track, ready to greet the couple whose arrival she expected very soon.

Chapter Thirteen

Ray Kirby enjoyed woodland. If he could have his life over again, he'd choose to be someone like Bear Grylls. His idea of heaven was spending time somewhere no one else wanted to be. As a younger man, he'd spent many a night under the stars, often on his own or with mates on those getting away from it all weekends. For stress busting, in his opinion, you couldn't better stuff like that. How the heck he'd ended up living in Surbiton, he really didn't know. Except, he did know, because that pointed to another life. Another lady. And the fact that when he hit his early forties, he decided the time had arrived to put down a wine cellar.

Funny how fate sometimes caused the frogs in the box to jump every which way. At this stage of his life it was he and Claudia who needed to put down roots as a couple and, whatever flip remarks he'd made to the Deacons' frosty friend, he felt secure with his partner of two years. Secure enough to buy a property with her. Although his gut feeling told him Claudia, bright and beautiful, with a voice which, whenever he heard it, turned his legs to treacle, maybe didn't feel quite so secure with him.

The amazing Cleo Dankworth was Claudia's heroine and role model, so she sometimes included *If We Lived on Top of A Mountain* in her performances. Three Roads nestled in a valley but was around 1300 feet above sea level with the mountain range looming even higher at one side of the village. Perfect. He let the words of the song run through his mind while he pictured Claudia, wearing one of her slinky dresses, standing on a stage, transfixing her audience. One newspaper reviewer had described Claudia as the possessor of a fabulous set of pipes. Claudia was fabulous, full stop. Enough. He glanced either side of him as he progressed.

Somewhere around here was an Outward-Bound centre. If this waterfall was all he'd heard it hyped up to be, surely there'd be safety restrictions in place? Youngsters and their instructors must come across it when trekking through the countryside. Was the enigmatic Ruth Morgan, not forgetting the Ms, trying to put him off the area, by any chance? If that was the case, she'd picked the wrong man for her scare-mongering tactics. Hazard was his middle name.

Ray Kirby marched on; black waterproof hat jammed on his head. High collar buttoned beneath. He burrowed his chin deeper as persistent rain lashed him. Not that he minded. But there wasn't a lot to look at yet. If you'd seen one leggy conifer, you'd seen them all. The Devil's Pool had better be worth this rather tedious trek. He'd take photographs and head back to the car ready for the drive back. At least his solo house hunting had led to a positive decision, but he'd stick to his word and keep schtum until he'd talked things over with his lovely lady.

Claudia would still be in bed in her cabin on the cruise liner. The ship was scheduled to leave Florida in a couple of days' time. Claudia. In bed. He savoured the image. Wondered if she was awake and thinking of him. He knew she'd tease him when he told her how he walked through bone-chilling, horizontal rain to take photographs. You could've searched on the internet, she'd say. Thinking about the woman who'd stolen his reason, if not totally his heart, Ray almost overshot the left-hand fork Ruth Morgan had advised him to follow.

Bethan beckoned to the driver to park by the front door. She waited as the car tyres crunched over the gravel and came to a halt.

The man at the wheel wound down his window. "Hi, Mrs Harley."

Jonathan Barnard possessed an unruly mop of black curls and a pair of dark brown eyes. Ray Kirby also had memorable eyes. In his case though, the phrase 'come to bed eyes' dropped into Bethan's mind. Maybe she'd been sleeping on her own too long.

"Not too difficult to find, I hope, Mr Barnard?"

"I do believe we're even on time for once. Mind you, my lovely wife tried to divert me from the Sat Nav by singing *Sospan Fach*."

Bethan chuckled and wished this pair had more collateral.

Mrs Barnard, wearing a crimson wool poncho with black leggings and ankle boots, hopped out of the front seat.

"I'm impressed, Mrs Barnard. You can give me a repeat performance if you like."

"Don't encourage her," said her husband.

Bethan waited to hear their initial reactions as the couple gazed at the property.

"Wow. This house looks really welcoming," said Mrs Barnard. "It's solid. Like you could depend upon it to look after you."

Bethan nodded. "You're right. I've always thought of its interior as its main attraction, but I agree the property has dignity."

"I like the way it sits in its own patch, with nobody overlooking it," said Mr Barnard. "Does the farmer use that gateway much? The one close by the gates to this house? I'm thinking about the right of way that's mentioned."

"Of course, but the entitlement is clear and I gather Mr Sartin is something of a loner, a one-man band with stock and a couple of fields to look after," said Bethan, employing her estate agent's tact. "I'm glad you like your first sight of The Sugar House. I'll just knock in case the vendors' house sitter hasn't noticed our arrival. I left a message on the answer phone, but she could be busy in the kitchen."

After two rings on the doorbell produced no response, Bethan inserted the key, pushed opened the door and called a greeting through the slice of air. "Are you there, Ms Morgan? It's Bethan Harley and I'm bringing Mr and Mrs Barnard in now. Okay?"

Nothing.

"Come inside," said Bethan, experiencing a ridiculous sense of relief. "I'll just check to see if the dog's here. She's a sweetie and if Ms Morgan has gone out, she'll have left Sparkles somewhere secure. Why don't you start your tour with the front room? That leads to the conservatory. Ignore the rain. Check out the fabulous view."

She left the couple to it and hurried towards the kitchen and utility room. Everything looked as though a Stepford Wife had done the business. She pushed open the utility room door very carefully, calling, "Sparkles? Are you there? It's only me."

No welcoming bark from a dog that definitely wouldn't be left outside in such lugubrious weather. So, either Ms Morgan had taken her for a walk or she and the Labrador were visiting locally. Either way, so far, Bethan couldn't detect anything designed to deter prospective purchasers. Unless she and the young couple went upstairs to the bedrooms to be confronted by a dead animal head staring glassy-eyed from a snowy pillow.

Bethan made a mental note not to let her imagination go into overdrive. It wasn't difficult to imagine her daughter saying 'Mu-um' in that way teenagers had. She hurried back to find her clients admiring the view as she'd suggested.

The tour of the house progressed to the point where the young couple had made all the right noises, asked questions and now, having raised their eyebrows at one another, were checking their watches.

"Have you seen enough?"

"I think so. How about you, darling?"

Mrs Barnard nodded her head. "I like the house very much. Could I ask why the vendors have put it on the market?"

"Ah, sorry, I should have said earlier. They want to live closer to their daughter in Wiltshire. They've been very happy here but I think they miss being around their grandchildren."

"That's understandable," said Mr Barnard. "So, are there many young families in the village?"

"There are a few," said Bethan. "Mostly the dads are forestry workers. The children are bussed to the nearby primary school. There's a community hall, though I'm not sure you'd be interested in bingo or ladies' keep fit classes."

"Well, maybe not the latter," said Mr Barnard. "My wife might, though."

She grimaced. "I'm not very good at joining in organised events. Walking's more my cup of herbal."

"Don't worry. She's not socially retarded," Mr Barnard ducked.

Bethan chuckled. "There are things to do around here but mostly they involve driving five, ten, or fifteen miles. It comes with the territory."

"It's one of the reasons we asked for a viewing."

"We're certainly not your average thirty-something couple about town," said Mrs Barnard.

"You can say that again," said her husband. "We'll be in touch, Mrs Harley."

Bethan moved towards the front door and opened it.

"By the way," Mr Barnard waited for his wife to step outside first. "I forgot to mention I overshot the turning to the house earlier. We realised our mistake and I used the lay by down the road to turn the car around."

"No problem. Lots of people do that," said Bethan.

157

"It's only that there was a vehicle already parked, with no one inside. I can't help thinking this isn't the kind of day to attract twitchers or ramblers."

Bethan frowned. "Can't help you there. It certainly isn't anything to do with my client list. I don't have any more viewings booked for today." She pulled the front door shut and checked it was secure.

"He's so nosey," said Mrs Barnard. "The vehicle probably belongs to someone walking their dog. Dog owners can't stop going out just because it's raining. Thanks, Mrs Harley. We need to do our sums, consider our options and get back to you soon."

"Thank you. Don't hesitate to get in touch if you'd like a second viewing. Take care." Bethan watched them get into their car. *Take care* – two words used so often these days but here in Three Roads, seeming to gain an extra resonance.

The Barnards set off down the track. Oh, please, she thought. Don't let that old witch be lying in wait. Surely even Ruth Morgan couldn't be evil and twisted enough to have cooked up some plot to spoil Bethan's day?

Sadly, she had a feeling this particular couple were batting a little bit out of their league. She might be proved wrong but her intuition didn't often let her down. On the other hand, sometimes the Bank of Mum and Dad offered salvation. The couple had obviously liked what they saw and Bethan, showing them round, felt far more relaxed without the house sitter lurking in the shadows.

She scolded herself for her lack of professionalism, secured the hood of her white raincoat and strode down the track to check out the parked vehicle Mr Barnard had noticed. Paranoid, she might be, but she couldn't drive away without doing so, however much she knew it could have nothing to do with the house sitter. There were too many question marks around Ruth Morgan's previous behaviour to allow Bethan to drive off regardless.

To her relief, she noticed nothing untoward, like an offensive sign. But, once on the main road, looking down towards the most populated part of the village, Bethan recognised the vehicle in the lay by. It wasn't only that it was a black Range Rover. It bore a memorable registration; the personal number plate RK 1973 announcing the presence of one Mr Ray Kirby. She wondered whether he'd chosen this because he'd been born in that year, and couldn't stop herself from calculating how many years older than herself he might be. Was he hoping to take another look at the house before he left the area? If so, why hadn't he rung the bell? He hadn't been sitting in the vehicle when Mr Barnard spotted it.

She told herself Ray Kirby might have arrived well before she had, called at The Sugar House but, having no luck with that, decided to go for a walk. If this man didn't let a curmudgeonly farmer's lack of consideration faze him, he wouldn't allow a rainy morning to deter him. But, realising he was out there somewhere, and the house sitter was also out there somewhere, Bethan sucked in air and shook her head. Why did she keep torturing herself with

159

these random dark thoughts? Even after such brief acquaintance, she'd a shrewd idea Ray Kirby played to win. No way could even Ruth Morgan get the better of him.

So, how would the house sitter have known he was in the vicinity? Ms Morgan hadn't been around on the day of Ray Kirby's viewing. She'd been in her own home, unless she'd been snooping and noted a strange vehicle in the lay by. Unless – unless she'd happened along the track just as Mr Kirby was about to come down it. He might even have approached her. Now that was a scenario Bethan knew she needed to check out, if only for her own peace of mind.

She walked back to her car. Seated behind the steering wheel, she tapped her fingernails upon it and knew her imagination wouldn't let her drive off until she called her office and confirmed her whereabouts, in tune with the Suzy Lamplugh effect. In fact, each of her admin assistants had been known to ring Bethan's mobile if concerned she was taking longer than estimated for a valuation or viewing. Her assistant answered on the third ring.

"Hi, Chris. Just letting you know I'm leaving The Sugar House and heading for The Devil's Pool." She paused. "No, not for a swim, thanks for asking. Our Mr Kirby has parked his car in the village and I've a feeling he's checking out the countryside. If he wants a second viewing, I'll let you know. Otherwise, I'll be a half hour or so."

Ruth trod the stony path winding through the forest, pushing on until she reached her target. To her annoyance, she found the bench surrounded by foliage. Fronds of tough grass

160

trailed around the seat. Thistles abounded. She clicked her tongue against her teeth.

"Good girl. Sit. Stay," she instructed the dog. "Nasty stingers!"

Sparkles gave her a mournful look but did as she was told and settled herself at Ruth's feet.

"Good girl," said Ruth again. She patted the Labrador's head and turned her attention to the swathes of wet grass and spindly gorse, pulling and tugging until the nearest armrest was cleared. She picked up Sparkles' lead and attached it to the wooden strut before fumbling in her pocket for a doggie chew and offering it.

"Silly girl," she scolded as the treat fell to the ground. "You'll have to winkle it out from the wet grass now, won't you? I shan't be long. Be good."

Ruth hurried off, picking her way, taking care where she placed her booted feet. Keeping to the overgrown but still discernible narrow path between the trees. She planned to be gone a matter of minutes. She didn't even know whether she could bring herself to carry out what she had in mind. All she cared about was keeping intact her life and future prospects. She was the one throwing the dice. She didn't intend letting anyone jeopardise her plan.

There were plenty of houses this Kirby man could buy. If he imagined he could ingratiate himself by offering her a bit of typing and possibly house sitting, he was very mistaken. Three Roads didn't need tainting by someone so brash as he. Perhaps a dip in a cold pool would put paid to his plans for a rural retreat.

161

She'd gone through a lot over the past days. A mere few days but each filled with so many events since the shock of discovering her friends' intentions. Friends! They needed to be taught precisely what true loyalty demanded. The more she contemplated Suzanne and Eddie's casual disregard of her feelings, the fiercer her indignation stung. Lemon juice on a cut finger.

She'd enjoyed the role-playing outside the offices of Baldwin, Caldwell and Balls. It gave her huge satisfaction to think the Harley woman had quit the premises while Delyth stood there, chatting with two house-hunters. The negotiator could never associate her with the elegantly attired auburn-haired woman to whom she'd probably given only a cursory glance. Ruth still gloated over that quick decision to look away, avoiding eye contact with someone who might have quashed her plan.

Valerie and Brad had lapped up her story of the unfortunate criminal's remains, with an awful fascination. To her knowledge, the couple hadn't even set foot in Three Roads.

The 'bomb' she fabricated had surely shocked and horrified Mr and Mrs Hunt when they drove into the village. It had proved simple to manufacture that bit of mischief but the incident's devastating and satisfying result was the placing of doubt in the minds of these particular house hunters. And no one could suspect her of being the perpetrator.

Kirby hadn't been such a pushover. Doubtless, had his bit of stuff been with him, he might have found her reaction

162

rather different. She could well have warned him not to laugh off the incident. Such happenings weren't that unusual in rural spots where some folk still mistrusted incomers and envied their ability to pluck the plum from the property tree.

Ruth had formed her own conclusion about Ray Kirby. He was adept at getting his own way. He hadn't yet learnt it wasn't all about who might be bigger and more physically powerful. If he came a cropper at the waterfall, it would be no one's fault but his own. She'd warned him. In return, he'd boasted about his outdoor skills.

Nor should those two doctors be thinking of Three Roads as their retirement place. They'd be as out of place as a pole dancer at a funeral. The placing of the field mouse in the conch shell was arguably Ruth's best trick yet. She'd timed matters to perfection and the canine presence in the house pointed to an obvious conclusion regarding the culprit.

The Harley woman had behaved less than charmingly. Once Eddie and Suzanne saw the error of their ways and removed their house from the agency's list, Mrs Smart Arse Harley would be on her bike. Sobbing over her lost commission.

Ruth caught a rattle of gunfire drifting on the breeze. Soldiers must be on manoeuvres on the plains across the valley. Her mouth twisted as she recalled Ray Kirby's mention of his military background. Maybe that was another reason for him to favour settling in the area. Well, he'd be out of luck if he tried to drive back through the village and take the ranges road towards the A40. The road was currently closed. She'd received notification of the date via the customary Ministry of Defence email to residents.

Ruth contemplated her next move. Could she really commit murder? Probably not. But could she engineer a happening that might well occur whether or not she instigated it, especially when it involved someone not paying sufficient respect to his surroundings? Yes, she could. So long as the stakes were high enough to tempt her and no one suspected her.

The stakes were high enough. There was absolutely no reason for anyone to suspect her. And surely there couldn't be anyone else wandering the woodland? The rain hadn't ceased. People around here talked about that thick, invasive drizzle permeating their bones, despite waterproof protection. Ruth, partially sheltered from the elements by the woodland, was so close to her prey, she could hear the waterfall roaring. Anyone stupid enough to stray that way might well receive much more than the satisfaction of capturing a few delightful images on a state-of-the-art camera. Those unforgiving rocks, jutting like sharks' teeth from the river's underbelly, would not be visible in any viewfinder.

Chapter Fourteen

Bethan convinced herself Ray Kirby would have headed for the scary falls as her daughter called the local beauty spot. She'd taken Poppy and her daughter's best friend for a picnic nearby a few years before and been warned not to take any chances, even on a calm, dry day. To discover the bench set back from and above the whirling waters was a relief.

Now she turned off the main road and drove as far as she could along a track used mainly by workers managing the land. Where had she left her car when she brought the girls? On one side of the road, there was a pull in area, marked with a Forestry Commission sign. She needed to park and check all was well with her client. For once, she didn't even stop to lock her vehicle, so intent was she on following her hunch.

If anyone asked what motivated her to set off like someone playing amateur detective, Bethan wouldn't be able to spell it out. An accusation based on a woman potentially dressing up and deliberately terrorising people viewing her friends' house, would be greeted with derision.

Who else but yobs would hurl such a putrid package at a Porsche's windscreen?

There was nothing sinister about an ancient farm tractor conking out and being abandoned until its one-man-band owner got around to sorting it. As for the last incident, how

and why would Mr and Mrs Deacon's dear friend produce a
dead field mouse and stuff it inside a decorative shell in the
downstairs cloakroom so it putrefied and discharged an eye-
watering stench?

But how stupid was Bethan going to look if and when
she came upon Ray Kirby happily waterfall watching? He'd
think she was some kind of stalker. Maybe even assume she
fancied him. Why else would she turn up in the woods on
the off chance he might be there alone?

Bethan stopped suddenly. She'd just taken a young
couple around The Sugar House without any problems
whatsoever. That happy fact hadn't really impinged on her.

Why?

Because she'd been jittery, that's why. Apprehensive.
Convinced the house sitter must be somewhere, waiting to
cause mayhem. But maybe Ruth Morgan had already left
the house before the answerphone message was left?

Bethan stood, twisting her wedding and engagement
rings around her finger. That dismal mew of a buzzard
always sent a shiver down her spine. The predator swooping
on some hapless creature was an aspect of nature, but the
wingspan of a jumbo jet plus the cruel beak took this big
bird into the premier predator league. She pictured the
buzzard swooping. Opening its maw. Soaring upwards after
it launched from the trees beside her. Other birds, tuned into
danger, scattered like ashes from a shovel.

Another sound made Bethan frown. Why would she hear
a dog barking? Might it be Sparkles? If it were, why would
Ruth Morgan take the old Labrador along, if intending to

engineer some malicious act? She judged the excited yelping to come from the woodland on her right and wondered if the buzzard had spooked the dog or vice versa.

Should she investigate or should she ignore it and continue what she came here to do? The answer arrived in the form of a golden Labrador, bounding through the undergrowth, lead trailing.

"Sparkles!" Bethan waited for the animal to reach her.

Clumsy as ever, the dog managed to tread on each of Bethan's feet and bump her bony head against both her human friend's knees.

"Where's your mistress, then? What's going on, girl?" Bethan felt her pulse ratchet to High Doh as she straightened up, clutching the leather lead firmly and tried to think logically.

If Sparkles was attached to her lead, Ruth Morgan must be in the area. What if she'd tripped and fallen? What if she'd hit her head on a stone and lay unconscious in the undergrowth? Irrespective of her dislike for the woman, Bethan knew what she must do. Treading carefully, she led the dog back the way it came.

"Hello?" She called as she followed a narrow track climbing towards a grassy plateau. On it stood the wooden bench she remembered from her only previous visit but which now didn't tempt her to sit down on it. There was no sign of the house sitter.

It didn't take forensic skills to realise the Labrador's lead must have been tied to the bench's arm. Sparkles had possibly been startled by the buzzard, become agitated and broken free. The wood must have rotted because of age and persistent wet conditions. But why tether the dog if the sole object of visiting the forest on a dismal day was to give her some exercise?

Bethan turned and rejoined the main track, still holding tight to Sparkles. If Ruth Morgan had suffered an accident off piste, so to speak, it would probably be quicker to locate Ray Kirby and enlist his help. She needed to express concern at noticing his vehicle in the village and wondering if he'd turned up, hoping for a second viewing. As a businessman, surely he understood her urge not to delay a possible offer. He might even have contacted his partner and received the thumbs up.

She heard the clatter of light artillery from the other side of the village. Could she also hear the rush of water?

Ray Kirby couldn't believe the jaw-dropping majesty of the landscape. He never failed to marvel at the magnificence so often found in Welsh scenery, coastal or inland. Yet who'd have thought such a gem could be concealed amidst massed conifers, each one seemingly a clone of its neighbour. Countless tourists, let alone county residents, must have passed the turning to Three Roads, oblivious of such riches within easy reach.

With no poncey gastro-pub in the village, no teashop with lovingly handcrafted goods to interest visitors, he could visualise making trip after trip to this secluded spot. What was its name again? He remembered the English version. The Devil's Pool didn't do this feature justice.

Claudia was going to love it. She'd be using the whoosh of water to inspire her next song. He'd be acting as soundman while she experimented with cadences. No doubt about that.

No one had thought fit to construct a viewing platform. He looked around for a seat but this miniature Niagara Falls didn't come with commercialism. Good. He and Claudia could bring folding chairs. Having walked down here, he realised he could park the car far closer than the village lay by.

It had even stopped raining. Almost. The clouds were skulking away. Shredding. Watery sunlight flooded the countryside. Could he capture that exquisite rainbow in his viewfinder? Ray reached for his camera. He could email the image to Claudia after he got back. Hey, lovely lady! How about that for your next song? Rainbow's End had to be the ultimate cliché but right at that moment, he believed it signified an astonishing omen for their future.

If he could only stand a little closer, he could obtain a better shot of the opalescence arcing above the waterfall. He looked down at his feet. Shuffled forward a bit. Not too close to the edge. He turned his attention back to his camera. Damn it. He needed to fish out his reading glasses, because he still hadn't totally got his head around this recently purchased gizmo. He'd better make sure he pressed the right buttons. Daren't go back without a few shots.

Red. Orange. Yellow. Green. Blue. Indigo. Violet. If he were only a different kind of a guy, he'd tell Claudia he wished he could give her the rainbow for a scarf. He smiled to himself. No way would she have chosen him, if she'd been seeking the romantic hero of her dreams.

Engrossed in the moment. Totally captivated by the wonders of Nature. He didn't even consider the possibility that he mightn't be alone in visiting The Devil's Pool on an autumn weekday, which began by overdosing on torrential rain.

Nor did Bethan, spotting him, realise Ray Kirby already had company. A rush of relief overwhelmed her and she surprised herself by her need to hold back tears. The choked-up feeling stopped her from calling out. Fortunately, perhaps, given his precarious position. But someone else had no such concerns. Sparkles barked, tugging her lead.

"Stay. Stay, Sparkles!" Bethan used both hands to restrain the animal from making a dangerous lunge.

Moving closer to the waterfall meant braving a quagmire. Bethan knew she daren't risk the dog causing her to lose her balance. Ray Kirby seemed not to have heard the commotion. His ears must be filled with the hammering of the waterfall, his concentration focused upon his viewfinder. She hesitated. And while she watched, she noticed something or someone materialise among the foliage close to the photographer.

Was it a trick of the light? Watery sunshine cast a disguise over the dark, brooding woodland. Bethan sometimes felt this part of mid Wales whispered secrets never to be revealed. But whatever lurked in the shadows had moved once more. Bethan blinked. The shape was now closer to Ray Kirby, who should know better than to allow his macho man image to threaten his life. The ground must be saturated where he stood and to yell a warning could bring danger. If indeed he heard her.

Bethan's mouth dried. Intent on the moment, she felt miraculously calm, despite her obsessive dark thoughts. The fear of someone moving in on the big man seemed entirely possible while he appeared so unaware of his vulnerability.

She didn't know whether to feel relieved or not when he shifted his foothold and looked across at her. Maybe she'd been imagining things after all because he didn't move from the spot but pointed to his camera and turned back, clearly determined to capture the image he wanted while the light was right.

Bethan blinked hard. Shielded her eyes against the sun. Whatever or whoever she thought she'd seen, was no longer in evidence. The Labrador had calmed down.

"Stay, Sparkles." She waited until the big man had taken enough shots of sky and water and picked his way back to join her on the stony part of the track.

"What are you doing here? Is everything all right?" His face showed a mix of concern and curiosity.

"Everything's fine," said Bethan. She wondered if her voice sounded as tremulous to him as it did to her. "Er, I've just been showing people around The Sugar House and happened to notice your car in the lay by."

His eyes crinkled. A smile softened what Bethan thought of as his tough guy image. "Yeah, that number plate's a bit of a giveaway."

"I wondered whether you were hoping for another look at the house before heading back to London. I had a hunch you might be here, so coming to check seemed the obvious thing to do."

His eyes widened. "But you've brought Sparkles. Surely that's beyond the call of duty? I met the house sitter taking the dog for a walk, when I was making my way here."

Bethan was about to tell him what she'd discovered when she heard a cry of surprise.

"Oh, my goodness. Oh, what a relief." Ruth Morgan emerged from the woodland only yards from them and hurried forward.

Bethan sucked in her breath. So, she hadn't been mistaken. The house sitter must have been skulking in the woods but with intent to do what?

Sparkles barked a welcome.

Bethan handed over the dog's lead. "She came bounding out of the woods, Ms Morgan. Luckily she ran towards me and I managed to grab her lead and stop her from getting too close to the water."

"She loves the water."

"I'm sure she does." Bethan took a deep breath. "But have you not noticed the state of the ground? It would be easy for an animal – or a person – to lose their balance."

She didn't intend spelling out the consequences. Ruth was glaring at her. Ray didn't comment. Possibly enjoying the show?

"As the dog was roaming around but you were nowhere to be seen, I was worried you might've had an accident. I

172

walked back the way Sparkles had come and saw the state of the bench." She held Ruth Morgan's gaze.

"But what were you doing here in the first place, Mrs Harley? Surely you weren't looking for me? I don't understand."

"I might say the same to you," said Ray Kirby. "Didn't you tell me you were heading home with the dog? You mentioned your knee was playing up. Wow, Ms Morgan, the England football manager would give his right arm for that kind of recovery time among his squad."

Fifteen love, thought Bethan, even if it was the wrong sport.

Ruth Morgan raised her chin. Her eyes gleamed. "Yes, I did set off back but couldn't help worrying about you being out here on your own. Despite your protestations, I agree with Mrs Harley. It can be undeniably treacherous in this area."

Bethan refrained from muttering 'In more ways than one.'

Instead, she answered Ruth Morgan's question. "I left a message on the answer phone to let you know I was coming over to show prospective purchasers around. You must have already left."

"You let yourself in, despite my absence?"

"Of course. As agreed with the vendors."

"Even so, common courtesy would decree you should have left a message asking me to ring you back and fix a convenient time. I worry about you bringing strangers into The Sugar House."

Bethan placed her hands on her hips. She knew she must plumb the absolute depths of her resilience or risk not maintaining her professionalism.

"That's a strange attitude, Ms Morgan, if you don't mind my saying so. The potential purchasers were passing through and read the particulars in the office window. Why on earth would I lose an opportunity to show them around, when the vendors have granted me full permission to enter their property?"

Ruth Morgan merely glared at her.

"Don't worry. I accompanied the couple every inch of the tour."

Ray looked at his watch but Bethan was beyond stopping.

"Anyway, why didn't you keep to the designated track? I'm surprised you can tolerate uneven terrain if your knee really is as troublesome as you make out." Bethan tried for the same impassivity as Ray Collins achieved when looking at the house sitter. She hadn't been quite so skilful with her confrontational comments.

Ruth avoided her gaze this time. "I... er, decided to leave Sparkles tied up at the bench for safety reasons, in case I needed to assist Mr Kirby. That dog may be old but she's still capable of pulling someone over, you know. She's quite a heavyweight."

Damn her. Score's fifteen all, thought Bethan.

"So that Lab's either clever with knots or you were never a Girl Guide, Ms Morgan?"

Bethan inwardly cheered. Thirty – fifteen, thanks to Ray Kirby. The house sitter from hell knew her way round these woods. She knew where to sneak up and pounce. Maybe to spook the big man. Maybe for a more sinister reason.

"Well, no harm done and everyone's okay," said Ray Kirby. "But I'm sorry my decision to check out the views has caused trouble for you ladies. I can't even offer you a lift back."

Bethan pulled her keys from her pocket. "My car's parked not far away. I'll drop you both in the village."

"That's really not necessary," said Ruth.

"We don't want you straining your knee any further, do we? I left my car in the forestry turning space." Surely forty – fifteen now?

They rode back in awkward silence. Ruth insisted Bethan park in the lay by rather than take her back to the house. The woman walked away, Sparkles lumbering beside her, leaving Bethan and Kirby standing next to his Range Rover.

"Rum old bird," said Kirby, watching the house sitter disappear from view at the corner of the track.

"She's not that old."

"She knows we're watching her so the limp's back. She fudged her way out of answering you back there though."

"So, you've been making her acquaintance?"

"I came across her when she appeared with the dog and I was about to climb the hill. I asked if I'd chosen the best place to park but she didn't suggest I drove closer to that track."

"I can't think why not. It would've been far more convenient."

"She seemed wary of me. So, being the gentleman I am, I introduced myself and she immediately said the Deacons had mentioned me. I get the impression she's like a mother hen with two rather elderly chicks. Likes to know what they're up to."

Bethan nodded. "Spot on. But you realise my priority is to concentrate on the business of selling a house, not to voice my personal views?"

He nodded. "Of course. That's why you took the trouble to discover what I was up to this morning. But it's obvious you don't like Ms Morgan." He held up his hand. "If you don't mind, I'd like to know more."

"Let's just say, your use of the adjective 'rum' is putting it mildly. I have certain concerns. Certain suspicions."

"Suspicions? Come on, Mrs Harley. I'm asking you to spill the beans. You needn't fear I'll drop you in it but I'm intrigued as to what's bugging you. Can you blame me?"

Bethan looked him in the eye. "These particular vendors seem to be experiencing a little too much misfortune regarding viewings."

He smoothed his hand over his chin. "Like when I turned up to find a dirty great tractor blocking access?"

"Exactly. There have been a few other incidents, enough to rattle my cage, even though I've made the right noises to my clients. I'm telling you this, Mr Kirby, in complete confidence and I'm aware I might be doing myself no favours."

"Go on."

She nodded. "Estate agents are always the baddies. But you're looking at one who likes to sleep at night and I have to say, if you're experiencing doubts about moving into Three Roads, I wouldn't blame you for driving off and telling your partner this one's not for you."

Kirby pressed his key to unlock his car, pulled off his hat and threw it on the back seat. "I meant what I said. I can sort out one cantankerous cuss of a farmer. No problem. But these other incidents you mention. How serious are they, on a scale of one to ten?"

"Mr Kirby, you're asking a lot."

"It's Ray. And you're risking a lot if you're not prepared to be totally honest, Mrs Harley. Something tells me I'm your best prospect when it comes to buying this property. Am I right?"

She couldn't stop herself twisting her rings around her finger again. "God, I need caffeine. Yes, you're right. So far, of course. And please call me Bethan."

He tipped his head in the direction of the house. "As there's no sign of baristas plying their trade around these parts, we could ask our friend there to fire up Mr Deacon's machine. Tell her I'm close to offering on her chums' house and in need of sustenance."

Bethan's laugh rang harsh. "And risk her poisoning us? I don't think so. As for your question, I'd say ten out of ten on that scale of seriousness you mentioned."

Ray Kirby didn't even blink. He lifted his wrist to check a watch that small boys and airline pilots would kill for. "If

177

I follow you back to town, may we talk privately in your office? But I warn you, Bethan, I want to know every single nasty detail."

Chapter Fifteen

Ruth took care to fake a limp after leaving the Harley woman with the equally irritating and macho Kirby. They were quite likely to check up on her. She seethed in silence as she approached the gateway, Sparkles padding beside her. Without a doubt, that bitch suspected her. She'd expressed concern over the possibility of Ruth getting into difficulties while walking but that was mere smoke and mirrors. All the estate agent cared about was her commission. What did it matter to Mrs Harley if Ruth's lifestyle and future prospects were crumbling around her?

She berated herself for failing to take the dog home before setting off. But that would have further delayed her arrival at the waterfall. And she might have run into the estate agent before she reached the woodland area. Either way she assessed the situation, the Harley woman was a nuisance, if a manageable nuisance. Whereas, Kirby...

Could she really have reached out and sent him flying? He might be built like a lighthouse but taken unawares while focusing on pretty pictures maybe his balance would have suffered. His feet might have aquaplaned, sending him sprawling helpless on the ground. Yes, he could even have tumbled into the deep waters.

Did he hold the cards to out her as a woman with a dubious history? To her knowledge, no one, absolutely no one else in the area had any inkling of how Julia Hayes had hit the Scottish newspaper headlines as the glamorous housekeeper who caused tongues to wag. Now, out there, imagining no third person in the vicinity, desperate to maintain her way of life and relationship with Suzanne and Eddie, she'd been inches away from teaching Kirby a lesson he'd never have forgotten. If indeed he had survived. Sometimes, she surprised herself with her own depravity. This was all the fault of the Deacons. How much longer would it take to convince them they should stay where they were?

Ruth had no intention of allowing the careful web she'd spun around her friends to be torn to shreds.

Back in Llanbrenin Wells, Bethan spotted a parking space, slapped her season ticket into view and hopped out to purchase a ticket for Ray, who'd parked further down the line.

"I got you an hour's worth." She handed over the slip.

"You didn't have to do that, but thank you."

They walked back to his vehicle in silence.

Bethan led the way up the ramp to the main street. "I appreciate your time. I also have a hunch you won't write me off as a hysterical female, gorging herself on crime novels."

"You; hysterical? That's one description I wouldn't apply."

"My daughter might disagree."

"So, you're married? Career, wife, and mum?"

Clearly, he hadn't noticed her engagement and wedding rings. "I… *we* are amicably estranged, if you must know."

"Sorry. I was out of order."

"I'm not precious about it." She indicated the shop. "Take away coffees? Sadly, I can't compete with Eddie Deacon's cappuccino bar."

"Take away black is fine. I'll get them."

When they entered the agency reception area, Bethan found her assistant dealing with a client. She called a quick greeting and ushered Ray Kirby into her office.

"I won't do you the discourtesy of tying this up in pink ribbons," she said when they seated themselves either side of her desk.

"Pink never was my colour."

"Okay. Here we go."

He listened carefully, sipping his drink while she gave him the facts in reverse order.

"That's about it," she said. "I have no solid evidence. I can only conjecture."

"Plus use your gut feeling."

"Indeed." She took a swallow of coffee. "That's better. So, it didn't take me too long to connect that woman I saw talking to Valerie and Brad, with Ms Morgan."

"Did you hear this – let's say, for argument's sake, this Morgan alter ego – actually speak?"

"No. But I distinctly remember her clearing her throat and raising her hand to stroke it. I saw Ruth Morgan do exactly the same thing when I was at the Deacons' house. Cue chill running down my spine."

181

"A nervous tic." He nodded. "I noticed it while we were walking up the hill together and she loosened her hood. But something like that is hardly conclusive, is it?"

"My daughter wondered if Ms Morgan might have a sister." She caught his eye. "Believe me, I don't make a habit of telling all and sundry about my clients and their peculiarities."

"Praise be for that."

She had no business liking the way his eyes sparkled but undeniably she did.

"I wanted to run my suspicions past someone. Poppy, my daughter, despite being only seventeen years of age, has a lot of common sense."

"You must have been a child bride."

She shook her head at him. Their relationship was shifting and she didn't know whether to be pleased with or wary of his slightly flirtatious tone. "I'm trying to make it clear that I do know the meaning of professionalism."

"Bethan. Watch my lips. I have no doubt whatsoever about that." He leaned back in his chair again. Crossed one leg over the other. He wore red socks. "Irrespective of that sighting and discounting your dislike of the house sitter, you appear to have good cause to suspect dirty deeds."

Bethan winced. "That whole business this morning stank worse than the dead field mouse that found its way inside a conch shell."

"You say, those two consultants didn't seem put off?"

"They appeared to be very keen on the house. But, given they've had no contact with the vendors, I find it inexplicable that Mrs Sarani rang to enquire whether there'd been any change of mind from the Deacons regarding their property remaining on the market."

"And your point is?"

"It makes me suspect Ruth Morgan might have got at them."

"Threatened them, you mean?"

"I didn't say that. Instinct tells me that isn't her style. I meant she could easily have fed them bogus information, hoping to put them off making an offer. In the same way that the mysterious stranger called Delyth took the trouble to visit a teashop with a couple she picked up in the high street so she could spin them the gruesome story of a local myth that might even have no foundation. I haven't got around to checking yet."

He grinned. "This really does get better and better." He threw up his hands. "Sorry, Bethan, but concentrating on that couple you showed around, how would Ms Morgan have known where to find them?"

"They were staying in the Queensbridge Hotel. Morgan knew that because Mr Sarani commented on the quality of its food. I heard him mention how much he was looking forward to his dinner that evening. She couldn't have failed to take that on board because she was in the kitchen at the time."

"So, our friend the delightful house sitter could have turned up, accidentally on purpose. Is that what you're saying?"

"That's exactly what I'm saying. Mr and Mrs Sarani could well have welcomed the chance of a chat with someone having insider knowledge of the area, especially as they'd already met her. Morgan could easily have drip-fed them negative ideas. Where else would they have got the idea that Mrs Deacon's mental health is less than robust?"

"Wouldn't they assume the house sale was an urgent matter, knowing the couple plan to move closer to their daughter? Wouldn't doctors, more than most people, understand how some people suffer more stress than others, when obliged to up sticks?"

"You'd think so, wouldn't you? I wouldn't mind betting the possibility of mental fragility was mentioned. That phrase can imply such a lot."

"Including lack of confidence about moving at the Deacons' stage of life?"

"Precisely," said Bethan. "I know for a fact that Eddie Deacon's anxious to get his wife back to civilisation, as he puts it. But his wife's, let's call it, nervous disposition is a plausible reason to describe to possible purchasers if I'm correct and Ms Morgan is actively hindering the sale."

Ray put down his coffee cup and folded his hands behind his neck. "If you're incorrect, it's obvious there's a hell of a lot to explain. Can't help thinking Mr Deacon doesn't know when he's well off though. Even in dreich weather, mid Wales has bowled me over."

"Okay," said Bethan. "You and he are at opposite ends of the spectrum. It's fortunate for me, and for the firm, that The Sugar House fits the criteria you have in mind. But the urge to live closer to family members as people reach their sixties and beyond is a popular reason for selling up. Moving on."

She rested her elbows on the desk. Clasped her hands beneath her chin. "I'm becoming more and more aware of how much Ruth Morgan enjoys being close to Mr and Mrs Deacon. It's not only a friendship thing. It's also, I think, about need. The woman acts as though they're her personal property and she has the right to make decisions on their behalf. I remember how you likened her to a hen with her chicks."

Ray gave a low whistle. "Yep, can't argue with that. Also, she did appear very negative when talking about the village."

"Her aversion to me's pretty obvious and goes far beyond lack of co-operation. I don't think it's a case of her disliking my signature perfume. I'm a threat simply because I'm trying to sell The Sugar House. Similarly, my clients are a threat because they might buy it."

Ray nodded. "Strikes me, our Ms Morgan has her feet under the table in more ways than one. Do you reckon she's got designs on the old man? How about she's planning to bump off his wife and become the next Mrs Deacon?"

Bethan stared back at him. "Oh. My. God. Are you serious? You are, aren't you?"

Ray wasn't yet ready to voice his suspicions about Ruth Morgan's past. He shrugged. "Think about it. If he became a widower, he'd be in shock. The status quo might strike him as more appealing than setting off on his own. We

185

know neither of his kids is living close by. So, initially, who's the one person he'd turn to?"

He raised his eyebrows but Bethan stared back at him, her face expressionless.

"The only person he trusts to let loose in his house, that's who. And that person might try to persuade him to stay put and let her look after him. Maybe she's convinced herself Mr Deacon's desire to move will fade if he suddenly turns into a lonely widower. She's not unattractive, you know. That spiky kind of zip appeals to some guys."

"Really?" Bethan shuddered.

He grinned. "I prefer someone more approachable."

Bethan avoided his gaze.

"But the woman's a powerhouse," he said. "There's a lot of repressed energy simmering. She could be near the edge."

"I couldn't possibly comment. I find her obnoxious... but let's not go there. I need to concentrate on facts and the way forward. I have to protect my clients' welfare, which means yours and that of any other prospective purchasers." Bethan narrowed her eyes. "I can't believe we're talking like this. You're probably wondering whether I've mislaid my marbles."

"Nah. As for the dreaded house sitter, I guess the jury's still out. But fact is often stranger than fiction." He looked at the flamboyant timepiece on his wrist. "I'd better shift myself and leave you to get on with your day." He reached for his wallet and took out a business card.

"I know my details are on your database but don't hesitate to ring me outside office hours if necessary. I know a lot of people, if push comes to shove and you need a little, shall we say, support." He handed over the card. "Bethan, don't fret. No bizarre old biddy's going to put me off your clients' house. The one to make the decision is my partner."

Bethan nodded.

"If Claudia decides the village is too remote for her or The Sugar House lacks the wow factor, I'm afraid that'll be it. But I have faith in her taste and I'd be surprised if she didn't fall in love with the place."

Bethan nodded again. Too many bitten lips didn't chime with her normally sunny personality. The Deacons would be back before long and Eddie Deacon would expect a full progress update. Who would he blame for the downstairs cloakroom fiasco? Ruth Morgan would doubtless put forward Sparkles, even though to push the tiny corpse inside the shell so snugly had to be beyond the old dog's ability. Yet, without tangible proof to back up Bethan's suspicions, where did she go from here?

Chapter Sixteen

"I don't know where we go from here, Eddie, and that's a fact."

Suzanne plumped herself down on a crimson chesterfield and stared through the hotel lounge window as if seeking inspiration from the stone cherubs gazing back at her.

"We're fine at the moment, thanks." Eddie nodded at the hovering waiter and settled himself opposite his wife.

He leaned forward and reached for her hands. "It's no bad position to be in, Suze. Think about it. We put our house on the market. We leave a trusted house sitter and estate agent to look after things while we swan off to view properties. Now we find each of us has fallen in love with a different house. That's progress, not something to agonise over, surely?"

"You don't seem to appreciate how close that beautiful bungalow I like is from Penny's place. The house on the coast is ten miles away and, in my opinion, the garden's unsuitable."

Eddie sighed. "Try not to let proximity to the family be your main criteria. You know Penny and Dec will be looking for somewhere bigger as soon as he comes back to the UK for good."

"I understand that, but they're still looking to stay in Salisbury or close by. Unless you know differently."

"I think it'll depend on where they find suitable to start a new practice."

"So, why are you rushing me into choosing a new home?"

"I'm not rushing you, Suze. We haven't sold our house yet and even when we do, we can find somewhere to rent if we still haven't made up our minds."

She nodded. "All right, but it mightn't be as easy to sell The Sugar House as you seem to think."

"We both know it could take months. We might even have to wait until spring before someone offers. If you could put the house down in Wiltshire, it'd be worth mega bucks. But even at the price Bethan Harley suggested, we all know it's still a terrific bargain. You mark my words."

"I hope you're right, Eddie. But I also hope we can move out of Wales and into a new home without renting somewhere first. To me that sounds too much like hassle."

"Moving house is never a picnic, my sweet, that's why I want to make things as easy for you as possible. You know Penny said you could stay with them and let me manage things at Three Roads ready for the actual moving day. It's easier for her to put up just one person."

"I imagine Ruth would enjoy having you to herself."

"Sorry?"

"Have you not noticed her attitude towards you?"

He shook his head. "Can't say I have. I've always considered her to be more your friend than mine."

"That's what she intends you to think. But ever since we put the house on the market, it's as if she sees me as an encumbrance. As if she'd like to see me out of her life but she'd very much like you still to be in it."

Eddie stared at her. "Are you serious?"

"I'm deadly serious. Think of her initial reaction to our decision. Now that had to be an 'if looks could kill' situation."

"You're over-reacting, Suze. Anyway, I take full blame for that blooper. I bungled it by not keeping an eye on things. I'm surprised the postman didn't say anything, anyway. Our friendly Knocker likes a chat with her before he goes on for his morning cuppa with Mrs Frame."

"He could have been running late. Maybe Ruth would have been even more upset if she'd found out that way. It was interesting how she turned on us, well me especially, but backed off again." Suzanne squared her shoulders. "I'm not ungrateful for all the help she's given us over the years. She's so good with the dog too. But we could manage without her if she was the one moving. I'm not so sure she feels the same way about us leaving."

"Can't think why. She must have coped before we arrived."

"How can I put this? Ruth's quite proprietorial, Eddie. And little by little, I can sense her trying to push herself between us."

"Oh, for flip's sake! Even if she did try that, it'd never wash with me." Eddie thrust away any fantasy he'd ever entertained of an illicit rendezvous with Ruth. There'd been a kiss. Once. He'd wondered afterwards but done nothing about it.

190

"Listen, Suze. There's nothing to keep us in Three Roads and the time's ripe for a new stage in our lives. I've enjoyed our years in Wales but our needs are changing. A decade or so can make a huge difference once you hit sixty. Ruth's younger than either of us. She knows more people in these parts than we ever will. Didn't her aunt live at Rock Cottage for years?"

"That's not the first time you've said that."

"About Ruth's aunt?"

"About Ruth being a younger woman than I am."

"I believe I pointed out she was younger than either of us."

"You also said not too long ago, that she'd make someone a good wife."

Eddie stared at Suzanne. He had an awful feeling the heat suffusing his face displayed his discomfort. But surely his wife didn't really imagine he had designs on another woman? On Ruth?

He considered his next words carefully. "Maybe you're reading things into the situation, darling. Living in a small community is bound to make us feel claustrophobic about certain matters. You don't have any other female friends, apart from her. Not close ones, anyway."

"To be honest, I'm wondering just how much of a true friend she really is. I'm starting to realise the extent to which she's been insinuating herself in my life."

"I know you're not keen on driving nowadays. But you don't have to feel obliged to ask her. I'll always take you wherever you want to go. You know that."

"Thank you, Eddie, but it's not only about chauffeuring me here and there. It's her carping comments about my choice of clothes and the number of times I want my hair done. If I'm wearing something she admires, she puts on the 'poor me' act about not being fortunate enough to indulge her tastes like I can. She went on and on about that amethyst and turquoise necklace I bought in Knightly and it was obvious she was hoping I'd hand it over."

"Why haven't you said something before?"

"I wanted to make sure I wasn't being hung-up over trivial incidents. But lately, and certainly since we put the house on the market, I'm convinced she's jealous of me. I might as well come out with it, Eddie. I'm not sure I want to go back to the village. I'm not sure I want to call The Sugar House home any more."

Ruth anticipated hearing from Eddie and Suzanne at any time. The morning after her catastrophic visit to The Devil's Pool she set off to Llanbrenin Wells with an important purchase in mind. She could have stopped off in Knightly but decided driving the extra distance to the larger town would be a safer option. Although, once she slipped into the ladies' toilets and dressed in her alter ego Delyth's attire, she believed no one who knew her would associate such an elegant auburn-haired lady with Ruth Morgan, whose usual denims and cords fitted days filled with gardening, preserve making and dog walking.

Nor was this market day when more people drove in from the surrounding villages. Fleetingly she thought of

Huw, her friend who lived a few miles away. But he shopped elsewhere and if he fancied a day out, he invariably drove to Abergavenny.

Often, when Ruth called at the arts centre or joined the fishmonger's queue on market days, she'd see a familiar face and maybe exchange a few words. The first time she adopted her Delyth persona, she'd not noticed anyone scrutinising her as if wondering if they'd met her before. She'd gloated over the realisation that her alter ego could face the world with impunity.

She tossed her red rucksack on the car's back seat, enjoying the knowledge that no one overlooked The Sugar House. She was on the verge of driving off, to check if her cat was at home and still speaking to her, when she thought of Bethan Harley. Given the chilly relationship between them, perhaps a courteous telephone call would be diplomatic. Ruth let herself back inside.

After a few rings she heard the voice of Briggs, Caldwell and Balls' admin assistant.

"It's Ruth Morgan, speaking from The Sugar House."

She waited for the woman to respond. "I'm ringing to say I shall be out this morning. Maybe you'll be kind enough to let Mrs Harley know? If she has anyone wishing to view, she's welcome to come over and let herself in."

"That's very thoughtful, thanks, Ms Morgan. Bethan is working at our Knightly office today but I'll pass your message on. As far as I know, we have no viewings scheduled for Mr and Mrs Deacon's property."

Ruth closed the call. Better and better. If the Harley woman was in Knightly, Ruth could relax while walking around Llanbrenin Wells in Delyth guise. If by chance Mrs Harley harboured any suspicions about the woman who'd talked local history to Valerie and Brad the house hunters, the odds on her clapping eyes on Delyth today were virtually non-existent.

Seated at her desk in the Knightly office, Bethan idly wondered what Tim might be doing. She and her husband found few opportunities to speak these days. His erratic hours and her peripatetic work style didn't encourage it. For the first two years he worked offshore, she'd missed having him around but became used to his absences until he returned home after one particular stint of duty and she realised how much she'd been thriving in the land where distance should make the heart grow fonder.

But it wasn't only her. Tim had confessed to seeing someone all the way up there in Aberdeen. Loneliness. A moment of madness. A chance meeting with a woman also dining alone in a restaurant, the affair fizzling out before it hardly began. Those were among the words he'd used to describe what she still considered his pathetic little fling. Bethan had been angry rather than devastated.

It would have been better if he'd said nothing. But no, he'd turned her into the classic wronged wife. Adultery figured high on her forbidden list but no way would she ever shatter their daughter's relationship with her dad by dwelling on it.

They strived to keep their slowly unravelling relationship from their daughter, but Poppy had inherited her mother's sensitivity to body language and atmosphere. Bethan knew the teenager understood what kept her parents together and what now tore them apart. Bethan knew she'd drunk too much white wine the night before but she remembered everything her daughter said. Realised how much she had to be thankful for. They'd be okay, she and Poppy, whatever happened between herself and Tim.

But her husband's announcement left Bethan in a wintry no man's land. Tim told her he'd do anything to keep the family together and, deep down, Bethan didn't want to draw a line beneath their relationship either. Yet. His confession had created a problem for her and she still felt the sting of rejection. But she realised that, apart from her daughter, her work was the main objective of her existence. How sad was that?

Financially, the family had no worries. But when Poppy went off to university, which was what everyone expected, how would Bethan prevent herself from becoming too immersed in the world of estate agency? Would she think about dating? Could she cope with all that after almost two decades of marriage? The thought of meeting someone through a website daunted her without even investigating the possibility.

She'd enjoyed her conversation with Ray Kirby. Apart from providing another opportunity to let off steam, Ray had taken on board her concerns and conjectures and made her feel her views were credible. Bethan enjoyed the company of men and was used to other women not warming to her. What was she supposed to do? She worked in a tough arena, aware how Briggs, Caldwell and Balls punched out of their league when competing against a couple of national agencies with branches in mid Wales. Nowadays some people looked to finding a house buyer online. As if the business wasn't difficult enough already.

But Ruth Morgan had erected a barrier of hostility. Bethan suspected, even if she'd been the kind of sales negotiator who looked like she worked in a library or health food shop, Ms Morgan would have behaved towards her in exactly the same manner.

Over and over again, she reran the sequence of events in her head. So far, the house sitter's plausible explanations covered everything Bethan found to question. Stripping away the excuses and examining the hard facts, Ruth Morgan could well be masterminding a campaign to prevent The Sugar House from selling but Bethan couldn't yet figure out how she'd engineered one or two of the stunts.

If Bethan mentioned this situation to her husband, what would he say? Bethan closed her eyes and told herself to focus upon not showing tolerance in any way. Her husband would insist she dared not assume Ruth Morgan was all right really, that she wasn't evil but merely misunderstood. Tim would be logical. He'd ask how a woman nursing an arthritic knee could scramble through undergrowth and perch on a steep bank, ready to hurl a missile. How would that same woman, on a different occasion, cover difficult terrain so speedily that she arrived in time to approach Ray

Kirby as he stood, poised above a dangerous drop into unwelcoming waters? Ray had made a jokey comment to that effect.

So maybe Ruth Morgan didn't suffer from mobility problems. If she was faking an ailment, who would dare challenge her? And if Bethan's suspicions were accurate, and the woman had disguised herself on one occasion, why shouldn't she adopt the same or even a different disguise, to sabotage potential purchasers? Three Roads didn't attract too many tourists at this time of year – at any time of year, to be honest.

Good point, Tim would say. And the dead field mouse? How would Ms Morgan contrive that incident, given it was probably in position before Mr and Mrs Deacon set off house hunting?

Bethan ticked off items on her fingers. She knew Ruth Morgan had a cat. Eddie Deacon had reported their friend would be spending each night at The Sugar House for the dog's sake. Ruth was a frequent visitor. What if her cat had brought a small dead creature in through the cat flap and Ruth experienced a light bulb moment? She could easily have wrapped up the vermin and carried it in her bag, placing it into that conch shell when visiting the cloakroom.

Bethan shuddered. Nursing that morning's second cup of strong takeaway coffee, her thoughts drifted back to Ray Kirby. How was she going to feel when she met him with his glamorous partner in tow? Animal magnetism. That's what that man had. In shed loads. The ease with which the term sprang to mind bothered Bethan. Someone else's man

197

was so not on her agenda. Why didn't she type Vocalist Claudia Kelsey into her search engine and really depress herself?

Her fingers took on a will of their own and clicked on the internet icon. But what did it matter to her whether Ray Kirby's singer partner was a pretty blonde or a dark, exotic siren? The phone shrilled. Bethan jumped and reached out to pick up her extension.

"Bethan? I'm having one of those mornings. Would you be able to meet a couple at The Old Mill and show them around?"

"Do you mean, like now?"

Her colleague sighed down the line. "If possible, please. I can't go myself. We're one staff member down today. You know how it is."

"I'll need to call in for the key on the way, won't I? You do mean The Old Mill just outside Llanbrenin?"

"That's the one."

"See you in twenty minutes or so."

All thoughts of Claudia Kelsey banished from her mind, Bethan called up the property on the company website and refreshed her knowledge. She didn't personally know this house, though she was aware that it has generated much interest but no offers. It'd be a coup to pull off a sale.

Bethan made good time and drove into a space close to the riverside car park entrance. When she arrived at the BCB office halfway down the high street, her colleague had the house key ready.

Moments later, she was through the agency door and back in the high street. There weren't many shoppers about but the sight of one particular person, down at the car park end of the street, caused Bethan to catch her breath. Could it really be? Barely able to believe her eyes, she was gazing at the woman whose image had left an indelible mark upon her memory.

"That's her!" Bethan froze. Had she really spoken aloud?

It must have been impossible for the woman she knew as Delyth to hear, given she was out of earshot, standing on the opposite side of the road, peering in a shop window. Yet, as if sensing someone watched her, the tall, elegant woman looked Bethan's way. Turning abruptly, she headed into the nearby coffee shop.

"Gotcha!" Bethan ran down the pavement, gaining black looks from early shoppers.

Heart racing, eyes fixed on the café entrance; she waited for the lights to change and the green man to bless the pedestrian crossing. There was too much traffic to risk dashing to the opposite pavement but when she burst inside the café and scanned the tables, she didn't see Delyth.

An assistant recognised her. "Hi, Mrs Harley. Are you meeting someone?"

"No, but I think someone I know just came in." Bethan's heart was still thumping and booming. Her mouth drying. She sucked in air.

"I was in the kitchen, but you might try upstairs. You know we've extra seating up there now?"

"Thanks, Elin. I'll dash up and check. I could have been mistaken."

As Bethan ran upstairs, her bag strap slid from her shoulder. She grabbed it, without breaking her stride. If she came face to face with the woman whom she suspected of being Ruth Morgan, how would she deal with her? She had an appointment to keep, her career to consider. But wasn't this all about her job, too? She daren't pass on this opportunity. If her suspicions proved accurate, Morgan would be up the creek minus the proverbial paddle.

On the upper level, her gaze fell upon three women sitting in the window. A raft of coffee cups, tablets and notebooks littering the table pointed to some sort of meeting. A smartly dressed man who might have been a sales representative, sat at a corner table, speaking on his mobile phone and flicking through the pages of a glossy catalogue. Bethan looked around in frustration before the reasoning part of her brain clicked into action.

She turned on her heel. Backtracked to the landing. Pushed open the access door to the toilets. Left for gentlemen. Right for ladies. Through the door painted with the garish pink female figure were two cubicles. Both were occupied. A walking frame stood nearby. She checked her watch. Bit her lip. She hated arriving late for a viewing. It was unprofessional. What's more, she'd made a total balls-up of catching Delyth.

The door to one of the cubicles opened to reveal an elderly woman with curly grey hair and Harry Potter spectacles.

She smiled at Bethan. "Would you mind pushing my walker over to me, please?"

Bethan reached for the frame. "I wonder, have you seen a tall lady with darkish auburn hair? Dressed elegantly."

The elderly woman nodded. "That sounds like the person I saw when I left the lift." She gave a disapproving sniff. "Awful woman could barely wait for me to get out before she shot in and pushed the down button. Shocking manners."

"The lift!" Bethan rushed away, doubtless leaving the elderly lady bemoaning her rudeness too. She clattered downstairs, looked around without much conviction and left, to scan the high street in both directions.

Not a hope in hell of finding her now. Bethan couldn't believe her bad luck. Cursing her own stupidity, telling herself she was only here because her job had taken her to Llanbrenin for an unscheduled viewing, she headed for the car park, her mind still fretting at the enigma. If she'd actually observed Ruth Morgan in disguise and Ruth had seen Bethan, wouldn't that explain the elegant woman's behaviour? People did call into catering establishments for the sole purpose of using the washrooms, but could anyone have reached the upper floor and vanished from view with quite so much speed?

Bethan got into her car. Smacked her palm on the steering wheel. What now? She started the engine. Her first priority must be to tackle the job in hand, but how she wished she could come face to face with the mysterious Delyth.

Chapter Seventeen

What now? Ruth, or rather Delyth, had sought refuge in a second-hand bookshop approached by an alleyway off the high street. She'd climbed the narrow stairway to the first floor and crouched at the far end, examining higgledy-piggledy piles of travel guides predating online holiday websites and social media links. Surely that bothersome woman wouldn't think of looking in here for her? Had Mrs Smart Arse Harley nothing better to do than follow a wild goose chase?

Ruth, convinced Bethan Harley couldn't possibly have penetrated her disguise, moved across to the window, holding an open book before her. She needed to remain positive. Confident. She could keep an eye on the alleyway and listen for the shop bell at the same time. Just in case the BCB sales negotiator was carrying out a check of all possible hiding places in the vicinity.

Even if Mrs Harley had no idea her quarry was Ruth in disguise, she might still be after sweet-talking Delyth, eager to question her knowledge of lurid local history. That couldn't be allowed to happen.

Despite the trickle of sweat running between her breasts, despite the nagging fear of discovery digging its claws into her jugular, Ruth couldn't resist smiling. Having reacted with such speed and quick thinking, she must merit the prize, must deserve a reward for evading confrontation. Her breathing steadied. She didn't take her eyes off the alleyway below. She heard no pinging shop doorbell. No murmur of voices as a question was posed.

Ten minutes later, she contemplated her next move, still mentally cursing Bethan. After taking the trouble to ring the Briggs, Caldwell and Balls office to leave a polite message, Ruth felt she'd been handed an unexpected gift and been gratified to discover the sales negotiator's base for the day. Mrs Harley had surprised and irritated her by turning up in the town where she shouldn't have been that morning.

Ruth congratulated herself on visiting the key cutter as soon as she'd changed into her Delyth outfit and thrown her rucksack back in the car. Today's visit had ensured possession of her own, undeniably precious, spare key to The Sugar House. She'd tucked it inside a pocket of her shoulder bag, convinced it would prove useful at some time in the future. In any case, surely it was her right to have her own key to the Deacons' property? Her lips set in a thin line as she reflected upon Eddie and Suzanne's negligence in not having handed her one in the first place. They so sorely lacked in many attributes Ruth would prefer them to possess.

These next few minutes could prove very tricky, if indeed she still risked discovery. Once out of the bookshop, she might walk straight into Bethan Harley. Who knew if her suspicious adversary still hung around this end of the high street, waiting to confront her? But Ruth believed she could still pull this off, as long as they didn't meet face to face. She debated the possibility of hurrying to her car and driving away without changing her clothing. She'd have to turn off the main road, follow the forestry track and park up somewhere, making sure no one else was around. She wouldn't take long to remove her wig and scramble out of her top layers and into Ruth's sensible quilted jacket, dark trousers and boots. If a forestry vehicle happened to come along, she would give a friendly wave because if the driver came from the village, he'd recognise her car and might stop to check she hadn't broken down.

A drift of Delyth's perfume assailed Ruth's nostrils, reminding her how much trouble she'd taken to assume her alter ego. All her careful preparation could be destroyed. It would be impossible to conceal her true identity from the Harley woman when in close proximity. Her adversary might even whip out her camera. These days, everyone carried those fancy phones that took pictures.

Ruth groaned. The bookstore owner had been on the telephone when she arrived. She'd used the shop now and then over the years and he'd certainly recognise Ruth. But would he recognise Delyth? Suddenly her confidence was wavering. She would buy a book and test her gentle local accent and her disguise upon someone with whom she had a slight acquaintance. If she passed this challenge, she'd have confidence to walk from the store and proceed to the car park. A sudden adrenalin surge boosted Ruth's courage as the elegantly attired Delyth walked down the stairs to pay for her purchase.

The bookstore owner greeted her cheerfully, took her five-pound note and produced change.

"No, I don't need a bag, thank you," she said in Delyth's lilting tones.

She said goodbye. She left the bookstore. She set off towards the car park. She kept her head down. She had no reason to meet anybody's gaze. The schoolgirl coming around the corner also had her head down, checking her phone as she progressed. The two collided.

"Oh, I'm so sorry." The girl's gaze took in the tall, stylishly dressed woman she'd almost bowled over.

"Why don't you watch where you're going?"

"I said I was sorry." The girl's cheeks reddened. "Um, are you like hurt or anything?"

Ruth cleared her throat. She watched the teenager's gaze focus on her fingers as her hand moved instinctively to stroke her throat. She frowned at her. "I'm not hurt. I'm in a hurry."

Ruth, diving for the pedestrian crossing, heard the leggy young girl gasp as a motorist braked hard to avoid mowing down a pedestrian. Once safely on the opposite pavement, Ruth hastened to her car.

Bethan took a plastic bag of supermarket stir-fry from the refrigerator crisper drawer, ripped it across and dumped the contents on her chopping board. She planned to add chestnut mushrooms, carrots, plus a chunk of white cabbage languishing in the vegetable rack. She heard the front door bang, heralding Poppy's arrival in the kitchen. Bethan picked up her wine glass and took a sip, briefly closing her eyes as she did so.

"Good day today, Mum? Not?" Poppy gave her mother a quick hug around the shoulders and opened the fridge to take out a bottle of fizzy mineral water. She slid on to a stool at the breakfast bar and perched, glass and bottle in front of her.

"Not the best day I've ever had but I may have helped sell a property not too far from here."

"Nice one. Anywhere I'd know?"

"It's the Old Mill."

"That's the pretty pink house not far from where Grace lives. Her mum says the deceptively spacious description is spot on." Poppy grinned.

"The description fits." Bethan couldn't help sounding defensive. "Kettle's not long boiled if you want a cuppa."

"You've had a hot drink and now you're on the wine? How long have you been back?"

"Ages. I finished work on time for once. And I'm not 'on the wine' as you put it. I'm merely enjoying a glass of Chardonnay. So, how did your study session with Callum go?"

"Good." Poppy slid off the stool and fished a teabag from the strawberry-shaped container beside the kettle. "Butter mint flavour? Will I like it?"

Bethan began chopping raw carrot into batons. "I should say so."

"Cool." Poppy swung around. "Ooh, I almost forgot. I think I might have bumped into your creepy lady in town today."

Bethan frowned. "In Llanbrenin? What were you doing out of school?"

"It's not a prison, Mum. I only went out to buy Grace and me a sandwich while she was in the library. We seriously fancied hummus and red pepper from the deli."

"So, what makes you think you saw someone you only know about from my description?" Carefully, Bethan scooped up sticks of carrot and placed them in a glass bowl with the other vegetables.

Poppy came to stand next to her. She lifted up the bowl and gazed at the medley of bright colours. "Looking good, Mum. So, what sauce are we having?"

"Packet mix, I'm afraid. You can choose."

Poppy doused her butter mint teabag with boiled water and retreated to the breakfast bar. "No worries. Whatever's in the cupboard will be fine."

Bethan wondered whether the pink cloud of love upon which her daughter currently floated, accounted for the sunny mood. She persevered. "This woman you mentioned? I take it we're talking about the one known as Delyth."

"Yeah, I wouldn't have given her a second look, except I used the quick way from school to the high street. This woman came rushing out of the second-hand bookshop like a whirlwind. We collided and I apologised but she was sooooo rude to me." Poppy rolled her eyes once more and shook her head.

"Why so?"

"Like it was all my fault we'd bumped into one another."

"What made you think it was Delyth?"

Poppy sniffed her butter mint tea. "Mmmm – yes, it's yummy. Because, Mum, I asked her if she was okay and guess what?"

Bethan picked up her wine glass. "I've no idea, Poppy."

"I think you will have. She cleared her throat and moved her hand upwards to her neck, exactly the way you described to me the other day. Like this – see?"

Bethan froze as her daughter demonstrated the gesture. "That's her. Oh my god, that's her!"

"Whoever it was, she raced across the road before the pedestrian light turned green. I thought she'd copped it but luckily the car coming past managed to stop in time."

"Did she say anything else?"

"No way. She did a runner. Off down the slope to the car park."

"Can you tell me how she was dressed?"

"Layers. Beige, maybe a kind of porridge colour. Coffee. She was carrying a big brown leather shoulder bag." Poppy wrinkled her forehead. "Her nails were painted. It was a shiny conker shade. Cool. I always notice people's nails like you notice scent, Mum. And this woman looked just like your description." Poppy stared at Bethan. "Mum, your face looks kind of ashen. The Delyth person didn't try and kill me. Maybe she has bad stuff going on in her life. Chill, why don't you?"

"I'm fine. You've been a great help, lovey. Thank you for telling me. Now, I'll get on with our supper."

Bethan boiled water for pasta, her brain replaying what she'd heard. When Poppy reported seeing the woman she'd collided with, throwing herself across the road in her eagerness to get away, light had dawned. If Ruth really was masquerading as Delyth, obviously she was, in her everyday life, faking a problem with her mobility, a form of cover that could, if necessary, become an alibi. She would be adding a different dimension to her alter ego in the form of agility. Her real self couldn't go dashing across busy roads or hurrying across uneven terrain. Her alter ego could.

Ruth Morgan didn't appear to use cosmetics. She certainly didn't apply nail polish and Bethan hadn't noticed any particular fragrance around her unless you counted a whiff of sensible toilet soap. Delyth exuded elegance as well as fragrance. Again, Bethan recalled a drift of sophisticated scent when she passed the knot of people outside the estate agency the other morning. Poppy had commented on Delyth's bronze nail polish. Yes! The pieces of the jigsaw were beginning to fall into place.

"Ray Kirby."

"It's Bethan Harley here, Mr Kirby."

"What's up, Bethan? Not trouble at t'mill, I hope? And it's Ray, remember?"

Bethan ignored the tremors induced on hearing that rich, deep drawl. His voice sounded much more intimate down the phone line. She tucked her legs beneath her. Settled into the sofa corner. "If you can spare a few minutes, I'd like to tell you something that happened today."

He didn't interrupt while she related the morning sighting of Delyth. How her daughter had encountered what

209

surely must be the same person, outside the second-hand bookshop, also in a hurry. A person so desperate to cross the road, she'd risked being mown down in full view of a dismayed Poppy amongst others.

"I see," Ray said at last.

"The woman my daughter bumped into has to be the one I've now seen on two occasions. That hand to throat gesture is the give away."

"Let's be absolutely clear about this. You're certain it's the same hand movement you've seen Ruth Morgan make?"

Bethan didn't have to think. She nodded, as though Ray could see her. "Yes. I've seen Ruth and Delyth each make an identical gesture. The day I did the viewing for those two consultants, I particularly noticed Ms Morgan making it. I didn't like her attitude regarding my arriving with prospective purchasers. She was on the defensive because of the putrid smell in the downstairs loo. The movement was slow. Unhurried. Likewise, that throat clearing which sounded to me like a nervous habit."

"I think I mentioned having seen her do the same thing? It was when she and I were walking up the hill from the village. Before she drew my attention to her arthritic knee."

"I remember you saying something. Did she seem edgy?"

"What struck me was her negative attitude about her friends' decision to sell up. She must have known I'd fallen for the house but she didn't seem too enthusiastic that the vendors might be making an easy sale."

"That would tally with my impression."

"She faltered while we were walking and she mentioned how difficult it was keeping up with me, because her knee troubled her."

"To gain sympathy, d'you reckon?"

"No. I think she wanted an excuse to get away from me and take the dog home."

"Which she patently did not do!"

"Correct. I still don't really know why she was creeping around the undergrowth leaving the Labrador tied up. I made it clear I could handle rough terrain and didn't need a nursemaid. Regarding this so say alter ego, you can't discount the possibility of Morgan having a sister in the area. That nervous habit might be a family tic."

"Agreed. But if that's the case, it doesn't explain why this Delyth acted as she did. She would have no idea who I was. That first time I saw her outside the Llanbrenin office, she very pointedly looked the other way, as if trying to avoid locking gazes with me."

"And you saw her shift in a way she couldn't have done if she had a gammy leg?"

"That's right."

"So, let's assume that was indeed Ruth Morgan in disguise. Are you quite sure she had no idea who you were, that first time?"

"I'm absolutely certain. She wasn't around when I visited the Deacons to carry out a valuation. But, when I left our office, dressed as I was, she might well have jumped to a conclusion and kept her head down, in case I was an employee."

"I'm playing devil's advocate here but why would she fear being recognised if she was in disguise anyway?"

"Perhaps she planned on pulling a similar trick while using a different type of disguise. But eyes are a give away. So are gestures a person makes without even noticing what they're doing. That sounds plausible, don't you think?"

His voice sounded warm. Amused. Affectionate even. "I'm impressed. That would indeed be a credible reason."

"It's difficult, trying to get into the mind of someone who I suspect of such appalling cunning."

"You're doing fine, Bethan. Here's another one for you. Ready?"

"Try me."

She noted the slight pause. Closed her eyes. All the better to picture him.

"Right. So, today, you think you see the same woman, once more trying to avoid eye contact. Next thing, she dives into a café. You follow. You hurry up the stairs only to find the bird already flown. If she's so cunning, why would she risk getting cornered in the first place?"

"I can't answer that. Maybe she acted on impulse, dashed through the first door she saw and realised, if I had suspicions, the obvious thing would be for me to follow her inside and confront her."

"OK. She rushed up the stairs ahead of you. Saw the old lady leave the elevator. Took a chance you were already heading up the stairs and judged it safe to use the elevator to get down again while you were stuck on the top floor. Gutsy."

"You sound as if you approve."

"Kind of. Morgan either gets off on being a female James Bond or she's seriously deranged." His laugh rumbled down the phone line. "It's all right, Bethan, don't worry. I am taking you seriously. And now you explain your daughter's experience, it does seem the elusive Delyth and the house sitter from hell are one and the same person."

"But how can I prove anything? Dressing up isn't a crime. I can't pin one single thing on Ruth Morgan, can I?"

"Hey, we need to think about all this. Can you leave it with me, please, sweetheart?"

When Bethan put down the phone, the endearment stayed with her. Whispering inside her head. Normally she'd have bristled. Felt patronised. But Ray had said he and she needed to think about all this, as if they were partners. Was he trying to reassure her? Living up to his macho image? If so, maybe she wasn't sending the right signals. If Ray Kirby thought she feared Ruth Morgan, he was mistaken. And sooner or later, she'd find a way to prove it. As for the affectionate term, maybe he used it to save having to remember which woman he was talking to at the time.

213

Chapter Eighteen

Eddie Deacon dropped his mobile phone on the satin bed cover. "She didn't pick up."

"Why didn't you leave a message?"

"I'd prefer to speak to her so she knows we're coming home tomorrow. In case she forgets to check the answer phone."

"Whatever you say, Eddie. I'm sorry I overreacted about going back. It is still our home, after all. It's only recently I've begun feeling unsettled."

Eddie walked across to where his wife sat in a chintz-covered easy chair beside the window. "It's my fault. I realise now how much I've railroaded you into all this." He kissed her on the lips.

Suzanne reached out to squeeze his hand. "It's probably a good thing we found out exactly what Ruth had in mind regarding her future."

"True, but irrespective of that nonsense, we both feel it's time to move on."

"Absolutely. Especially as Penny's told us Declan's new practice is 99% certain to be in the Salisbury area."

"That's a definite bonus, even if we still can't agree which house we like best." He yawned and stretched. "I think I'll take a shower before dinner."

"I'll try our number again in a bit. See if I have better luck than you. If I know Ruth, she'll be looking for a glass or three of your Merchant's Choice red wine before too long."

"Meeoww!"

Suzanne chuckled. "I'm right though, aren't I?"

"It's good to see you feeling calmer again."

She watched her husband shuck off his clothes and shrug on the complimentary towelling gown. He looked in pretty good shape for a man his age. Had he been totally faithful to her throughout the years of their marriage? Probably not. But no way had she ever accused him of infidelity. Nor would she, now or ever, fret about random indiscretions he might or might not have enjoyed in the past. At this stage of their lives, Eddie appeared content. These last few days, she'd co-operated when he declared the time had come to turn back the clock and reclaim something missing from their relationship. She'd almost enjoyed the resumption of their intimate relationship. Almost.

But, feeling the unease she did, regarding Ruth, she knew these next weeks and God forbid, possible months, might prove challenging. Sometimes, if she was feeling too wide-awake, she'd lie beside Eddie, who could sleep for Britain, going through her 'what if' list. No way could she bear her husband even to think about straying in that particular lady's direction. Somehow, Ruth had rattled her. Had introduced a feeling of insecurity, slowly but slyly, over the last weeks. Why had she not noticed this sooner?

Suzanne reached for her expensive hand cream and squeezed the tube, allowing a small pool to ooze into the palm of one hand. She began massaging the lotion into the

215

back of her hands, stroking the fingers as if pulling on a pair of gloves, while thoughts tumbled through her head. Soon she and Eddie would return to The Sugar House, maybe for not too long a stay, if all went well. She'd make sure she concentrated upon keeping him happy. This would tie in with the very necessary start of a cooling off period regarding Ruth. It was time for her to show she too had teeth and could use them when necessary. She'd need every ounce of her strength.

The fragrant lotion soon soaked into her skin. She inhaled the scent of vanilla and almonds. Reached for Eddie's phone, smiling at the sound of him singing the big song from his favourite musical show. When she punched in her own telephone number, she heard it ring three times before the call was picked up.

Their house sitter had returned.

"Hello, Ruth," said Suzanne, in cheerful mode. "All well, my dear? I'm ringing to let you know we're driving home tomorrow morning. I'm sure you'll be pleased to hear you'll soon be relieved of your duties."

From the bathroom, Suzanne could hear her husband warbling, *Do You Hear the People Sing?* The woman on the other end of the phone call appeared temporarily flummoxed by Suzanne's announcement.

"Ruth? Can you hear me properly? I said we're coming home tomorrow. Perhaps you'd like to get your things together and return to Rock Cottage after breakfast so the rest of the day's yours."

Bethan settled herself behind her desk in the Knightly office and fired up her laptop. She focused on an email received from Ray Kirby sent late the previous night. Either he'd quizzed his partner about her schedule after his conversation with Bethan, or Claudia Kelsey had contacted him with her news. The message heading read *Proposed Viewing.*

My partner's due back in London tomorrow. I'd like to request a viewing of The Sugar House for Saturday noon. Is that OK? You do realise, if Claudia says the magic word, I shall make an offer? If your clients accept, you'll no longer have to worry about the wicked witch of the woods. But in all fairness, I feel I must advise Claudia about recent events.

Best regards, RK

Bethan typed a brief response, confirming date and time and informing him she would meet him at the property. She also told him she'd no intention of informing the house sitter of the appointment, given the Deacons had awarded her carte blanche in the form of a spare front door key.

She sat back in her chair. How would she feel if she was Claudia? Returning to her lover after weeks of absence? Bethan felt her cheeks heat as too vivid a scenario tantalised her mind's eye. She swallowed hard. Tried to concentrate. Tried to forget the intimate tone of Ray's deep voice when they spoke on the phone. Tried to blank out that full upper lip blessed with a curve to make a woman yearn to trace its outline with one finger.

She tried to imagine hearing how a deranged neighbour was allegedly trying to interfere with the sale of Mr and Mrs

217

Deacon's home. How much would that influence the glamorous Claudia, especially when she knew how heavily Ray had fallen for the place?

She'd temporarily forgotten the farmer and his cavalier attitude to the right of way attached to The Sugar House. According to Eddie, Ruth Morgan had been delegated on two different occasions to coax the man to see sense. Her excitement mounting, Bethan recollected the morning she drove over to make sure she was around when Ray Kirby arrived for his viewing. How credible was it for the blocked driveway access to have been engineered by one Ruth Morgan and not Mr Sartin?

Bethan had never met him, yet could imagine how easily Ms Morgan might manipulate the farmer to do what she asked. Especially if she played the sympathy card and stressed how Mrs Deacon needed a quiet life with her good friend close by to ease matters along. She might even have warned him how new people coming to live so close to his land might be much more intrusive than the current owners. Things were clicking into place.

Bethan contemplated the various events conspiring to make her suspect the motive of the woman who called herself the Deacons' best friend. There had to be something linking these seemingly random happenings.

Bethan uttered a four-letter word she forbade her daughter to use. Realisation flooded her. How could she not have realised the common denominator? The encounter with Brad and Valerie Childs must have been pure chance but they'd been set up. The couple had been so much in the

218

thrall of friendly Delyth with the gentle Welsh cadence to her voice, they refused even to set foot in Three Roads. No one would have known about Delyth's intervention had not Bethan coaxed Mr and Mrs Childs to reveal the truth behind their aversion to the property that ticked their set of boxes.

When the Deacons received news of their first viewing, they must have told their friend, of course they must. Maybe they even informed her on purpose, so she wouldn't call and interrupt. That knowledge offered Ruth time plus the perfect opportunity to plan a malicious, premeditated attack. In the unlikely event that someone from the village had spotted her accessing her vantage point above the road, they wouldn't have given it a second thought. People would know such a keen cook and gardener might well comb the woodland for wild herbs, berries and the like.

What were friends and neighbours for, if not to share triumphs and woes? Ruth would have feigned disgust when she learnt of the mindless prank, presumably carried out by yobs and which caused Mr and Mrs Hunt to cross The Sugar House off their shopping list.

The big freeze towards Bethan had manifested when she rang to report she was bringing Mr and Mrs Sarani to view. Morgan had been unable to conceal her animosity. She'd stalled for extra time. But that dead field mouse must have been put in position before the Deacons left home. She'd taken a chance there would be further viewings while they were away and she was proved right. But, as had Ray Kirby, the Saranis accepted such things could happen – especially in the country and with a dog in the house. Since then, however, the two consultants appeared to have formed a perception that didn't quite fit. Why?

Bethan still had Mr Sarani's mobile telephone number saved in her own phone. What if she gave him a call on the pretext of touching base? Maybe the Saranis could provide another clue towards this sinister puzzle's solution.

But wasn't she being thoughtless? This was a working day when a busy consultant would be up to the proverbial eyebrows with patients and impossible demands on his time. Maybe she'd try him during the evening and hope to catch him at home. At worst he'd think she was desperate to achieve a sale. On the other hand, she might learn something to her advantage.

Jalil Sarani stretched out on the battered rust corduroy sofa he defended with his life when his wife threatened to book a skip because his sanctuary contrasted with her beloved decor. His noise-cancelling headphones acted like an umbilical cord connecting him with the sublime sounds of Rachmaninoff's Piano Concerto Number 2. His wife occupied the armchair opposite, her feet in soft suede moccasins, propped upon a jewelled leather pouffe. Jalil suspected she was probably watching *Coronation Street* but, insulated against domestic disputes and lovers' tiffs, Jalil closed his eyes and let the music wash over him, taking him far away from memories of another day of examining X rays, making diagnoses, breaking startling news: in all, doing what he was paid well to do.

His phone throbbed in his pocket. Jalil opened his eyes, paused the music and rose from the sofa. Zoyah glanced away from the TV screen. "Do you have to answer that?"

Jalil shot her a wry grin and left the room. In the hallway, he checked the caller's identity and pressed the green button. "Jalil Sarani."

"Mr Sarani, I'm so sorry to interrupt your evening."

He smiled. "Mrs Harley. My wife and I must be a great disappointment."

"Not at all. I'm not ringing with a sales spiel. But I would appreciate it if you'd allow me to ask a question or two."

"No problem. So, what kind of questions?"

"I'm facing a rather delicate situation."

"I'll help if I can." Jalil waited again.

"Thank you. What I really need to know is whether you've had contact with Mr and Mrs Deacon's house sitter since viewing their property." Bethan's words tumbled out in a rush. "I'm talking about Ruth Morgan."

"In a word, yes," said Jalil. "We had a chance encounter with the lady and her gentleman escort at our hotel that evening." He hesitated. "I don't feel comfortable in disclosing details of the conversation that took place in the bar, Bethan. I wouldn't risk my integrity by revealing information regarding anyone's health issues, whether they were genuine or as perceived by a third party."

Health issues! "I understand," said Bethan. "Please forgive me, Mr Sarani, but I have certain suspicions. If proved accurate, there could be serious repercussions."

"You have my full attention."

"Could I enquire whether whatever you heard from Ms Morgan caused Mrs Sarani to ring BCB and check whether the vendors might be likely to change their minds about selling?"

Again, he hesitated. Bethan waited, anxiously chewing the end of a stray strand of hair.

"I have to say, yes, it did. But this disclosure is strictly confidential and, all in all, events conspired to make us decide to let the dust settle. Off the record, my wife and I were somewhat nonplussed by the house sitter's attitude towards the sale. We received mixed messages. On that basis, I'm afraid we would be highly unlikely to make an offer on the property."

Bethan closed her eyes.

"We very much like that house, Bethan. But as you know, we're in no particular hurry. Your office of course has us on the mailing list so you may yet find us parachuting onto your patch."

"I do hope so, Mr Sarani. Please give my regards to your wife."

Bethan closed the call, her feelings a mix of anger, regret and satisfaction. She called Ray Kirby straightaway.

"You caught me cracking open a bottle."

She grinned. "I forgot to visit my wine merchant on the way home."

"That's tough. Since you've already responded to my email, I imagine something else has happened?"

She gave him a swift précis of her conversation with Mr Sarani, referring to him as a prospective house purchaser.

Ray gave a low whistle. "That's pretty conclusive, though I appreciate whoever it was wouldn't wish to give a verbatim report of that cosy little chat."

"I wouldn't want to urge him to contact Mr and Mrs Deacon, that's for sure. As you know, this is an extremely delicate situation but clearly Morgan has put the boot in."

"At least we know there really is cause for concern and your speculation has substance."

"So, do I now go to the Deacons and reveal all? Or do I allow enough rope in the hopes that a certain person might hang herself?"

"You could take the easy option and wait until I've brought Claudia to see the house."

"I just don't trust Ruth Morgan, Ray. What if she finds out about your visit and pulls out all the stops to put you off?"

"That's not going to happen, Bethan. My card is clearly marked and, in any case, she has to be running out of stunts. I don't want to tell you how to do your job but have you alerted your staff? Made sure they don't divulge information about future viewings? I wouldn't put it past Morgan to ring your office and get all pally with one of your admin people."

"I've instructed that anyone who calls regarding The Sugar House, whoever it might be, is put through to me or asked to leave a number so I can ring back."

"Excellent, Miss Moneypenny."

"You sound more Billy Connelly than Sean Connery. Anyway, isn't it time Miss Moneypenny became a Ms?"

"Nope. I'm an old-fashioned kind of guy." He chuckled into Bethan's ear, making her smile. "So, any news of the Deacons returning?"

"Not so far. I have to carry out a valuation the other side of Three Roads tomorrow so I plan to call on my way back. See if anyone's home. Make sure no taps have been left running in the bathroom, etc. Mind you, Ms Morgan would have to pick up the tab if she pulled that trick."

She heard him click his tongue.

"Just watch your back, Bethan. I imagine you have safety procedures regarding being on your own when you're out of the office?"

"Well, of course. You're thinking of poor Suzy Lamplugh, aren't you?"

"Now you mention it, yes, although that was a long time ago and this is an entirely different situation. However, I'm not at all sure we're dealing with someone operating on all cylinders. I really need to do some research."

"On mental health issues?"

"Nah. Something's been niggling at me ever since I met this lady. I'll get a colleague to check it out. Have you ever heard of a Julia Hayes?"

Bethan thought. "I don't think so. Should I have?"

"I'll explain when I see you. It could be nothing."

"Anyway, Ray, what if I text you after I leave? Ms Morgan might not even be there but obviously I'll alert the office as to my progress after the valuation."

"Okay. If we don't speak again, I'll see you on Saturday at high noon."

"Why do I get the feeling you're enjoying all this?"

She waited two beats. Sometimes he liked to take his time before responding.

"I think we make a good team."

Ruth still smarted from Suzanne's flip comment when making her brief phone call the evening before. *You can get your things together and return to Rock Cottage after breakfast!* What kind of an attitude was that? Even Ruth's offer to stock up with fresh vegetables and whatever other items their highnesses might require, met with a negative response, Suzanne simply stating their intention of stopping to do a big shop on the way through Abergavenny.

Ruth had completed a tour of the house, checking everything was in order. She'd stripped her bed but, with a flash of malice, dumped the used linen in the John Lewis laundry basket. Her original offer to wash the bedding hadn't seemed to impress Suzanne. Thoughts of retaliation simmered and seethed. She was annoyed because the Deacons hadn't allowed her sufficient time to prepare an appropriate welcome home calamity. She'd originally intended to devise a situation to dismay the couple and allow her to ride to the rescue, thereby basking in the resulting sunshine. She'd been caught on the hop.

The amethyst and turquoise necklace was back in the jewel box. The frock she felt fitted her shape so well, and which she'd worn to meet Huw at the hotel, dangled, spineless, from a rail in Suzanne's walk-in wardrobe. All empty wine bottles, including a couple discarded by Eddie in the kitchen bin, were placed in her car boot, destined for recycling.

All appeared to be in order but she still disliked the way in which Suzanne had ordered her out and off home. She'd wanted to be in residence, prepared to welcome her friends on their return. Ruth rather enjoyed throwing open the front door and standing back to allow the couple access. She'd done that several times in the past. What could be the reason for the very deliberate put down this time?

Eddie and Suzanne had been quick to butter her up when he'd arranged for them to go away and needed a favour. Now, with her future and theirs poised for change, there must be some means of regaining her former place in the couple's affections. She longed to regain control. Or at the very least the comfortable routines she'd enjoyed before.

She was startled by the sound of the doorbell. Ruth strode across to the hallway, almost forgetting to slow her pace and favour the leg she'd elected to afflict with phoney arthritis. She decided there was probably a parcel delivery service vehicle parked on the driveway, as Suzanne often ordered paperbacks and DVDs from an online bookstore. Ruth opened the door to find herself face to face with Bethan Harley.

Chapter Nineteen

The Deacons had reached Suzanne's favourite supermarket. They sat in the coffee shop, Suzanne jotting down necessary items on a memo pad. Eddie, fingers awkward as uncooked sausages, was haltingly composing a text message to let their daughter know they were back in Wales, an easy drive from home, and would ring that evening.

"I may as well stock up with coffee beans while we're here." Suzanne gazed at the service counter without taking in the scene.

"Good thinking," said Eddie. "God, how I hate predictive text."

Suzanne took a sip of her cappuccino. "Poor you. I've got my phone set so it lets me do the work."

"All right, Clever Clogs. It's sent now." He reached across the table and picked up his wife's shopping list. "Can you write bottle of brandy on there?"

"Medicinal?"

"No. Something smooth. Like I get in for Christmas. And I fancy a pack of those Medjool dates." He looked up at her. "Also like we have at Christmas."

"Any special reason?"

He shifted his position on the plastic chair and grimaced. "Doesn't the driver deserve a treat after a long journey?"

"Of course you do, darling." Suzanne took back the list and scribbled the items on it.

She looked up at him. "I thought I'd choose a really special box of chocolates for Ruth. Maybe Belgian or Swiss. As a thank you."

Eddie's eyebrows shot up. "Whatever for? I thought we agreed to give her cash this time. She's always insisted she helps us out of friendship but now it's different. We both know we don't want or need that feeling of being beholden."

"To her or to anyone else, in fact."

"Absolutely. Oh God."

"What is it?"

"I haven't given a thought to it until now."

"Eddie, I haven't the foggiest what you're on about."

"Nor should you have. Before we came away, I noticed a weird kind of smell in the downstairs loo. I felt a bit guilty, leaving Ruth with a potential problem."

"A smell? Why on earth didn't you say something?"

"We needed to get away. It's not as if Ruth's incompetent. I completely put it out of my head."

"It couldn't have been anything too awful, surely? We'd have got an emergency call."

"You're right."

"So how much money did you have in mind for Ruth?"

"I thought £75 would be appropriate."

"Aren't you being over-generous? We've only been away a few days. She'll have been living out of our freezer and drinks cupboard."

228

"Which is what we suggested she do. Think of the money we've saved by not having to put Sparkles in kennels."

"I suppose so. All right, Eddie. But I think I'll still get the chocs."

"Now who's being over-generous?"

"No," said Suzanne. "Not any more I'm not. You wait and see." She drained her cup. "Let's grab a trolley and get this done. It's time we went home and picked up the reins again."

"That's my girl." Eddie kissed her on the cheek, clasped her hand and led her to the trolley rank.

Bethan noted how the house sitter remained expressionless when she opened the door and saw who stood before her.

"Mrs Harley. To what do I owe this honour?"

"Good morning, Ms Morgan."

"Surely you haven't brought more prospective purchasers?" Ruth peered over Bethan's shoulder.

"Not this time. I've just completed a viewing the other side of the village so decided to drive back this way. I'm calling to make sure everything's all right."

"Why wouldn't it be?"

Bethan shrugged. "Well, we both know there have been a few odd happenings around the sale of this property. And your leg has been troubling you. You and I didn't get off to the best of starts, did we?"

"I really don't have the time to stand chatting."

"I understand how busy you are and I shan't keep you. But it would be reassuring to hear you haven't been troubled by any other odd occurrences." Bethan watched the house sitter's eyelashes flutter and the eyes swivel away from her gaze. Up went the hand. Bethan held her breath as she heard the nervous throat clearing.

"Everything's in apple pie order. Mr and Mrs Deacon are due back later today, so if you don't mind, I need to get on."

Bethan nodded. "Mr Deacon sent me a text. You'll be moving back to your cottage now, of course." She lowered her voice, hoping to sound confidential, singling out the Deacons' friend as the privileged one, chosen as first recipient of glad tidings. "Your friends may have cause for celebration soon. I'll say no more. We both know there's many a slip—"

The house sitter's face contorted. She raised her right hand, long fingers spread, as if about to slam the door in the sales negotiator's face. Bethan flinched. The movement had revealed something that rocked her. Stunned by the significance of this carelessness on Ruth Morgan's part, she gathered her scattered wits and stepped back on to the gravelled drive.

"I, er, I'm sure you'll be pleased to return to your own home again." She turned away.

Behind her, the door slammed. Resisting the urge to run as though fleeing demons, she walked back to the lay by where she'd left her car. She got behind the driving seat and tapped out a text to Ray Kirby.

230

Just left RM. Little fingernail R/H bears bronze nail polish trace.

Bethan pressed send and sat, waiting, eagerly anticipating a swift response. She wasn't disappointed. Smiling, as if opening a long-anticipated gift, she cracked open the newly arrived message on her phone.

Yay! Respect. CU 2morro. RK

Funny. She wouldn't have taken him for the kind of person who used text-speak.

Bethan set off towards Knightly, her emotions strangely mixed. She really shouldn't have wound up the house sitter with her teasing titbit of news. She'd wanted to drop the hint as a veiled warning that despite devious tricks on Morgan's part, there could be an interested party on the verge of making an offer. But what if the woman flipped and ordered a ton of hardcore – or something worse – to be dumped outside the Deacons' gate? You heard of such malicious behaviour, especially when jealousy showed its fangs. Discarded wives had slashed Armani suits. Poured vintage wine down drains, their minds deranged at the thought of another woman warming their husband's bed.

This was a different kind of emotion. But, if the house sitter did play some malevolent trick, wouldn't the telephone or online ordering system identify the originator's whereabouts? And Ray Kirby now retained as much information on Ms Morgan's perfidy as did Bethan.

She couldn't believe her good fortune in spotting that vital confirmation of Ruth and Delyth being one and the same. A careless application of nail varnish remover had blown Ruth's carefully contrived cover. It didn't matter if the mistake was noted and the bronze streak removed. If Ray Kirby arrived tomorrow to find the Deacons wringing their hands over yet another unforeseen calamity, he and Bethan could sit them down quietly and explain exactly how the two of them had tracked the behaviour of their so-called friend over the last week or so.

Care was needed now. Bethan would make Mr and Mrs Deacon aware of Ray Kirby's second viewing scheduled for next day, but she would warn them to remain silent. Bethan should also alert them regarding any telephone call purporting to be made by an employee of her agency. She wouldn't put it past Ms Morgan to carry out a voice disguise scam but Bethan needed to consider all opportunities for mischief making. A simple password would suffice.

There was a small research task she needed to carry out before tomorrow. Several times, she'd been on the brink of typing Claudia Kelsey's name into her search engine and each time decided against it. Now she felt she should take a look.

Bethan caught her breath as the glossy image appeared on her screen. Deep inside her, molten heat triggered the wrong kind of response. She calmed herself by imagining how the beautiful, dazzling vocalist would dress for a late September trip to damp, misty, mid Wales.

Eddie drove along the track towards his house and found the gates already open. A sharp sucking in of breath from

Suzanne accompanied his own groan. Ruth's car stood at the side of the forecourt. Somehow it would even have been better if she'd shown no consideration and left her vehicle in the place he always used. That way, she might have hurried out to explain she was just on her way.

"I thought I made it clear there was no need for her to wait for us," Suzanne said.

Eddie swung the car around so the rear was closest to the house. "She could be giving Sparkles a last walk before leaving. I'll go through the front and open up the back ready to unload the shopping."

He went ahead of Suzanne, unlocked the front door and stepped into the hallway, giving an apprehensive sniff. "What a relief!" When he went back to help his wife from the passenger seat he was beaming. "The hall smells of flowers and furniture polish. No peculiar odours, thank goodness."

"I wonder how many strange pairs of feet have crossed the threshold while we've been away," said Suzanne. "Unless it's all been quiet."

Eddie chuckled. "I expressly stated I didn't want you bothered by feedback but now we're home I can tell you there have been several viewings. We both needed a break, didn't we? Ready to face the music."

"You were right, Eddie. I feel so much calmer now about everything, though I did wonder why Ruth hadn't been in touch. I'm sorry I threw that little wobbly."

"Forget it, my sweet."

The couple stood still, leaving the door open. They looked up at the sound of light footsteps along the landing towards the head of the staircase.

"Welcome home! You made good time, then. I haven't even started the coffee yet." Ruth descended the stairs. Slowly. Long fingers skimming the banister rail, feet clad in suede moccasins treading in turn on each step of the expensive cream carpeted staircase. The carpet they'd chosen and which now, Suzanne felt, Ruth seemed to appropriate with every new step she took.

She recovered herself first. "We haven't long had coffee, thanks, Ruth. It's sweet of you to have waited but we really mustn't keep you any longer than necessary."

"That's right," said Eddie. "Many thanks, Ruth. Is the back door unlocked? I may as well bring the shopping in that way."

Ruth reached the hallway. Stood at the bottom of the staircase like a gatekeeper. "It's locked, of course. Shall I go through and unlock it? I can help put the groceries away."

"Don't trouble yourself, my dear. I'm fine."

Ruth turned her attention to Suzanne. "Why don't I carry your case upstairs and unpack for you? You look tired, dear. All this stress is making its mark."

As Ruth saw Suzanne's mask of politeness shift, she cleared her throat, reverting to her nervous habit, stroking her throat as if it was the comfort blanket of her childhood. She waited for the other woman to respond. Would Suzanne accede to her wishes or would she stamp her authority? She heard the sound of Eddie's feet crunching on the gravel path as he headed for his car. It was a pivotal moment, but did Suzanne recognise it as such?

"I'm not in the least tired, thank you. In fact, I feel better than I have in months. You should think about taking a few days away too. We'd always pop down and feed the cat."

Ruth watched her friend. Mistress of the house, Suzanne had recovered from the deliberately spiteful comment and looked sleek and in control. As if she'd returned with batteries recharged. This wasn't the way it was supposed to happen.

"How were Penny and the children? I'd love to see them again." She remembered too late that she'd met Suzanne's daughter only once and that was before her children were born.

But Suzanne's expression relaxed. Her own experience was much more important. "It was wonderful spending time with them. I'm so pleased Eddie convinced me we should put the house on the market. It's the right thing to do, at this time of our lives."

Ruth glanced towards the kitchen door and decided not to pick a fight. This was not the right moment to hint Suzanne might find a long-term relationship with her grandchildren more exhausting than short, sweet bursts of quality time. She longed for a way, any way, to extract from the couple the return to their semi dependency upon her that she craved.

As if on cue, Eddie reappeared. "Place is immaculate, Ruth." He held out an envelope. "Here you are, my dear.

Before I forget. We're very grateful to you for helping us out. Hopefully we shan't need to bother you again before we move."

Ruth stared down at the envelope. Raised her arm to take it from him. The sensation of being paid off like a redundant employee permeated her whole being. She felt a wave of giddiness. Her body was giving her clues. Swaying a little, she closed her eyes. Crumpled to the floor where she lay, waiting to see what the couple would do next.

Back at the office, Bethan stared at the monitor before her. She'd wanted another look at the website. Words leapt out from the impressive CV of one Claudia Kelsey: *Dynamic. Passionate. Sophisticated. Providing entertainment with class and elegance. Creating an intimate atmosphere. Whether it's a romantic ballad or something to make your toes tap, Claudia brings her own very special magic onstage.*

On screen, the golden girl's hair gleamed like polished ebony. Blue violet eyes smiled at the world. Her legs began at her shoulders. Her pleated silver gown clung here, rippled there. No wonder Claudia's besotted lover longed to buy her a hideaway home. Did he aim to make her fall in love with Three Roads and the comfortable nest he planned so he could keep her for his eyes only, away from her adoring public? Would such an exotic creature wish to bury herself in the Welsh countryside?

Bethan closed down the site. Why did she feel such bleakness? What did Ray Kirby's love life have to do with her? She already had a husband. Sort of. She should concentrate on rebuilding what she and Tim once had and stop harbouring dangerous, hungry thoughts that nibbled and gnawed at her reason. Such thinking could only bring heartbreak.

Somehow Bethan endured the rest of her day. Sifting inquiries passed on by her staff, arranging to make three valuations next week. She needed to concentrate. Her professionalism came to her aid. She learned the people she showed around the Old Mill at short notice had made an offer which satisfied the vendors. The regional manager emailed her.

It was no good. At around four o'clock she decided to ring and check whether the Deacons were home.

"Hello, Bethan." Eddie's voice sounded cheerful. Excellent. Maybe he'd kicked the witch into touch.

"Is this a good time?"

"Absolutely. We've been back several hours. Unpacked. Washing machine in action as we speak. I think my wife has taken on a new lease of life."

"That's brilliant news." Bethan chose her words carefully. "If I could update you as to what's been going on—?"

"Feel free. Our house sitter has left everything tidy. After we left, I had a guilty feeling there might have been a slight problem in the downstairs cloakroom but Ruth explained what had happened. Naughty old Sparkles, ay?"

Bethan gritted her teeth.

"Anyway," Eddie continued. "Ruth said those two consultants were charming. Any hope of them making an offer?"

"Apparently, Mr and Mrs Sarani are in no hurry." Bethan decided not to pursue this thread. "There's also a young couple who love your house but probably can't afford it, though you never know. What's really promising is that Mr Kirby has requested a second viewing."

"Hey, that's good news. Well, we're up for it, Bethan. Is this so he can bring his lady love to check out the place?"

Fleetingly Bethan wondered how far Eddie Deacon's eyes would stand out on stalks when he clapped them on Claudia. "I believe so," she said. "He was obviously impressed after his initial visit."

"Old Sartin behaving himself, is he?"

"As far as I'm aware." She couldn't put it off any longer. "I've arranged to meet Mr Kirby at your house tomorrow at noon. So, there'll be three of us descending on you. I hope that's in order."

"Of course. Suzanne and I will look forward to it."

Bethan heard the note of hesitation in his voice. "Is there something you want to tell me?"

"My wife and I have seen a couple of properties we like so we really need to push on with our sale. Or should I say, you do?"

"Understood. That's what I'm here for." She paused a beat. "We have to hope Mr Kirby's partner falls in love with The Sugar House."

"Indeed. Before you go, I wonder whether I should ask Ruth to warn our farmer friend about this second viewing? Mark his card, so to speak."

Bethan sucked in her breath. "If you don't mind my being totally frank, Mr Deacon, I'd advise you not to say anything about this appointment, either to Ms Morgan or to Mr Sartin."

"But the old devil takes notice of Ruth."

"Surely you don't anticipate a problem? You told me there have been only two isolated incidents since you moved into the village."

"That's right. So, you really don't think I should say anything?"

"Mr Deacon, please trust me for now. If necessary, we can have a little chat tomorrow. I apologise if I sound mysterious, but believe me, I do have my reasons." She hesitated. "I'm sure Ms Morgan would understand if she happened to call and you politely asked her to return at a time when you could enjoy her company in a more relaxed manner." She held her breath.

"Whatever you say. Suzanne or I will ring her later, as she left here saying she felt a bit under the weather. But if it's what you want, we'll keep this second viewing under wraps."

Eddie put down the phone, feeling puzzled. He wandered out to the conservatory where his wife sat reading a glossy magazine she'd pounced upon at the supermarket. The dog snoozed at her feet. The scene radiated contentment.

He lowered himself on to the wicker chaise longue opposite. "That was Bethan Harley ringing for a chat."

"How did she know we were back?" Suzanne peered over the top of her reading spectacles.

"I sent her a text."

"You've done a great job of sheltering me from all this, haven't you?"

Eddie shrugged. "Now we're back, that won't be so easy. Are you sure you're feeling as refreshed as you look, my darling?"

She laughed. "According to our dear friend, I look tired. Suffering from too much stress."

"Ignore her. So, what really was going on there, d'you reckon?"

"The fainting fit? I'm not sure, Eddie. She made a big, heroic thing of insisting she was fine to drive herself home. I think there are many sides to Ruth. Also, she could be going through that particular phase of life when her hormones are all over the place."

"Or she could have been swinging the lead, as my old dad used to say."

"I had the feeling she was playing to an audience."

"But why pretend to faint? I'd just handed her a cheque. Should I have bought a bouquet of roses to go with it? Oh, damn it, you didn't give her those chocolates you insisted on buying."

"They'll keep. As for the fainting, I don't know. All I know is that for a while now, her attitude to me has been strange."

"Believe me, Suze, I haven't encouraged her in any way. She hasn't a hope in hell of sidelining you, my angel."

"I wonder if that is what's behind all this. She does have a habit of trying to undermine my confidence. *Our* confidence, if I think back to the first time we shared our plans with her."

Eddie nodded. "She can have a possessive attitude, I agree."

"There was absolutely no reason for her still to be here today. She offered to carry my case upstairs and unpack for me. I probably sound like an ungrateful old biddy but I'm not in my dotage quite yet!"

"You're certainly not. She wanted to help put away the groceries too. Going it a bit, I thought."

"Honestly, Eddie, when Ruth appeared on the staircase, I actually felt like we were the live-in domestic staff returning from a break and she was Lady Ruth, bestowing a gracious welcome."

Eddie gave a short mirthless laugh. "I don't know about that but there's a cold, calculating look about her eyes that I haven't noticed before."

"Tell me what Mrs Harley said."

"Something very encouraging. You'll be pleased to know that big guy Kirby is due here tomorrow with his lady friend."

"I meant to ask you to find her on the internet."

"I'll take a look later. The main thing is, Bethan has asked that we don't tell anyone about tomorrow's viewing."

To his astonishment, Suzanne nodded.

"You don't find that surprising?"

"Not in the least. While we were away, I had time to think back on those few days after Ruth learnt of our decision. Remember how she suddenly put on a good face after that initial frostiness?"

"To be fair, Suze, we should have broken the news to her before the sale sign went up."

"No one gave us a knock to say they'd erected the board. If you remember, that evening, we battened down the hatches soon after you let Sparkles out for a wee."

"All H2O under the bridge now. But what else were you mithering over while we were away?"

"I don't want to sound paranoid but I can't help remembering certain things. Before we went away, Ruth was very keen to be kept informed when people were coming to view. In her place, I wouldn't dream of insisting on such a thing."

"Well, we did leave her in charge while we went away, Suze. She needed to know what was what."

"No, Eddie. I mean right in the beginning. Personally, I thought it a little odd, considering you gave Mrs Harley a door key and permission to bring prospects even if we weren't here. It's about as odd as Mr Sartin choosing the precise morning we had a viewing to abandon his tractor right in front of our gate."

"But Ruth chased around looking for him. She went out of her way to help."

Suzanne pursed her lips. Gave a slight shake of her head.

"Am I missing something here?"

"Possibly. But not something I can back up with evidence. It's a gut feeling. A kind of unease."

Eddie shrugged. "Fair enough, but I can hardly ban the woman from calling, can I? That would really be rubbing salt in the wound."

"There's one other thing I'd like to say. It'll sound ludicrous. Trivial. But I can't help feeling uneasy."

"Suze…?"

"It's about when Ruth was lying on the floor and I went to fetch a glass of water. You helped her sit up and she took the tumbler from me. That's when I noticed a very out of character thing."

"You'll have to spell it out. As in men are from Mars and women from Venus."

"I wouldn't expect you to notice but she had a streak of metallic varnish on one fingernail. I've done that myself. Removed old nail polish in a hurry and missed a bit."

"What's the big deal? I don't understand."

"Ruth never, ever, uses nail varnish, Eddie. Seriously! In all the years we've known her, even when she's come here to a drinks party or Christmas Dinner, her nails always look clean and scrubbed but unpolished. Doesn't that make you wonder why she'd suddenly take to varnishing them?"

"Maybe she decided she was missing something. Maybe she borrowed some of yours, to see how she liked it." Eddie's voice surged with the triumph of suggesting a neat solution.

"I never buy anything remotely close to that shade. All my colours are pinks and purples. Do you not notice? Oh, silly me, of course you don't."

"Where's this leading, Suze?"

"I'm not even sure, myself. All I can say is, when I saw that scrap of leftover polish on Ruth's fingernail, I felt as shocked as if she'd suddenly pulled a gun."

Chapter Twenty

On Saturday morning, Bethan dressed with extra care. She selected a short-sleeved vivid emerald jumper with a charcoal skirt suit and sheer black tights. Her appearance didn't go unnoticed.

"Heels? Perfume? On a Saturday morning?" Poppy looked up from her breakfast muesli as her mother headed for the kettle. "Mum, if you're dressing up like a footballer's wife, you should wear the silver locket Dad gave you for your anniversary."

"Oh, I should, should I? I'm going to work, dressed to look professional, not as if I'm off to lunchtime drinks later."

"You could've fooled me." Poppy mumbled through a mouthful of oats and seeds.

"Do you want a lift to Callum's? You weren't sure last night."

"Change the subject, why don't you?" But Poppy smiled. "You look great, Mum. And no, I don't need a lift thanks. I have an essay to finish."

"I'm impressed by your early start. And thanks for the compliment."

"Callum's calling round later. There's a photographic exhibition on at the Arts Centre. 1960s stuff. Sounds cool. What time will you be back?"

Bethan sipped her herbal tea. "Not sure. Officially I shouldn't be working but I'm anxious to attend this particular viewing."

"Ah. This is the guy with the partner who's a singer, right?"

Bethan nodded.

"So will that creepy woman be, like, hanging there too?"

"Goodness, I sincerely hope not. What I'm hoping is that Mr Kirby and his lady decide to make an offer so the Deacons can get away well before Christmas. And I can stop worrying about what might happen next."

Poppy slid off her stool. "Do they know any of the stuff you told me about?"

"I haven't said anything yet but I felt I should warn them not to say anything to their friend about this morning's viewing."

"Wow."

"Don't worry. I managed to say as little as possible but I imagine I'll have to explain myself later."

"Shall I do you a slice of toast, Mum?"

"Yes, please, darling."

Poppy fed two slices of bread into the toaster. "What if that creepy woman decides to spy on the house?"

Bethan shuddered. If Ruth Morgan rang the Deacons to suggest they met up later and received a negative response, would the woman suspect something was going on and decide to set up another of her little jollies?

"I was only joking." Poppy put her arms around her mother.

Bethan smelled citrus fragrance drifting from the lustrous hair and warm, young body. Tenderness swelled inside her as she hugged her daughter back.

"I know. But I don't want you worrying about me, sweetheart. There'll be plenty of people around this morning."

"I can still remember feeling scared that time I overheard you and Dad talking about what happened to that estate agent."

"You must have been eavesdropping at a tender age! We wouldn't have meant to frighten you about something that happened so long ago. But we all learned a lot from that tragedy. And Suzy Lamplugh's mother has left a legacy for us all."

"It's scary to think of someone doing the same job as you, going off alone to keep an appointment with a stranger in an empty house. I'm glad you text the office before you go inside an empty property."

"Nowadays, mobile phones make all that easy." Bethan's imagination dragged her from safety precautions and flashed an image of close-cropped dark hair, broad shoulders. Powerful thighs in tight black jeans. She felt a jolt of unexpected pleasure. Far from being a lone female, on the occasion she accompanied Ray Kirby on his first visit to The Sugar House, the vendors were sitting downstairs in their conservatory while she carried out the tour. But any woman would feel safe if Ray was around, whatever the situation.

In the master bedroom, Bethan had kept her eyes on the big man as he unlocked the veranda door, having asked if he might step outside to enjoy the view. She'd been enjoying her own view. On that morning, hadn't she experienced a swift physical jolt, similar to the one hitting her now? She'd imagined those powerful hands exploring beneath her severely-styled jacket. Would she have pushed him away? Or would she have welcomed that intimacy? Once initiated, how badly would she have craved more? Would she and Ray Kirby have given in to the spark of attraction she knew each sensed in the other but determined to ignore?

Poppy was watching her curiously. The ping of the toaster rescued Bethan from her erotic and totally unprofessional fantasy. Reaching up, she took a jar of creamy Welsh honey from the shelf.

"Callum seems a nice boy. But it's early days and he's a year older than you. Have some lunch here by all means but maybe you could tell him you're not sure when I'll be back. Spell it out to him I could walk in any moment."

"Gross, Mum! What's that all about?"

But Bethan felt she'd hit the right note with her too gorgeous for her own good daughter.

Ruth Morgan reached into the bottom drawer of the dark wood desk and took out a notebook that she placed on the leather-bound blotting paper holder before her. If she tugged the yellowing, ink-smudged paper gently away from one corner, she could see the original pristine white of the sheet set in position by her late aunt, years before.

Ruth read her notes through once again. She'd recorded everything connected to the sale of the Deacons' property, including her thoughts. The information ran from the moment she set eyes on the sale board to the morning she moved in ready to house sit for her friends. The next section described actions taken while in residence, visits made, telephone conversations with the Harley woman, culminating with the return of Suzanne and Eddie and the gauche way in which they'd paid her off.

Having made these notes using the Pitman shorthand she'd successfully studied in college years before, Ruth needed to read slowly. But the symbols upon the pages reported everything as clearly as if she'd handwritten the words. Each curve, stroke, hook or tiny circle, whether thinly or thickly inscribed, was meticulously crafted, to contribute to the story of a woman on a mission.

She scanned what she'd written, frowning as she stumbled over one less than perfect outline. Relaxed again as soon as she realised she'd written the word 'metallic.' Delyth possessed only three bottles of expensive nail varnish in her cream leather vanity case. One was in a tasteful shade of peach. Another reminded Delyth of milky coffee. The third and most recent one gleamed like beaten bronze. All had either been purchased online, or bought surreptitiously while Suzanne Deacon was having her hair styled by Paul or Josh, or whoever was judged worthy of cutting and blow-drying or sometimes colouring the well-regarded client's pampered locks.

Ruth blinked, taken by surprise at what she noticed next. For a moment her vision blurred. Her head swam. She closed her eyes, supported herself, hands palm down on the desk. Sucking in air. Holding it for moments before huffing it out again. When she felt the dizziness fading, she reopened her eyes and examined the nail of one little finger. How could she have been so slapdash?

She rose. Stalked towards the bathroom and reached for the bottle of acetone pushed to the back of her medicine cupboard. Swiftly she dealt with the telltale streak at one side of her fingernail. No one could have noticed it, surely? The last time Delyth made an appearance in Knightly, the Harley woman had been hanging around but fortunately hadn't been allowed to get too close for comfort. The owner of the second-hand bookshop had barely seemed to register the tall woman dressed in subtle shades.

The only other close contact had been the old dear pushing her walking frame out of the lift into Delyth's path as she waited impatiently to enter. That had been a lucky escape. Even that gormless teenage girl intent on her mobile phone and not on where she was walking, hadn't stopped Delyth in her tracks for long.

Suzanne would have been sure to comment, had she noticed the offending finger nail. Certain to enquire what had made Ruth start paying attention to such a frivolity at this stage of her life. She'd maybe ask whether Ruth had renewed her relationship with her former tennis partner in Llanbrenin Wells. She'd ask because she could never quite comprehend why Ruth didn't actively seek someone with whom she could share the rest of her life.

Suzanne's existence centred upon a man. Doubtless it had always been the case, as the stick of candyfloss blonde progressed from being Daddy's adored princess to some spotty youth's pawed-over girlfriend. Finally, the blonde had achieved the top prize by acquiring a fiancé in the form of Edward Deacon, son of a hotelier, but as revealed by Suzanne in a careless moment, not quite the excellent catch her daddy would have envisaged for his darling daughter.

Ruth knew so much about the Deacons. Much more than they knew about her. She preferred it that way. So did Delyth. Neither of these two women could handle being thwarted in any way. This cooling off which Ruth had noticed, particularly on Suzanne's part, needed dealing with. She walked out into the cottage's tiny hallway and picked up the telephone. A few words of warning from a friend should find their mark, unless she was totally misjudging the situation.

She didn't believe that was the case. Ruth had perfected the art of seeking out vulnerability. She had the Deacons' landline number on speed dial. Seeds of doubt might lie dormant for a while but how easily might they blossom, given encouragement.

Suzanne's voice sounded hesitant when she answered Ruth's call.

"Good morning, Suzanne." Ruth smiled as she spoke, kept her voice light and friendly.

"Oh, it's you, Ruth. I hope you've recovered from your funny turn."

"I have, thank you."

"So, did you leave something behind?"

Ruth narrowed her eyes. "I haven't noticed anything missing. No, I was wondering whether you'd like to walk round for a chat so we can catch up."

"Um, Eddie might want an early lunch. I think there's probably rugby on television."

Ruth brimmed with glee. There was no rugby match on the TV schedule. Suzanne should have mentioned golf or racing. No matter.

"Perfect! Can you not leave him some of that quiche I made for you? Come on your own and we can have a lovely gossip. Maybe a glass of wine, just the two of us. I'm longing to hear all about your trip."

She waited for Suzanne to break the silence. Compressed her lips, sensing a quandary.

"It's very kind of you, Ruth. But I really should begin sorting through books and other bits today. Start clearing the decks while we're waiting to sell the house. We do intend to downsize."

Ruth kept her voice relaxed. "You know I'll happily give you a hand, any time you like. But to be quite honest, there's something bothering me and I wouldn't be doing my job as your closest friend if I didn't confide in you."

Ruth sensed Suzanne was intrigued. Struggling to keep her distance.

"Can you not tell me over the phone?"

A little catching of breath. An almost sob from Ruth. "My dear, I really do think this would be better said to your face."

"I hope it's nothing too dreadful. Are you all right?"

"Health wise, yes. But there is something you need to know – something for your ears only. I'm sorry to sound mysterious but I'll expect you in a half hour or so. Your favourite treacle tart will be out of the oven by then. And if Eddie's watching the pundits talking before the rugby match kicks off, he'll barely notice you're not there."

Ruth felt a tremor of anticipation fizzle through her body as she put down the phone. Suzanne would be speculating as to what was going on. She'd conjecture as to whether this was a female only confidence or something to do with the community hall and the committee upon which both she and Ruth served. She'd merely tell her husband she was going to Ruth's for a chat.

Bethan heard nothing from Ray so assumed he must be on his way from London without hold ups delaying him. She pulled up in the Deacons' driveway and reversed her car, easing it side on to the hedge, leaving plenty of room for him to manoeuvre his Range Rover beside the couple's BMW. She would have to expect a different Ray Kirby today. He would have morphed into one half of a couple, intent on watching his other half's reaction, hoping for her to approve his choice of a home for their future together.

In this kind of situation, her personal safety was far from Bethan's mind until she opened her side window. The magnificent shrubs and thick evergreens surrounding the garden would provide a haven for someone wishing to slip like a shadow into the foliage. There might even be an opening in the hedge, enabling entry to the garden from the neighbouring field. Had the Deacons ever checked this might be a possibility? Bethan wasn't normally a nervous kind of person but this jittery thought gave her an anxious frisson. She recalled the dark shape moving closer to Ray as he concentrated on his camera at the waterfall that day – so much had happened since then.

A bird flew from the shrubbery and shot past her windscreen, making her jump. Bethan told herself to stop such stupidity. Told herself to text the office mobile and confirm her arrival.

She looked at her watch. Several minutes remained until noon. All seemed quiet. She'd wait until the appointed time before ringing the doorbell. The Deacons were probably in the conservatory, unaware of her presence. The sudden advent of golden autumn weather would draw them to sit at the rear of the house and enjoy the sunshine. She knew the couple would be totally prepared to show off the property on which they'd lavished such loving attention.

Her stomach lurched at the sound of an approaching car. The black Range Rover nosed its way through the gates and the driver parked in the space left for him. Bethan occupied herself by picking up her folder and leather shoulder bag. She got out of her car and pressed the key lock. Even in the environs of any house she visited, she never left her vehicle unsecured.

Feet crunched over the gravel towards her. Bethan looked up, bright smile in place, prepared to shake hands with Claudia Kelsey and her man.

"Bethan. I hope I'm not late."

He surprised her by leaning forward to kiss her cheek. She caught a drift of sandalwood and some other indefinable scent. Her chest tightened. Where was his partner?

"You're not late, Ray. But I thought you were bringing Ms Kelsey?"

He grimaced. Ran a big hand over his cropped hair. Bethan's fingers tingled with the urge to do the same but she held her ground, waiting for his explanation.

"You're not the only one. It's a long story but I'll make an excuse to the Deacons and maybe you and I can talk later?"

She swallowed. "Of course." Her mind buzzed with what ifs. Did he mean he'd driven all this way just to tell the Deacons in person that he was no longer interested? Of course not. That wouldn't be his style.

Eddie came to the door just as Bethan was about to ring the bell a second time.

"Here I am. Please come in, both of you. I was just topping up the dog's water bowl. It's too warm for her in the conservatory so I put her in the utility room for now."

Why was he gabbling? Bethan smiled at him. "You remember Mr Kirby?"

"Of course." Eddie closed the front door and held out his hand to the big man. "Good to see you again. Have you driven from London this morning?"

"Good to see you too, Mr Deacon. Yes, the motorway wasn't a problem but it was pleasing to cross the Severn Bridge and know my junction wasn't far off."

Eddie peered around. "You're on your own?"

"I'm afraid so. My partner's feeling unwell and couldn't face the journey."

"I'm sorry to hear that."

"We could have rescheduled." Bethan looked enquiringly at Ray.

"Thank you but it's not necessary. I want to check out a few things. Pending that, I shall make a decision without Claudia being here."

His face was impassive. Bethan knew better than to probe further but her thoughts churned, distracting her.

"As it happens, my other half has deserted me too." Eddie chuckled. "She sends her apologies but it seems our friend Ruth sounded somewhat distressed when she rang earlier." He spread his hands in a gesture of bewilderment. "I had no say in the matter. It would have been churlish to put my foot down, don't you think?"

Bethan sucked in her breath. "You're saying Mrs Deacon will be alone with Ms Morgan during our visit? At her cottage?"

"Apparently. I don't know where the fire is but Suzanne said there was something Ruth wanted to get off her chest. Beats me."

Bethan glanced at Ray. His face remained expressionless. "Mrs Deacon won't mention anything about Mr Kirby coming for a second viewing?"

"I passed your message on and I can't see why she'd let it slip, Bethan. But if she does, surely that's not a problem? Ruth wouldn't come running over here when she has Suzanne in the house already."

Bethan locked gazes with Ray. "Of course not." Something wasn't quite right. "Where would you like to start, Mr Kirby?"

"Upstairs, if that's all right?"

"Feel free," said Eddie. "I meant to prepare coffee. Shall I do that now?"

"That would be brilliant, Mr Deacon," said Ray. "I'll go on up, then."

"Would you prefer to be left on your own, Mr Kirby?" Bethan watched the big man hesitate at the bottom of the staircase.

"I'd like to inspect the loft first. You may wish to stand guard."

"Shall I show you how the ladder works?" Eddie hovered in the kitchen doorway.

"Don't worry. I'll yell for help if I can't suss it out."

Ray winked at Bethan. The tiny gesture sent a slow wave of warmth throughout her body.

"Come and keep me company, Mrs Harley."

Bethan followed in Ray Kirby's wake. She had health and safety issues to bear in mind. Needed to subdue her curiosity as to Claudia Kelsey's absence. More importantly, she needed to say the right things to Eddie regarding her cryptic announcement of the previous day. She tried not to question why Ruth Morgan's presence seemed so marked, hanging like a pall, despite her being nowhere near the house.

"It's good to spend quality time with you, Suzanne. Yesterday, I was a little puzzled by the way you wanted me out of your house in such a hurry."

"I think both Eddie and I felt we'd imposed upon your generosity enough without keeping you hanging around any longer."

"You should know by now, I'm only too pleased to help. Do have another slice of treacle tart. Or try the quince jam with a scone."

"I'm fine, thanks." Suzanne pushed her empty cup aside. "What did you want to discuss? I should get back."

"Oh dear, I don't like doing this, I really don't." Ruth wrung her hands. Turned her head and gazed through the window.

Suzanne frowned. "Has something happened while we've been away? Did you break something? Spill wine on a rug? If so, it's not the end of the world."

"It's nothing like that." Ruth heaved a sigh. "I very much fear your husband may have wandering eyes."

"Sorry?"

Ruth leaned forward, fixing her gaze upon Suzanne. "For a while now, I've been conscious of the way Eddie looks at me." She cleared her throat. "Not on every occasion he sees me, of course, but enough times to make me feel slightly uncomfortable."

She raised her hand and stroked her throat.

"Uncomfortable?" Suzanne frowned. "But everyone knows my husband's a flirt. He can't resist chatting up the ladies but he means no harm by it. Surely you realise that by now?"

Ruth shifted in her seat and lowered her gaze as if afraid to meet her friend's. "This isn't quite the same. Oh, dear, this is difficult, Suzanne, but I've had the feeling for a while now that he'd quite like to proposition me."

"I see."

"I did wonder if your attitude towards me lately could have something to do with Eddie and me. That maybe you were afraid his friendship with me might develop into something else. Something more intimate."

Suzanne stood up, scraping the kitchen chair legs on the wooden floor as she did so. "I don't have time for this. Nor do I intend discussing the details of my marriage with you."

"I'm trying to help you, my dear. In terms of weighing up your future, I wouldn't want you to suspect me of trying to steal your husband."

Suzanne opened her mouth and shut it again. "I don't think for one moment your suspicions are correct. I suggest you find some other male on which to focus your fantasies. What about that nice man you used to play tennis with? As for me needing help to weigh up my future, as you put it, please don't trouble yourself."

Ruth continued to sit still, watching Suzanne. Without a doubt she'd rattled her composure. Suzanne would walk home now, seething over the innuendo, anger dissolving into anxiety as she cast her mind back to various occasions when maybe her husband and her friend had looked too cosy at the candle-lit dinner table when Suzanne returned with dessert or cheese board.

There had been one occasion when Eddie had walked Ruth back to her cottage after an evening of wine sampling. Maybe Suzanne had wondered what on earth had taken him so long. He'd instigated a rather drunken fumble while still outside the back door. Ruth hadn't in the least enjoyed this but it had served a purpose. Given her stored ammunition. Suzanne would have looked at the clock and wondered what was keeping him. Maybe that memory would come back to haunt her now.

Suzanne placed both hands on the back of her chair as if waiting for a slight dizziness to pass. Ruth watched her with eyes narrowed. When Suzanne pulled on her soft purple fleece and picked up her handbag, Ruth rose. Slowly.

"If he's like that with me, someone who's your friend and who knows how to handle him, what will he be like in a new environment? Think about it, Suzanne. Who knows you better than anyone else in the world? Those friends of yours you hanker after have never put in an appearance, have they? They've probably never given you a second thought since you left Sussex. You should stay at Three Roads. Take your house off the market." She grabbed Suzanne's arm.

"You're going to need support, my dear. I'm ready to give both of you that assistance. Think hard what a move would mean at your time of life. It's not fair to burden your daughter with two aging parents when she has young children demanding her attention."

She saw a spasm cross Suzanne's face. She relaxed her grip. Watched the other woman walk to the back door and open it. She didn't walk through it.

In three strides Ruth was there. She closed the door and drew Suzanne back to the table.

"Do you really think we've made the wrong decision, Ruth? Do you think I'm living in cloud cuckoo land?"

A sense of triumph flooded Ruth. She helped Suzanne back into her chair and seated herself opposite again.

"I think Eddie's at fault for playing on your emotions. I've seen a lot of family dynamics over the years, mainly when I've worked as a companion housekeeper. Each generation has its own agenda and that's how it should be."

Ruth reached for Suzanne's hands and clasped them across the scrubbed pine surface. "Your delicate constitution needs tender loving care. Your daughter, bless her, cannot possibly cope with the burdens that come with age."

"We're not that decrepit," said Suzanne.

Ruth noted the flash of spirit. "Of course not. And these peaceful surroundings will help you stay that way. How does that part of Wiltshire you visited compare with this village, Suzanne?"

"I did notice the roar of traffic when we were looking at one particular house I liked."

"Precisely. You need to compare what you actually have with what you think you need. Choosing a new home is exciting. It's easy to get carried away by that initial enthusiasm. It's rather like the first heady days of a love affair."

Ruth kept her voice low. Her words soothing. "Life's too short to keep upping sticks. Moving saps anyone's energy. You know I'm right, Suzanne. Trust me. We were absolutely fine, all three of us, weren't we? Before Eddie got fidgety?"

Suzanne didn't appear to have heard her. "I'd better get back. I need to talk to him. Tell him I'm not sure about all this. Mr Kirby might still be there. He's the one most likely to make an offer on the house."

Ruth felt a flash of fury. Somehow, she managed to keep her voice calm. "I didn't realise you had a second viewing this morning. You should have told me, Suzanne."

"Mrs Harley told Eddie not to say anything to anyone about this viewing."

"But I'm not just anyone, my dear." Ruth got to her feet. "I'll drive you back. Come on. I've said what needed saying and now it's up to you. Don't let yourself be bullied, Suzanne. Bring your doubts to Eddie's notice."

After Ruth dropped her friend at her gate, she drove back to her cottage, a slow smile buttering her face. Did Mrs Harley really think she could get the better of her?

Maybe she wouldn't need to open her Pandora's box again. If only she could hear the conversation between husband and wife. She'd opted to go for the jugular and succeeded in startling Suzanne out of complacency. Given her plenty to think about. The expression on the other woman's face had inspired exquisite pleasure in Ruth. What delicious effects the right words could produce.

"Are you all right up there?" Bethan called from the foot of the aluminium loft ladder.

"I'm good, thanks. I wanted to check the load-bearing joists. Your agent speak isn't euphemistic – this space *would* make a perfect studio."

"The Deacons had the roof windows put in as part of their original renovation."

She saw his face appear from on high. A grinning face. "You don't need to do the hard sell. I'm totally hooked on the house, but you already know that."

"I could have emailed answers to your questions and saved you driving all the way on your own. I do feel awkward about this."

"Well, don't. I wanted to come back, and not only to take another look at the house. I'm coming down now."

She moved away from the ladder as Ray Kirby went into reverse and planted one well shod foot after the other upon the rungs. She needed to keep his trim rear out of view. Out of her thoughts. That set her wondering what he meant by saying he had more than one reason for visiting mid Wales today.

"I've never thought to enquire but do you and your partner have children?"

"No, Bethan. Not last time I checked, anyway."

He sounded amused. What had made her ask that? Feeling silly, she turned around and watched him flip the sturdy ladder up and away into its resting position. One twist with the metal rod and the loft flap fitted flush with the ceiling.

"Mr Deacon called upstairs to ask if you'd like coffee now."

"I certainly would." He stood back to allow her to descend ahead of him.

In the kitchen, Eddie looked up from his laptop. "Are you a sports fan?"

"Do you mean me or Mrs Harley?"

Eddie chuckled. "Either of you. Big golf tournament this afternoon."

Ray Kirby nodded. "I play now and then. And enjoy telling the top golfers how to take a shot when I'm watching on television."

"You're a backseat driver, old chap?"

"Afraid so."

Bethan fidgeted.

Eddie got to his feet. "I'm forgetting my manners. Please sit down, both of you. Coffee's ready to pour."

"Shall I fetch milk from the fridge?"

"That would be great, my dear."

Ray looked around him. "I feel at ease here. Even if a property has all the mod cons, it doesn't necessarily possess the right atmosphere."

"There are no ghosts in this house, as far as I know."

Bethan, opening the refrigerator door, resisted the urge to comment.

"My only quibble is the lack of a garage," said Ray. "I like somewhere I can tinker. And on winter mornings, I detest having to defrost a windscreen before I set off. Not that I'll often be driving for work purposes."

"We did contemplate converting that old shed." Eddie sounded defensive. "But we don't normally venture out when the weather's bad and I certainly don't tinker with the car. Mechanics isn't my forte."

"Mr Deacon comes from a family of hoteliers." Bethan hovered at Eddie's elbow. "Milk, Mr Deacon? I know Mr Kirby likes his black."

Immediately the words were out, she wished she hadn't said them. Eddie's swift glance at Ray met a deadpan gaze but a hotelier would be used to interpreting body language and intuiting subtext hidden by a seemingly innocuous remark. She decided to allow vendor and prospective purchaser to circumnavigate this kitchen table scenario.

"That would work," said Ray. "So long as there was a door at the rear to access the kitchen door."

"I can't foresee any problem there." Eddie helped himself to sugar.

"So, have you found somewhere you'd like to move to, Mr Deacon?"

"We've seen two houses which would fit the bill. Trouble is, I favour one and Suzanne much prefers the other."

"Which of you is the better negotiator?" Ray Kirby's expression was quizzical.

"Jury's out on that one," said Eddie. "I think my lovely wife might get her way. But of course, this is all in the lap of the gods."

Bethan looked up at the kitchen clock.

Ray Kirby drained his cup. "I must complete my tour or I'll be interfering with your TV watching."

"Not at all. Take as long as you want. Have a good wander round."

"I'd like to go outside via the kitchen door. Suss out the possible garage conversion and check whether the patio would accommodate a hot tub."

"Help yourself. A hot tub, you say? That'll give the villagers something to chew over!"

The big man strolled towards the kitchen door. Bethan heard him speak to the dog. The Labrador made a friendly little sound in return. If she'd been a cat, Bethan would have described it as a purr. She sensed Eddie's eyes upon her. Turned towards him and smiled brightly.

"So far so good. I'm sorry to have missed Mrs Deacon."

"I've no idea when she'll be back. Here, let me show you the house she fancies. I've saved the particulars in my favourites."

Bethan stood, replaced her chair neatly under the table and walked around to join her client. She was leaning in

266

when Eddie's hand shot out and rested on her arm. Comfortably, like an old friend, confident his action wouldn't be misunderstood.

"There it is. What do you think?"

"Wow. It's gorgeous." Bethan's blonde head almost touched Eddie's snowy one. "Let's take a look at the master bedroom."

"I wish!" Eddie roared with laughter. "Known the time, my dear."

"What's this about?" Suzanne walked from the doorway and stood, hands on hips, her gaze taking in her husband and Bethan, who immediately sensed the tension.

"Hi my darling. Mr Kirby is prowling around, checking out exciting possibilities. I was just showing Bethan this house you like. Have you had a good gossip?"

"Are you all right, Mrs Deacon?"

"I've been better, Mrs Harley."

Bethan pulled out a chair for Suzanne. "I don't think Mr Kirby will be much longer. Unfortunately, his partner couldn't join him as planned but there's no doubt about his enthusiasm towards your house."

Suzanne sank on to the chair and stared blankly at her.

"Shall I help you off with your coat?" Eddie kept his eyes on his laptop.

"Let me," said Bethan, moving towards the older woman.

"This is all too much," said Suzanne. "I'm not sure I can cope."

"I know how distressing it can be, having a stream of strangers coming and going." Bethan spoke soothingly. Gently she helped the older woman slip her arms from the sleeves of her fleece.

"Kirby seems a good guy. A bit John Blunt but that's no fault. We could be on a winner here, Suze."

Suzanne slumped in her chair. Shocked, Bethan saw an old woman, tired and frightened, behind the smartly dressed, elegantly-coiffed silver fox and felt compassion for her client.

"Has someone given you bad news, Mrs Deacon?"

Bethan saw Eddie snap to attention at the sound of her words.

"Suze? Has something upset you?"

"Let me leave you two alone. I'll wait in my car."

"No, don't go," said Suzanne. "Mrs Harley, do you truly think we're doing the right thing by selling our house?"

"Suzanne, please!" Eddie reached out to his wife. "We've gone through all this before."

"Mrs Deacon, I know you've been visiting Ms Morgan." Bethan hesitated. "I wonder, has she said something to upset you?"

Bethan watched Suzanne's face crumple.

"That bitch!" Eddie snapped. "Has she been stirring things again?"

"No! You're wrong, Eddie. I think Ruth has our best interests at heart. Maybe we are too old after all. I mean, too old to cope with the upheaval of setting up home in a new part of the world. Didn't we agree the move to Three Roads should be the last one? Everything's happening in too much of a rush."

Bethan watched Eddie look at his wife as if she'd turned into a stranger.

"I think we should make tracks." Ray Kirby's powerful frame filled the doorway. "Sorry to have taken up so much of your time, Mr Deacon, Mrs Deacon." He nodded at Bethan. "We'll see ourselves out."

Chapter Twenty-One

Ray Kirby leaned against his vehicle and folded his arms across his chest. "This is a bugger's muddle, isn't it?"

"How much did you hear?"

"Enough."

"I swear I'll swing for that evil piece of work!" Bethan sighed.

"Why the feck did Mrs Deacon schlep down there, anyway? You'd think, with a second viewing booked, she'd want to be at home with her husband. Why did he let her go, I wonder?"

"She thought Morgan sounded distraught on the phone. I'm thinking emotional blackmail where their so-called friend's concerned. Morgan's playing Suzanne Deacon like a harp. Knows just when to tighten the strings and when to relax them. I wouldn't mind betting she's fed Mrs Deacon all kinds of poison, parcelled up as friendly advice."

"Sheesh. It doesn't make my position any easier."

"No."

"I could use a stiff drink."

"You and me both."

"Why don't you come back to my hotel?"

She stared at him. For moments the earth tipped on its axis.

"For a drink? Maybe a bite to eat?" He sounded hesitant.

"I'm not sure. I should go straight to the office, in case Mr Deacon rings. He's got the job of calming his wife down."

"Where I'm staying's on your way. Your vendor has your mobile phone number, surely?" Ray didn't allow her time to reply. "In fact, why don't you ring him now? Go on! Tell him I'm prepared to offer the asking price."

"Are you serious?"

"I never joke where money's concerned. If it's the uncertainty that's worrying Mrs Deacon, what better way to calm her down than remove the offending factor?"

"You're quite certain?"

"Are you in the business of bricks and mortar selling or not?"

"Originally, you said you wanted your partner to approve your decision."

"I want this house, Bethan. I'm gagging to get my paws on it, with or without Claudia."

Bethan ignored the gigantic lurch inside her stomach and pulled out her mobile. "Right. You're either going to make Eddie Deacon's day or totally trash it. Either way, it will be an unforgettable moment."

Ray nodded. Kept his eyes fixed on her. Kept them so focused, she almost rang her own number. Had to start again.

"Two hundred and ninety-nine thousand pounds?"

"That's what your website stated last time I looked. Go on, make his day, why don't you?"

Bethan selected the correct number this time. Waited for the call to be picked up. "Mr Deacon? We're still in the village but about to drive off now. I'm ringing to give you good news. Mr Kirby has offered the asking price for your property."

She didn't need to look up, to know Ray Kirby still kept his eyes on her. She didn't know how much Suzanne Deacon's emotional outburst had affected her husband's decision-making process. But when she heard Eddie Deacon pause a beat before giving his verbal agreement to the offer, she felt several things. Relief. Triumph. Professional satisfaction. Not to mention a huge amount of joy that owed nothing to the commission achieved from selling a heap of bricks and mortar in an idyllic location.

She smiled at her purchaser. "It's a yes. Do you want to go back inside?"

"Nah, let's leave them to it. He'll calm her down. Still fancy that drink?"

Bethan followed him back to Knightly. He drove carefully, obeying every speed restriction sign.

His hotel stood on the town's outskirts, approached via an ornate gateway and a winding drive. It overlooked one of several rivers that helped make the area so appealing. Vehicles belonging to local businessmen dotted the car park. She recognised a personal number plate belonging to the owner of the nearby country store, a business that drew customers from miles around. This was green welly country. Lots of people kept horses, goats, chickens and dogs. The Royal Welsh Showground was an easy drive from here. Ray Kirby parked at the side of the building and she drove into the adjacent space.

He pulled a dark grey holdall and a laptop case from the rear of his Range Rover.

"I stayed in Llanbrenin on my first visit." He zapped his key lock.

"At the Queensbridge?"

"Yup. I thought the food was excellent."

"I'm surprised you didn't want to go back."

"I thought Claudia might prefer this place. The spa's undergone a facelift but I imagine you'd know all about that."

"I like to keep my eye on the ball."

He looked around. "You wouldn't think we were so close to the town. Such as it is."

"Isn't its size and quirkiness part of Knightly's charm?"

"I wasn't trying to wind you up. Hell's teeth, I might have an urgent need to buy a set of wind chimes one of these days."

Bethan laughed. "Or Chinese massage balls. They're supposed to be very therapeutic, according to my daughter."

They walked towards the entrance, and she felt the temporary closeness of being part of a couple that were not a couple. He held open the swing door and she entered the lobby ahead of him.

"I'll tell them I'm here. It's too early to check in."

He approached the desk and spoke to the receptionist with that easy charm which so belied his tough guy appearance. The woman looked across and recognised his companion.

"It's good to see you again, Mrs Harley."

Bethan responded, confident the hotel employee would recognise she was here as part of her business duties and not because of an assignation. She was equally aware how her feelings towards this particular client had ratcheted to an inappropriate level totally unrelated to a business transaction. The knuckles of her left hand brushed against Ray's quilted black jacket as she walked beside him towards the lounge bar. She drew her fingers away, clenching them as though they'd brushed against the logs burning brightly in the enormous fireplace.

The ringing of her mobile snapped Bethan back to reality. She checked the caller's identity.

"My daughter. Do you mind if I—?"

"How about I order a half bottle of champagne? Seeing as it's still your working day."

She nodded. Accepted the call. Watched him march up to the bar, his long legs devouring the distance in a few strides.

"Mum, can I stay at Callum's tonight? His sister's boyfriend's coming over and we want to get a takeaway and watch movies."

"Will his parents be there?" Bethan waited for the familiar 'Mu-um' to echo in her ear. She didn't hang around for long.

"They're going to someone's house for dinner. They'll be back by midnight. Callum's sister says I can crash in her room. Satisfied?"

"Yes, darling. Have a lovely evening. I'll see you in the morning then. Text me when you want a lift."

Bethan walked into the bar where Ray had been chatting with the barman.

"I'm sorry about that. My teenager's social life is far more interesting than my own." Again, too much information. "So, champagne? You haven't even exchanged contracts, yet you're celebrating?"

"It's you as well as me, surely? You've worked hard. Put up with a lot of flak. You deserve a glass or two of bubbly."

He led her to a table beside the window. Bethan didn't intend dampening his enthusiasm with the usual warnings about potential delays and unforeseen blips and turned her attention to the river, its peaty brown waters tumbling and splashing over a weir. A heron perched motionless on a flat white stone, remaining so still one might be forgiven for accepting the long-legged bird as a stone garden sculpture.

Ray Kirby's voice broke her reverie. "I don't often get to drink champagne of a morning," he said.

"Nor do I." Her last taste of the bubbly stuff had been at a colleague's wedding reception. She and Tim's attendance at another couple's nuptials hadn't halted the advancing chill of their own marital breakdown.

"Actually, it's no longer morning."

"True," she said. "It still feels like it though. You must have made an early start."

"I'm used to getting up at sparrow-fart." He raised his eyebrows. "You know, it would have been a downer, spending the rest of the day alone, having made such an important decision."

Bethan recognised a chink in his armour. She burned to ask if he intended at least ringing his partner. Perhaps he thought Claudia might still be sleeping.

"Maybe you're thinking of driving back today to check your partner's all right?"

"Nope. I shall honour my room reservation. Get some plans on paper. Drink more champagne…"

He was watching her. She looked away. Looked around the lounge. Looked anywhere but at him. "They have a big screen TV. You could watch sport all afternoon. That golfing thing Eddie Deacon mentioned."

"I could, couldn't I?"

She heard the smile in his voice.

"Do you work every Saturday, Bethan?"

"No. Officially today is my day off."

He raised his eyebrows. "I'm flattered."

"I was determined nothing would interfere with – well, you know."

Ray kept silent while their waiter popped the cork and poured fizz into two crystal flutes. He raised his glass to clink against hers. "We're not out of the woods yet. I'm not that naïve."

"The Deacons can move out without too much delay. Mr Deacon has a couple of possibilities lined up but said he was prepared to rent somewhere if necessary. You're a cash buyer. That's always a favourable situation."

"You know what I meant." He drank from his glass and put it back on the table. "If our suspicions about the witch of the west are accurate, as you and I know they are, she might yet pull all the stops out to try and prevent the sale going through."

"Maybe Mr Deacon will drive his wife back to the daughter's place to keep her out of the line of fire."

"If Mrs D leaves the village, won't Mr D be a full-on target for the scheming Ms Morgan?"

Bethan fought the temptation to reach for a strand of her hair to play with. "Do you think I should go and see him? Make it clear exactly what happened while he and his wife were away?" She tried to imagine herself describing Ruth Morgan's Delyth persona; watching her client's eyes widen in amazement.

"I'd say leave it for now. It mightn't ever be necessary. Morgan the Fey might decide she's done her worst."

"Let's hope so. She obviously doesn't worry you. Many people in your position might have decided not to offer on the property."

He shrugged. "I feel sorry for that woman, as it happens. She shouldn't be living where she does. Some people thrive on isolation. Others self-implode. As for me, I plan on contacting a solicitor first thing Monday. I won't allow anyone to interfere with my plans."

Bethan looked at him and wondered if she'd glimpsed a flash of regret in the powerful man's eyes. "I'm sure your partner will fall in love with The Sugar House when she eventually sees it."

"If she sees it." He emptied his glass. Motioned to hers. "Top up?"

Bethan stared at him. What was going on? "I'm fine, thanks." She picked up her glass and sipped the chilled wine, unsure how to react to his comment. What difference should it make to her?

He picked up on her uncertainty. "Make no mistake, Bethan. I shall move into Three Roads, with or without Claudia. At the moment, it looks very much like without."

Bethan hid her hands beneath the table so she could clench her fists. Feel her fingernails biting into each palm. "If she's poorly it's probably wise that she didn't come with you. She's probably feeling very sorry for herself and longing to have you back again."

"There's a lot going on I don't know about, is all."

Bethan picked up her bag. "I really must get back, Ray."

"They know you're with a client. Can I not persuade you to join me for a spot of lunch?"

The description sounded bizarre, coming from the big man.

Bethan shook her head. "Thanks, Ray, but duty calls. Enjoy the rest of your stay."

"I'd enjoy it more if you'd agree to have dinner with me tonight. Or is a date with a prospective purchaser a no-no?"

Thrown, she clutched her handbag strap like a lifeline. "I've never thought about it. It's the first time a client ever asked me out."

"I find that difficult to believe. Why don't you think about it? You can always give me a call later. I shall probably order a ploughman's and go for a walk before I sketch out some plans. I need to stretch my legs after this morning's driving."

On her return home from the office, Bethan, still with reservations about the situation at Three Roads, sent a text message to Eddie Deacon's phone, hoping for a swift response. While she waited, she changed into black leggings and yellow sports vest, with a lightweight sweatshirt tied around her waist. She did her usual stretches and bends, placed her Yale key inside her money belt and let herself out of her front door just as her phone rang.

It didn't take long to outline her fears about Ruth Morgan, although Eddie, she sensed, didn't seem too bothered. Who could blame him, having received an offer on his asking price? When Bethan jogged through the small residential estate only a mile from the hotel she'd visited that morning, the afternoon still drifted, golden, gentle, and far too delicious to waste on housework or batch cooking for the freezer.

Even one single glass of champagne slid too easily into her head. It had been a considered decision, not to accept a second. Ray Kirby's invitation had caught her off balance. Tugged at her emotions, never mind other more physical portions of her anatomy. She'd wanted to accept. Wasn't she home alone that evening? It would be so easy to call his mobile and say yes. But would that lead to a complicated few hours? What did they have in common save their joint suspicions regarding Ruth Morgan and determination that Ray should become the new owner of The Sugar House? She'd do her utmost to grease the wheels on the conveyance machine, having recommended a local solicitor with whom she'd gone to school and who prided upon his non-procrastination skills.

There'd also been that odd mention from Ray of a Julia something or other. He said he'd explain when next he saw her. Anything that might explain the actions of Ruth Morgan was important to Bethan. Maybe, having dinner with him would be helpful in that respect.

As for being attracted to the guy, he had a live-in lover and Bethan had a husband. Which part of that did she not understand? For the first time in years, her body was trying to override her scruples, rather than allow her brain to function, as she'd prefer.

Bethan left the quiet estate, upped her pace and began an easy loping run, moving confidently. Passing the small retail park enjoying a sunny Saturday afternoon business boost, and heading down the quiet residential road leading out of town. She would turn down the first forestry track. The scenery couldn't compete with that around The Devil's Pool but the terrain was far gentler.

It had been a good morning, apart from that one big blip. She needed to unwind now. Needed to push herself in a different way from that in which she reacted to the challenges of her professional life.

She heard the distinctive call of a buzzard as she progressed. A quick upward glance showed a pair of birds. Not too many miles away was a Red Kite feeding station, where she and her husband had taken Poppy and her friends, or weekend visitors, on several occasions. The thought of her estranged husband brought Ray back into her thoughts. She and he did, after all, have in common their precarious love life situation: he unexpectedly ambivalent about his partner's place in his future plans, and she undecided as to whether she wanted to remain married to Tim for Poppy's sake, or for her own.

Being a single mum when your child's father was supportive and generous wasn't too bad was it? She enjoyed her job. Usually. Poppy was happy at school and now she was working towards a university place. The house would be quiet without her but she was often out a lot anyway, studying with one of her friends, and these days spending time with her boyfriend at weekends.

The leaves in front gardens were turning. Falling. Too damp to shift in the breeze, they lay, giant freckles plastering lawns and patios. In the distance the sun dappled conifers with gold. Bethan continued to run at a steady pace. She passed the town boundary sign.

She saw the big man walking from the forestry track back to the main road as she covered the final stretch of pavement. She could easily turn back the way she'd come. Maybe he hadn't noticed her. Somehow her legs kept on propelling her in his direction.

Ray Kirby stopped walking as soon as he saw her. Why had she not chosen the other side of town, with its riverside footpath, for her afternoon exercise? She might have known a stranger to the area, in search of a walk in the fresh air, would leave the hotel and head away from the town. Her hair was pulled back into a ponytail, her clothing chosen for comfort not fashion. She didn't need to glance down to know dampness darkened the front of her T-shirt. She slowed down and faced him. She couldn't stop staring at his mouth.

"Why don't you come back for a swim? We can have tea at the health club bar. I'll put you in a taxi afterwards and you can ask the cabbie to collect you at seven."

Eddie poured himself a large gin and tonic over a couple of ice cubes. Suzanne stood at the worktop, whisking eggs. He watched the golden mixture thicken and bubble as she beat. Her favourite omelette pan, which he knew cost more than her last half-day session with the hairdresser, was heating on the hob.

"How about a drink, my darling?"

"Maybe in a bit."

"I'm glad you seem better." He perched on a nearby stool, admiring her neat way of working. She hadn't lost any of her culinary flair.

"I'm fine, Eddie. I don't know how I got so wound up. As soon as we heard about Mr Kirby's offer, I felt much calmer. You know how much I hate not knowing what's going to happen."

"I think we both know the reason for your returning in such a state. I need to keep you away from Morgan le Fey."

"From whom?"

"You know very well whom! Arthurian legend and all that."

"You mean the enchantress?"

"Some said sorceress."

"Do you find her enchanting, Eddie?"

"Morgan le Fey?"

"Ruth."

He clicked his tongue against his teeth. "Isn't it time you told me what rubbish the woman's been spouting?"

"I asked you a question."

Eddie frowned. "She's far from being enchanting, though I think it's fair to say she's in reasonable shape for her age. Apart from that arthritic knee she goes on about. But she's not my type." He tried to reiterate, seeing his wife's lips tighten. "This is crazy! Why should I want to fool around when I've got you? You don't honestly believe I'd be unfaithful at this stage of our lives, do you? Perhaps I should feel flattered, an old geezer like me."

"I'll have that glass of wine now, please."

He went to the fridge and took out a bottle of Suzanne's favourite Semillon. "I wish you'd tell me the real reason why you returned from Rock Cottage in such a state."

"I wish you'd tell me how many people viewed our house while we were away. And what went on." She poured the beaten eggs into the smoking pan. Tipped in fresh herbs and chopped mushrooms. Raked the mixture with a wooden spatula.

Eddie put a glass of wine on the counter top beside her. "You don't want to be bothered with all that. We've received an offer. Fingers crossed the sale will go through smoothly."

"We didn't make the best of starts with the viewings. I still shudder when I think about Mr and Mrs Hunt's experience."

"Forget it, Suze. Water under the bridge."

"I'm amazed Mr Kirby came back again after that business with the tractor."

"Be thankful he did and go with the flow. Lunch smells good."

"Part of the reason I get so nervous about things is that you conceal so much from me."

He sighed. "I can't see the point of going over it all. If you must know, Bethan Harley and Ruth didn't exactly hit it off. Ruth appears to have become very territorial. Possessive even. Mrs Harley was pulling out all the stops to achieve a sale and found Ruth not as co-operative as she'd have wished or expected her to be. That's about it."

"Ruth has made some unpleasant insinuations about you."

"Has she indeed! Is this about what I think it is?"

Suzanne switched the hob control to zero. "You tell me." She waited several moments and flipped the omelette on to a plate. Picked up a knife and turned towards her husband.

He flinched as the light caught the sharp steel blade. "Over the years we've known her, there might've been times when I've—"

"Been tempted?"

"No! Please let me finish." He stared at her. "All right. Maybe one occasion when we'd both had too much to drink and I kissed her. Or she kissed me. Whatever. We all know that sort of thing happens between consenting adults sometimes."

Suzanne cut into the omelette so one helping was bigger than the other. "Define sometimes." She placed the smaller portion on a second plate.

"Remember those late-night shindigs at the hotel? Smooching on the dance floor with someone else's spouse?"

"Perlease! That was usually dancing cheek to cheek and always in full view of everyone else."

"If you say so. Sometimes you can be a little naïve, my darling."

They began their meal in silence, the atmosphere heavy between them. Eddie, struggling to find the right thing to say, said nothing at all.

"I don't intend to make a big thing of this," said Suzanne at last.

He reached his hand across to touch hers. "There is nothing going on. I swear on my mother's memory."

"Thank you. And I'm sorry for doubting you. I realise there have been times when I haven't been as loving towards you as I should be."

285

"Do you know what I think?"

"I will when you tell me." She laid her fork down.

"Here we go then. My opinion is that Ruth wants to take us over. I've done a lot of thinking while we've been away. Some of the things you told me show how she's trying to control you in particular. That business about us all living together one day – I reckon it's all down to the loneliness she dreads if you and I leave Three Roads."

"What? The woman with all the friends and local contacts?"

"Think about it, Suze."

"I'm thinking more about the way you said 'if you and I leave Three Roads.'"

Eddie swallowed hard. "When! I meant to say, *when* we leave."

"I think you should tell me absolutely everything Bethan Harley has told you."

He reached for a chunk of baguette and spread butter upon it. "All right. But it sounds like a run of bad luck to me. For starters, I've never heard a bizarre tale about a murderer being buried somewhere around here. Have you?"

Chapter Twenty-Two

Bethan couldn't believe how good she felt. The gentle lunges and limb stretches before her leisurely run followed by the silky feel of the water stealing up her body as she descended the steps into the hotel pool. The smooth lengths achieved while Ray Kirby ploughed up and down in an impressive crawl from deep end to shallow end. Wrapped in a towelling gown over a borrowed swimsuit, she reclined in a wicker lounger beside him in the conservatory.

"Do women in their late thirties or forties still get crushes?"

She felt her heart skip a beat. "What kind of a question is that?"

Determination not to look at him didn't stop her from sensing his amusement. She reached for her cup of Earl Grey and watched the lemon slice swirl as she stirred the tea.

"Okay," he said. "I'll try not to dig myself into a deep hole here. I think Claudia has fallen for some guy and might be mistaking rampant lust for that old thing called lurve."

"I don't think age comes into it if people are attracted to one another. But seeing those images on the internet, Claudia doesn't look anywhere near forty to me." Hastily she gathered her thoughts. "I hope you don't mind. I mentioned her to my daughter and Poppy found her website and clicked on the audio button. Claudia has a beautiful voice."

"Why should I mind? That's what it's there for. But you, more than anyone, should know how to tart up a few photographs for a website."

"I'll ignore that remark on the grounds it might incriminate me."

"Claudia may be drop dead gorgeous but she's 39 years of age and well-used to guys coming on to her."

"Has she ever been married?"

"Yeah. Married at 20. Divorced at 23."

"Wow."

"Wow indeed. And in case you're wondering, I've been married too but my innings lasted a hell of a lot longer than Claudia's."

Bethan decided not to probe in that direction. "Dare I ask if this crush you mention happens to be focused on someone she met on the cruise?"

"The gentleman in question is a musician, a saxophonist to be precise. He joined the ship's orchestra for this last trip and seems to have found the right harmonies extraordinarily quickly."

"You must have always been aware of the risk. Having a beautiful partner who's so much on show. I'm sure you mentioned something to me." Bethan's voice tailed away. Where was this leading? The big man didn't strike her as the type to need an agony aunt.

"Yeah. I've always maintained, if someone swept her off her feet, I'd have to accept it. Odd how I envisaged, if it happened at all, it'd be a fling with a passenger. Silly really, as there aren't usually too many straight, single males taking the kind of cruises Claudia works. The customers mostly consist of Baby Boomers celebrating retirement or significant anniversaries."

"I'm sorry," said Bethan softly. "Just at the time when you probably least expected it."

"That's life. Ironic really, Claudia having decided not to work any more cruises after the next one. Who knows, now? Maybe I shouldn't have imagined I could have it all."

"Getting back to basics, I think a woman that sort of age is no less prone to experiencing a crush than a woman in any other age group."

"You think this might burn itself out?"

"It's possible."

"Has it ever happened to you? Or is that question way too personal?"

No flattering banter about her not being old enough yet to know, but cutting straight to the chase. She met his gaze. "It has happened to me, yes."

He stared at her. Swore softly under his breath as his mobile phone demanded his attention. Bethan drained her teacup and decided to make a move.

Ray checked his message. "I should respond to this."

"I must get dressed and continue my run."

"No cab?"

"No cab."

"Then write down your address for me and I'll arrange for a driver to pick you up at seven." He pulled a pack of post-it notes and a pen from his towelling gown pocket.

"Very organised, but are you quite certain you can put up with my company again this evening?"

"One hundred percent, ma'am."

His smile transformed his face. His eyes drew her to him. She had to clench her fists to stop herself leaning over and kissing him. Stupid. Stupid. *It's just a little crush.* The words of the song taunted her. Ray loved Claudia. And Poppy's dad was still Bethan's husband.

"I'm not sure those two consultants would be the right people for this place anyway," said Eddie.

He and Suzanne had moved into the conservatory and were sitting, watching the birds squabble and flutter around the feeding table. He'd freshened his glass and topped up his wife's wine.

"Why on earth not?"

"Think about it, Suze. Bethan said they were lovely, cultured people whose family was scattered all over the world. They shouldn't be contemplating a move to mid Wales. It's just not practical."

"It's not like it's the Outer Hebrides. Driving from here to London isn't that big an ordeal."

Eddie shrugged. "A couple like that, coming up to retirement, surely need somewhere with easy access to theatre and cinema and restaurants. Isn't that what we're after?"

"Amongst other things. I'm still mortified at the thought of the stench Mrs Harley described. I do wish I could apologise to the Saranis personally."

"Well, you can't, so don't worry about it."

"But what on earth was Ruth thinking of, not checking the cloakroom?"

"I can't help thinking there's something odd been going on."

"And that young couple. Did Ruth meet them too?"

"Apparently not. But Bethan had a feeling, budget wise, they were out of their league."

"I still think Mr and Mrs Hunt would have been ideal."

"For the love of God, Suzanne, can't you give it a rest?" He rubbed his eyes. "That's irrelevant now, isn't it? Ray Kirby has come back and offered the asking price and we've accepted."

"You've accepted, you mean."

He groaned. "What am I supposed to do? Ring Bethan and say we've changed our minds? Do you really want to stay in this little rut? Not too long ago you were moaning about the way Ruth was sneering at you. Criticising one thing and another. One minute you want out of here, the next, you're running down to hers for girly gossip, then coming home in tears. The lord only knows what Bethan and Kirby must have thought."

"Bethan this, Bethan that. You're obsessed with that woman. I wish you wouldn't drink gin. It always makes you belligerent."

"Ah, you want to control my alcohol intake now, do you?"

"I'm only reminding you that red wine suits you better. You always say it mellows you."

He got to his feet. "I'm going out. While I'm gone, I suggest you do some serious thinking."

"Are you taking the dog?"

"No. I need some male company, Suze. Watch my lips! When I come back, I need to know what you really think about moving. Not what I think. Not what Penny and Declan think. And especially not what that bloody harpy down the road thinks!"

She stared up at him. "But where are you going?"

"To the golf club."

A green woodpecker alighting on a tree branch above the feeding table snagged his attention. "It's beautiful here, of course it is, but maybe one can overdose on fantastic scenery when there's not much else to concentrate on. I fancy a change, Suzanne. I want to feel alive. And to be honest, I can't stand the thought of even just one more winter in Three Roads. If you truly don't feel the same, we're going to have to make other arrangements. Face up to it."

He left her alone. At her feet, the dog opened her eyes and looked up at her mistress.

"I'm such a failure, Sparkles. I'm not sure now what I want and that's a fact."

Eddie grabbed a jacket from the utility room. Sparkles, who'd followed him, waited patiently.

"Not this time, old girl. Sorry." He ruffled her ears, guided her gently back into the kitchen and closed the connecting door. He left, banging the backdoor behind him, something he hadn't done in years, except if the wind intervened. He did sometimes take the dog down the track and around the village, but on this occasion he needed to get out from under. Something had gone very wrong. He didn't understand why he couldn't seem to please his wife, whichever way he played it. Maybe all this indecision meant she was heading for a nervous breakdown? That would put a different complexion on things. Matters might have to go on hold.

He got into his car and closed his eyes, gathering his thoughts, recalling something one of the forestry men had said to him a while back. It was far easier to buy into this area than it was to sell up and escape. In fact, the man's comment had been blunter than that. Easy to get in but effing hard to get out! Now Eddie had a buyer lined up and amazingly this hadn't taken long to achieve, despite his original fear that the series of viewings and almost viewings might be jinxed.

Ray Kirby personified the ideal successor to take over The Sugar House. Someone younger might have feared the novelty would wear off, but Kirby sought tranquil surroundings. He seemed in good health, active enough to enjoy good walking country. He worked from home and didn't seem bothered about the village's adequate rather than super fast Broadband speed. He possessed a partner so wouldn't suffer from loneliness.

He certainly wouldn't tolerate Ruth, or anyone else for that matter, interfering in his life. He probably wouldn't join in the meagre programme of community activities but that wasn't Eddie's problem. Suzanne was Eddie's problem. These days his wife changed her mind more frequently than her expensive silk knickers.

He sat up straight. Started the engine. There were a couple of guys at the golf club who might well listen to his troubles over a drink in the bar, but how could he voice his feelings when they were so confused? One of his mother's favourite sayings when faced with a dilemma had been, 'if in doubt, don't.' Upon reaching adulthood he decided that kind of attitude never got anyone anywhere. Risk-taking sometimes paid off. Having made the decision to put their house on the market, shouldn't they persevere? Bethan Harley said Kirby wanted the sale to go through with minimum delay.

Bethan. She'd be sympathetic. She'd probably seen this kind of thing before. He liked her and he trusted her, even though no one was supposed to put their faith in an estate agent. Reading between the lines, he'd soon twigged she didn't have much time for Ruth. More importantly, Bethan was present when Suzanne returned from her visit to Ruth's and had seen the kind of behaviour currently worrying the life out of him.

It all boiled down to the fact that Suzanne had been blowing hot and blowing cold. She'd perked up while they were away. They hadn't tried to find a property right on their daughter's doorstep as the little family would relocate, even if only a few miles, when Declan left the Army and began his new venture. Eddie was prepared to go along with his wife's preferred choice of new home.

But she'd got herself in a stew over returning to Three Roads. She'd expressed concerns about Ruth, acted like a kid afraid to face going back out into the playground. When she calmed down again, he'd been relieved. Yet the way she reported her telephone conversation from the Wiltshire hotel with their friend and house sitter, had amazed him. She'd sounded calm and confident. Back home again, she seemed to crumble. Why hadn't he put his foot down and prevented her from jumping to Ruth's command and going to Rock Cottage? What kind of a husband was he?

He drove slowly down the track. If only he could pack Suzanne back in the car and drive her to their daughter's. But he couldn't do that to Penny. Her mother's current state was far too fragile for his liking. Perhaps he should arrange a GP appointment. That was more like it. Perhaps he should calm down and treat Suzanne's agitated state as he would a cold virus or sprained ankle. It needed the right treatment and time to rest. He wouldn't share his concerns with anyone but would let the property sale wheels go on turning. He needed to stay positive.

Hopefully, his wife would have gone upstairs for a rest. She'd niggled at him over his drinking. Well, maybe she'd had a little too much wine. It was quite possible she and Ruth had drunk sherry or wine together earlier. Come to think of it, hadn't this crazy notion of Ruth, Suzanne and him ending up as a triumvirate begun on an evening when Suzanne admitted to bashing the booze with Ruth? She'd probably have put up her hand for a double helping of cold sago pudding, the amount she must have taken on board.

Eddie already felt much better. Calmer. This had been a good idea. Getting out. Taking a breather. It wasn't at all a bad afternoon. Maybe he'd been right in the first place when he wondered if Suzanne should get medical help. A little sedative would do her no harm. He'd ring the GP surgery first thing on Monday.

Ruth ate her solitary lunch of wholemeal bread and canned tuna in sunflower oil. She had Radio 4 for company and half-listened to callers phoning in to state their views on education, television reality shows, and the recent sale to the Japanese of an obscure, obscenely expensive oil painting. Her mind couldn't stop dissecting recent events at The Sugar House.

She cast her mind back to the day when she walked up the hill with Ray Kirby. Not too much later at Pwll-y-Diafol, the Harley woman had turned up like one of those strident female police officers in a television drama, thus preventing the natural progression envisaged by Ruth. It hadn't seemed in the least wrong to make her way stealthily through the woodland and check up on the confident house seeker who considered himself immune to risk.

So, hard-nosed Mr Kirby had turned up again to take a second look at the house he'd so set his heart on?

Unfortunately, he'd chosen to visit on the day after the Deacons' return. She wondered what had prevented the couple from bubbling over with news of a second viewing by the big man from London. They must surely have had advance warning, unless Eddie forgot to inform the Harley woman of their return and she'd turned up again, key in hand.

Suzanne had blurted out the information in the end; although too late for Ruth to arrange some kind of mishap. But Suzanne, with her innate fragility bolstered by Eddie's pandering to her every whim, would hopefully, by now, have scotched any offer made by Kirby. Sometimes people needed to accept they couldn't necessarily have tumble into their hot little hands something they desired with such intensity.

Dylan shot through the cat flap like a pantomime imp and dropped a dead field mouse at her feet. Ruth took a sizeable chunk of tuna and put it on the floor in front of her cat. He sniffed. His tongue shot out. He wolfed the fish. She rose, found a rubber glove and flung the corpse in the compost bin beside the back door.

No need now for tricks and disguises. She stood alone against the opposition: Eddie and Suzanne, the Harley woman and Ray Kirby. The demise of any one of these four could seriously affect the dynamics of the situation around The Sugar House. The Harley woman was a minion and more than likely a tart. She had that hungry, searching look, doubtless motivated by money. She wore rings but Ruth felt sure they counted for nothing. Was she sleeping with Ray

Kirby? Or had he brought his glamorous partner with him today?

Ruth seethed. The words that had so impressed her when she studied Milton's *Paradise Lost* at school fell like scattering confetti into her consciousness. Impotence. The night hag. The Portress of Hell gate had replied, *'Hast thou forgot me, then; and do I seem now in thine eye so foul?'*

Everything was falling into place. Eddie and Suzanne needed to acknowledge Ruth's importance in their lives. She refused to allow them to cast her off like some fallen angel. She'd invested too much. Too often. Too carefully.

Whether Ray Kirby made an offer on the house or not, Ruth knew what she must do. Deep in her thoughts, she suddenly became aware of her ringing telephone but elected not to answer. It might be Eddie calling to ask for her help in calming Suzanne. Maybe for once she should play hard to get.

She needed to face certain facts. It was unlikely she'd cross Ray Kirby's path. She'd lost her chance of his undergoing an unfortunate accident so must move on. He might even decide the house in the nowhere place that called itself a village, wasn't for him after all. Mr Kirby could easily find some other vendor's hands to fill with cash.

The sales negotiator wasn't worth thinking about. Bethan Harley's exasperating manner would be of no consequence once the sale board vanished. That left the key players. How much had Ruth been able to play on her

298

impressionable friend's mind? Perhaps she should have picked up that phone call after all.

When she crossed the room and entered the little hallway, she punched in 1471 and listened to the electronic voice. The number she heard belonged to her old friend Huw. She clicked her tongue. He surely couldn't want another meeting so soon after the last one? It wasn't worth pursuing. Not with all she had on her mind. Sometimes, people asked her why she didn't make use of the answer phone service. Ruth's theory was, if someone really wanted her, they'd ring back. And back again.

The thought of what might be happening between the Deacons pecked at her like a bird tearing at carrion. But she didn't intend ringing them. The situation had become volatile and she needed to wait and let sown seeds germinate. Meantime, it wouldn't hurt to take a stroll.

As she let herself out through her front door, she heard the telephone ring again. Ruth sighed. She'd ignore it. The urge to discover what was happening at the other end of the village burned too fiercely for her to withstand it any longer. Her fingers reached into her right-hand pocket and touched the replica key to the Deacons' house that she had cut on her last trip to town. It might prove useful. Vital even.

She set off, adjusting her pace, feigning a slight limp yet taking care not to overdo her pretended mobility problem. When she came within sight of the Deacons' turning, she slowed her pace further so she stood right beside Phil Sartin's gateway. She moved on to his bumpy bit of driveway and took refuge beside his fence, out of sight. If she climbed up on the bank, she should be able to see the back of Eddie's car and if so, establish he was at home.

Ruth smiled to herself. The vehicle wasn't in its usual place. Perhaps he'd left the lady of the house home alone.

Chapter Twenty-Three

She didn't tiptoe. She didn't skulk. She eased the newly cut key from her pocket and into the Yale keyhole. Satin-smooth. The safety lock had not been applied. Relieved, she pushed open the door and closed it again. Very quietly. In tune with a house holding its breath. The jewel colours of the asters she'd plucked so recently lit up the hall table. The kitchen door stood ajar. She held her breath, straining her ears, anticipating the click of claws on wooden floor. Nothing. The dog must either be shut in the utility room or outside in her play area. She took a deep breath, relishing the idea of materialising in Suzanne's afternoon as if she'd walked through the wall.

First of all, she needed to bolt the front. Suzanne hadn't put the safety chain in position and this blip was something Eddie often nagged her about. It might also mean she'd drunk too much wine at lunchtime and gone upstairs for a nap. Fortune smiled upon Ruth.

Keep a cool head. Go through and bolt the back door too, why don't you? Check the dog's whereabouts. Take the phone off the hook. It mustn't ring and disturb Suzanne while you're still on your way upstairs.

When she was ready, she climbed the stairs. Slowly. Once upon the landing, she cleared her throat. "Hello? Suzanne dear, are you up here?"

Her friend took a while to answer. Long enough for Ruth to tiptoe towards the door of the master bedroom and knock tentatively. "Don't be alarmed. It's only me, Ruth. May I come in?"

She heard the sound of rustling, as though Suzanne was resting on the bed.

"Ruth? How ever did you get in? Has Eddie come back?"

"No, my dear. I met him as he was walking up the hill. He told me he'd left the back door unlocked. Asked me to call and check you were all right."

"Did he indeed? You'd better come in."

Ruth pushed open the door and stuck her head round. "I hope you don't think I'm intruding but Eddie mentioned something about the two of you having a bit of a domestic. He seemed quite distraught. I'm worried about you, dear."

Suzanne sighed. "Come in, Ruth. I feel terrible. I can't seem to stay on an even keel for long. Sometimes I wish Eddie hadn't suggested the idea of moving. But then I think of Penny and I feel disloyal. Guilty."

"Hush now." Ruth moved closer to the white satin ocean liner of a bed. "We can't have you making yourself ill. Could you drink a cup of tea if I go and make one?"

"That'd be wonderful. After Eddie stormed out, I came up here to try and think things out."

"You really should rest. Try and relax. I'll be fast as I can."

Ruth flew downstairs to the kitchen. She set about making tea, found a tray, placed items on it. Took a pillbox from her pocket and tipped two tiny tablets into one of the rose-splattered, gold-rimmed cups. She poured milk into a little jug, poured boiling water into the teapot and carried the loaded tray upstairs.

The door to the master bedroom still stood ajar. "Only me. I hope you don't mind my joining you for a cuppa before I leave you in peace."

"I could do with some company." Suzanne still stared into space. "He said if I didn't agree with his plan, we'd have to make other arrangements. I don't know what that means exactly. What do you think?"

"I think you shouldn't let yourself get worked up. There's plenty of time to talk things over."

"But that's just it. There isn't time. Mr Kirby has offered the asking price for the house and Eddie has accepted."

Crockery rattled as Ruth's hand shook. She paused, then poured tea into one cup and added a sugar lump. She gave a good stir, placed the cup beside Suzanne on the bedside cabinet and filled the remaining cup.

"Ruth?"

"Suzanne, it's the weekend, remember? Solicitors' offices don't open again until Monday. In any case, if you tell Eddie you disagree about selling up, he can't go ahead. Not without your consent, he can't."

Ruth kept her eyes on Suzanne, who was sipping her tea. She took much more milk than Ruth did. How fortunate. This cooled the hot liquid and soon Suzanne would feel the urge to close her eyes. To sleep her problems away.

"Why don't I wait here until Eddie returns? You might even take a little nap. I can make sure Sparkles is all right. I'll let her into the garden for a while, shall I?"

With the house to herself, Bethan did a twirl in front of the cheval mirror she and Tim had come across when browsing antiques in North Wales soon after their marriage. She'd stood entranced in front of the looking glass, wondering how many decades of women had checked their appearance in it. Maybe it had come from a mansion where it held court in the lady of the house's bedroom, reflecting shifting patterns in her life. Witnessed her silhouette changing through childbearing and the lifestyle of a well-off Victorian matron with servants to run her errands and prepare her food.

The glass remained unmarred by scratches or blotches. The wooden framed rectangular mirror still perfectly balanced between two barley-sugar twist struts, their feet firmly placed upon the soft pink and green carpet transforming Bethan's bedroom floor into an impressionist meadow.

Tim had decided she should have it. Somehow, they managed to load it into the boot of their car, wrapped around with an ancient tartan rug, plus woollen sweaters pulled hastily from their suitcases. They still had two more nights before their honeymoon ended. On the road home, Bethan had crossed her fingers while Tim negotiated geometrically impossible bends and twists. He'd laughed at her and told her to trust his driving.

Seven years later, she'd stood their daughter before the cheval mirror so Poppy could see herself in her first school uniform. Solemn eyes. Light brown hair styled in two plaits tied with navy blue ribbons. No Victorian satins and velvets, but a crisp white blouse and short pleated skirt. White socks and Mary Jane black patent shoes. Yet another image absorbed and contained in that looking glass.

Now Bethan stood, examining her reflection, preparing to meet with a man who wasn't her husband. Her stomach lurched yet again. Why was she doing this? Easing on misty grey gossamer tights, a cheeky little black dress and high-heeled black shoes. She'd chosen to leave her hair loose. Around her neck she wore the silver locket Tim had given her. It rested just above her cleavage.

Poppy would approve the wearing of her dad's gift, but be furious to think of her mother dressing up to eat dinner with a man she barely knew. Teenagers could be incredibly puritanical where their parents were concerned. Bethan knew that from comments made by her friends as well as from personal experience.

How conveniently she'd forgotten the constraints of her position. Earlier, at the moment when the receptionist's gaze travelled from Ray Kirby towards his companion, Bethan had seen a flash of curiosity in the woman's eyes. She'd assumed her presence would be construed as part of the duties of a sales negotiator smoothing the way for a prospective purchaser. Doubtless when Ray checked in later, the receptionist would have asked him casually if he was visiting the area on business or for pleasure. She'd have

305

explained this question was designed to help the hotel company judge the percentage of tourists against those staying for reasons other than viewing ruined castles, waterfalls and wild bird feeding centres.

The hotel employee must have wondered what was going on when Bethan reappeared that afternoon. She occasionally used the spa facilities but wouldn't accompanying a hotel guest into the swimming pool spark curiosity? Hopefully, the same woman wouldn't still be on duty that evening. Bethan contemplated the possibility of telling a fib, maybe inventing a fictitious relationship. Ray might be Poppy's godfather or an old school friend of Tim's?

She turned away from her reflection. People could think what they wished. She hardly ever went anywhere in the evenings, unless it was with her daughter or a female friend to use the gym, stopping off afterwards at her friendly local pub for a quick beer or glass of wine.

She had to face facts. She was attracted to Ray Kirby and they were both on their own, thrown together by circumstances. There were question marks around his romantic situation. Bethan's own relationship remained in limbo. Her daughter wasn't at home to censure her actions. Bethan wondered what the text Ray had received was all about. She suspected it was from Claudia but she could be wrong. A businessman like Ray didn't adhere to a nine to five routine. If Claudia hadn't got in touch with him, surely he would have contacted her? That might well depend upon how much he cared.

What did Ray now expect from Bethan?

She walked downstairs and picked up a knitted wool coat she'd bought from a local boutique. Hazy greens and blues mingled with thin strands of pewter grey. The coat transformed her in a way she couldn't explain. It wasn't a coat for wearing to the city. She could have walked into any smart hotel in Cardiff or London and her stylish black dress and accessories would have provided a passport to anonymity. The coat, designed and made by a local craftswoman, belonged to mid Wales. Its body and soul spoke of hill slopes and heritage. She wondered whether Ray would notice and approve. She wondered what he was thinking and again she wondered what the evening would bring.

The ringing of her doorbell made her jump. She left her house with a pull of the front door and a grimace at the blast of drizzle sweeping from the mountains. The golden autumn day had dissolved into chill greyness. In no time at all the taxi pulled up at the hotel entrance.

"Give us a bell when you want picking up, Mrs Harley," said the driver.

She'd sold a starter home to the man's daughter. That's what living in this area entailed. You moved in circles, each of which touched another sphere, whose edge in turn blurred into another and another. Local farming families intertwined. You rubbed shoulders with people you'd known in school and people you'd met because your children were at school with their children. She liked it. Was accustomed to it. It had driven Tim nuts at times.

Bethan walked through the swing doors and scanned the foyer. She'd wondered if Ray would be waiting in the bar but saw him sitting in a chair near the reception desk. He unfolded his long frame and came forward at once.

"You look stunning."

"Thank you. I wish I'd worn a raincoat."

"Thank God you didn't."

"I should leave my coat in the ladies' room."

"What would you like to drink? Champagne?"

"What are you having?"

"Champagne of course. I did warn you."

"So you did. Count me in."

"I'll be in the bar."

Standing before one of the mirrors in the pink and gold room marked *Ladies*, Bethan patted her hair. It was barely damp but she fluffed it a little. Her reflection stared back at her. A pair of elderly women pushed through the swinging door, chattering in Welsh. Bethan smiled at them. You didn't hear too much of the native language spoken in these parts. She picked out a word or two. They'd enjoyed their dinner and were looking forward to visiting Powis Castle the following day.

When she walked into the bar, Ray turned and watched her every step as she approached.

"There's a table free by the window. I said we'd eat at eight. I hope that suits?"

"That's fine. Thank you."

He pulled a chair out for her. "We've just avoided the rush. A coach load of senior citizens came out of the restaurant and are at this very moment about to enjoy an evening of Bingo in the function room."

"I may have met two of them in the ladies' room. They were speaking Welsh. I tried to eavesdrop."

"Were they talking about you?"

She chuckled. "Of course not. They'd enjoyed their sherry trifle."

"I'm impressed. It's not a language I know much about."

"The ladies were speaking a kind of Wenglish."

"Sorry?"

"They spoke a mixture of the two languages. The words 'sherry trifle' were mentioned in the midst of the Welsh."

"Is it spoken much around here? Triflish?"

She laughed. "Hey, don't mock. The answer is, not as much as in other parts of the principality. You'll be fine."

"Do you speak it?"

"Just a smidgeon. Poppy's Welsh is pretty good."

"That's your daughter? Do you have other children?"

"No."

"Sorry. I keep barging in." Ray shook his head.

"So, do I."

"Why don't we make ourselves comfortable at our table?"

Bethan followed him across the room, keeping her gaze on Ray's broad back. A waiter hurried to pull out her chair and by tacit agreement, neither she nor Ray mentioned Three Roads or any of its residents.

Each of them sat back when the wine waiter arrived.

"This is getting to be a habit." Ray laughed.

309

"I wish." Bethan shook her head at him and speared a green olive, unable to believe her gaucheness. She was so out of practice with this kind of social sparring.

"Make a real wish," said Ray when the waiter left. He picked up his glass. "And I'll do the same."

"You're full of surprises, Mr Kirby."

"Aren't I just? Well, I shall make a wish." He closed his eyes for moments. Opened them again and drank some of the delicious white wine chosen to accompany their meal.

"I can't think of anything."

"You must be a rare kind of woman."

She thought hard. Wished for Poppy to be offered a place at the university of her choice. Picked up her glass too.

"I spoke to Claudia earlier."

Bethan smiled. "How is she?"

"Feeling much better, apparently."

"That's good."

"Yeah." He looked down at his hands as if unsure whether to continue.

Bethan thought how different he looked. He'd changed into a dark suit, pale blue shirt and a safe kind of dark blue and grey tie. She waited for him to speak.

"Do you mind if I talk to you about her? I'd appreciate your take on this."

Bethan hesitated. "I'm not sure how much help I can be, considering I've never met her."

"Don't worry. I probably need to get it off my chest if you don't mind my boring you."

"I can't imagine you ever being boring."

His smile lit up his face again. "Now that's a challenge if ever there was one. Maybe we'd better find something we have in common to talk about."

"Save that for dinner. You might enjoy your meal better if you tell me what's bothering you first."

"Good thinking. Though I apologise if some of this puts you in mind of your vendor."

"Mrs Deacon?"

"Yep. Sounds like Claudia is tearing herself apart, though in her case, she's trying to decide whether she really does want to bury herself in the countryside – with me – or whether she'd prefer to remain in London."

"It's none of my business but I take it you intend on keeping the London property?"

"I own the apartment. I intend using it when I need to. My son stays there now and then."

"I thought you didn't have children."

"You asked if Claudia and I had children. I answered your question."

She resisted the urge to make a sarcastic quip.

"Joel and I don't really see much of one another." He spread his hands. "He's 22 years of age and to his credit tries to visit his mother as often as he can, given my former wife lives in Western Australia."

She longed to know what had gone wrong with his marriage. Wondered how old he'd been when his son was born. Decided to go for a safer option. "Do you know where the saxophonist lives?"

"Milton Keynes. Wouldn't you just know it?"

She chuckled. "Nothing wrong with Milton Keynes."

"There is now."

"At least you and your partner are speaking. That's always good."

He raised his eyebrows. "Do I detect a note of bitterness?"

"We're supposed to be concentrating on you and Claudia."

"What really bugs me is the speed at which she's cottoned on to this guy."

"It's understandable you should feel like that." Bethan thought back to Tim's confession and his insistence that the marital indiscretion was a one off. She'd told him it was still infidelity. She had no idea if he'd seen the woman again and didn't intend asking. Did that mean she didn't care? Was that why she was here this evening?

"Claudia and I have been together for two years." He picked up his glass and drained it. "I thought we had the ideal set up. Each time I returned from a trip overseas, if she was between cruises, it was like a honeymoon. Do you know what, Bethan? I've been like a little kid, longing to show her the house I wanted for our future."

"Of course. It might still all come right for you both in the end."

His face set in grim lines. No way should this man ever play poker. He was open and honest and blunt and kind and…

312

"Maybe I've pressurised her." He paused. "Okay, that's enough about my situation. I appreciate your listening but you really don't need me droning on about my love life."

"It's important where property decisions are concerned. You don't need me to tell you that." She watched while he refilled her glass.

"I can assure you I shan't withdraw my offer. My plans haven't changed as far as that's concerned."

"You've already made it clear you still want to go ahead. But offers made on a weekend come with a built-in cooling off period."

"Not in my case. I can't wait to start my new life."

"Well, that's good." She leaned back and smiled at him. Some time, he was bound to ask about her status. She wasn't sure she was ready to talk about Tim. The wronged wife wasn't a role she enjoyed playing. Didn't it always take two?

"I'm not planning on asking you about your marriage, Bethan. I just don't like to see that look of resignation in your eyes."

"That's something I'm not aware of." She bit her lip. He knew, without being told, she didn't have a man to go home to.

He leaned forward. "Do you believe in fate?"

"Goodness, another strange question." She stared at the chandelier above them, shimmering like a thousand lit candles. "In a way it would be comforting to believe in destiny but I believe human beings have to make their own decisions. I believe in luck too. I find coincidence fascinating. Is that okay?"

"I've heard it said there's no such thing as coincidence. Would you say we've been drawn together for a purpose? And no, that isn't a chat up line."

"The fact that you and I have met owes nothing to coincidence. I'm an estate agent. You decided to find a property in the area within which I operate. End of."

He grinned. "I'm glad you explained that."

"Why so?"

"Because all at once your eyes lost that look of resignation. They came alive. You came alive. You're a beautiful woman, Bethan. End of."

They sat staring at each other. A squawk from Bethan's phone broke the silence.

"Saved by the bell."

She watched his lips twitch. "I'm so sorry. You know how it is…"

"You don't have to tell me."

She viewed the text message. Frowned. Placed the phone on the table between them. "You'd better take a look at this."

She still reeled from what he'd said before the text came in. And she could tell by the expression on his face that Ray could read her feelings. She knew the two of them were blurring the boundary between professionalism and the reactions of a man and woman temporarily adrift in an emotional sea.

He looked up from the LCD display. "Decided not to accept my offer, ay? So, what now, Bethan?"

"We can't fight someone's state of mind."

"Suzanne Deacon's or Ruth Morgan's?"

"Both, maybe," said Bethan. "I'm so sorry, Ray."

He shrugged. "This message may come via Mrs Deacon's phone, but I'd bet next month's salary she didn't send it."

"I'll try Eddie Deacon's mobile first." Bethan waited. Left a voice mail message. Tapped her nails on the table. "Land line next and if he doesn't pick up, I'll leave a message saying I'll ring first thing Monday morning."

"I guess that's all you can do. The plot thickens."

But Bethan was frowning. "I'm getting the unobtainable tone. I wish I could think that was down to absentmindedness on the part of one of them. But I can't."

Ray leaned across the table and took both her hands in his. "You're not the Deacons' nursemaid. You're not at work. You're with me and this is a chance to enjoy each other's company. What may or may not happen between us in the future is up for discussion. But nothing's going to happen tonight, so relax. Forget Three Roads. I shall need to drive back to London tomorrow but I'll be in touch on Monday morning. In a personal capacity as well as in my house purchasing mode."

She felt a small surge of joy. "Thank you. And, you're right of course – the Deacons have to sort out their own problems."

The waiter hovered, two large menus in his hands.

Ray's big hands gave her slender fingers one last squeeze. He looked up at the young man. "So, what do you recommend?"

Bethan waited until their meal was ordered before reminding Ray of his promise. "You mentioned something about a woman called Julia. What was all that about?"

He nodded. "Weird. That time I walked up the hill with Ruth Morgan, there was something about her that seemed familiar. So familiar that I asked her whether she'd ever worked in Edinburgh."

"Why?"

"Because, a while back now, I spent a couple of years in the city. A scandal hit the headlines – maybe not shocking enough for national coverage but there was stuff in the local papers. A couple of retired doctors, a younger, glamorous housekeeper and the husband's sudden death. I don't have to spell it out?"

Bethan frowned. "Well, no, but what has this to do with our friend the house sitter?"

"It wasn't so much that Ruth Morgan's face reminded me of Julia Hayes, the housekeeper under fire. This was a while back. Maybe a decade. It was that throat stroking gesture that triggered something. You know what I mean? Plus her build, though this woman was a blonde."

"How difficult is it for someone to change their hair colour! Ray, this is worrying." Bethan, leaned forward.

"Isn't it just? When questioned by local police investigating the sudden demise of the husband, the housekeeper admitted certain facts proving she was either stupid or extremely clever."

"Like?" Bethan took a sip of champagne.

"Julia admitted the husband became infatuated with her but she'd always withstood his advances because of her fondness for his wife. The old chap suffered a fatal heart attack one morning and collapsed on the landing between the marital bedroom and the room used by their housekeeper."

"So the housekeeper didn't murder the husband?"

"Some of the wilder theories doing the rounds were that he might well have met his end within the steamy confines of Julia's bed and that she'd dragged him out to the landing while his wife still slept. It didn't take long for someone to point out that her housekeeper could easily have added a little something to the bedtime drinking chocolate. Julia 'discovered' the body at seven o'clock, after showering and dressing ready for breakfast preparation."

"So there was nothing to prove any wrong doing on the housekeeper's part?"

"Exactly," said Ray. "She'd washed up all the crockery and stated the wife was awake when she took in her morning tea before sitting down and breaking the sad news. I remember thinking how clinical this sounded but Julia professed her grief and her loyalty to her remaining employer and stayed until the widow moved into sheltered accommodation, having rewarded her faithful housekeeper with a generous golden handshake."

"How come you know so much?"

"A colleague of mine was a former patient of the husband, that's how. He was dining out on the tale."

Bethan shook her head. Slowly. "I suppose I'm prejudiced but I can well believe that housekeeper was the woman we know as Ruth Morgan."

"As you say, our opinions are coloured by our suspicions but it's something to keep under our hats for the time being, don't you think? Even though the husband's death was pronounced as due to natural causes, if Ruth Morgan really is the woman I've read about, the last thing she'll do is admit it." He paused. "And who knows what else she's capable of?"

Chapter Twenty-Four

When she was certain Suzanne was no longer wakeful, Ruth collected the tea things and laid the tray down outside the door so she could lock Suzanne in. The poor woman needed a proper rest after all she'd gone through.

But, if she should happen to wake later and Ruth was elsewhere in the house, would her friend panic? Suzanne's attitude towards Ruth veered from warm to frigid and back to warm. Ruth needed her on her side. Keeping his wife imprisoned might offer too much ammunition to Eddie, once he discovered he was barred from his own home. He might decide to return with a doctor or some kind of ridiculous mediator. Ruth unlocked the door.

She went downstairs, unloaded the tray and washed up in the kitchen sink, ignoring the dishwasher. Eddie might return any time. He'd receive quite a surprise when he tried to come in through the back door. He'd assume Suzanne had bolted it and would probably go to the front door and take out his key. He kept all his keys on one ring, including that of his car. But it didn't matter. Both doors were bolted.

Everything had clarified. The Deacons must not move and leave her alone in Three Roads. If Eddie came to his senses and agreed things should return to the way they were before the sale board appeared, Ruth would let him into the house. But he'd have to sign the letter she was about to compose. She walked into the drawing room and across to the bureau where Suzanne kept her notepaper. How typical that it must be stationery purchased in London's Bond Street.

Ruth pulled out the antique chair and sat down. How right it felt, to be sitting here. She uncapped Suzanne's fountain pen and tried a few strokes on a scribble pad. The pen needed refilling. She reached for the bottle of Mediterranean blue ink and watched the pen's belly consume the dark liquid.

She began writing a brief letter for Eddie to sign. Suzanne could sign it too. Whether or not she'd returned to full consciousness. Ruth's lips stretched into a satisfied smile. Everything would be all right. She wouldn't crowd them for the time being. She'd stay at Rock Cottage, unless of course Eddie decided Suzanne needed more attention than he could give. He had his golf. His camera club meetings. His ability to lose several hours in front of the television set, watching Wimbledon or winter sports or whatever currently took his fancy.

It would be good to drive Suzanne around again. She would no longer tease her about having expensive tastes. She'd share in them. Eddie would be grateful and would increase his gifts of wine. She'd let Suzanne continue paying for meals and drinks they enjoyed while out together. There'd still be visits to the arts centre and she could suggest an occasional outing to Cardiff. If Eddie made her a named driver on his insurance policy, she could drive them all back. She didn't have a problem with night driving but suspected he had. Or soon would.

320

Everything would work out to perfection. She smiled again as she composed the brief but important letter. This time, she'd have something tangible – a permanent reminder of the bond between her and the Deacons, rather than a half-remembered remark, carelessly spoken and conveniently discarded by Suzanne.

She'd completed the letter and was on her feet when she heard the ring of the doorbell. She took a quick peep through the window and saw Eddie Deacon, hands on hips, standing on the front step. His face stony, he stared at the door as if willing it to open.

She strolled through to the hallway and, leaving the safety chain in position, peered out at him.

"What the hell's going on? Open the frigging door this minute!"

"In a while. First we need to establish ground rules."

"I'm trying to keep my patience. Joke's over."

"It's not a joke, Eddie. You seriously upset Suzanne. Fortunately, I've been able to calm her down so please don't do anything foolish like ring the doorbell again."

"Where is my wife?"

"Resting upstairs."

"Thank you. Now, if you'll kindly open this door, I shall relieve you of your responsibilities."

Ruth sighed. "Oh dear. You just don't get it, do you? You're no longer in control here, Eddie. Suzanne is in no fit condition to cope with moving house. But, please don't worry. I'm here to help you adjust to the situation. I've already contacted Mrs Harley to let her know."

"You've what?"

"We must get your hearing tested, my dear. I've been wondering whether to drop a tactful hint about it."

"You cunning cow. Let me in or I'll ring 999."

"Not a good idea, Eddie. Not with your vulnerable wife in the house, traumatised by your behaviour. I think you'd find the police wouldn't wish to disturb her as long as a responsible adult was present. I also think you might be well advised to drive into town and find a hotel for the night. Come back in the morning when you're in a less belligerent frame of mind."

He vanished from view. She pushed the door closed. Waited. Walked back into the sitting room and sat down in Eddie's favourite armchair to watch television on the big, widescreen.

Bethan and Ray had chosen their starters and main courses when her mobile buzzed into life again.

"Don't mind me," said Ray.

She mouthed an apology. He leaned back in his chair, watching her face as she listened. She knew he saw her body stiffen. Knew he was watching her free hand twirl a strand of hair.

"Mr Deacon, I'm so sorry. I understand how you must feel. You have my word I shall disregard the instruction you know nothing about. I did try to ring you."

She listened, nodding.

"So that's tantamount to a hostage situation. How do you intend on dealing with this?"

Bethan listened again, gaze fixed on Ray who now sat bolt upright in his chair, his eyes focused upon her.

"Give me time to think. I promise I'll ring you back soon. In the meantime, why not go and sit in your car? Or is there a neighbour you could visit? Mr Deacon, are you still there? Hello?"

She closed the call. "He's gone."

"I take it Morgan's in the house with Mrs D and Mr D is out in the cold."

"Yes. Morgan gained entry while Eddie was out. She's refusing to let him in and he's decided not to call the police."

"Good decision. He's the one outside and Morgan's the one inside and she's nothing if not plausible. The police would, with justification, side with the two women."

"I just hope Suzanne Deacon's come to no harm. I've had bad vibes about those two ever since that text message."

"We'll go over there. Now."

"Really? But neither of us should drive."

"I'm not over the limit, Bethan. Scout's honour." He got up and strode to the headwaiter's desk as she watched. "Something's cropped up, I'm afraid. We need to take a rain check on dinner. I'll ring you later. Charge what you need to my account."

Bethan raced off to fetch her coat. When she emerged, Ray was waiting at Reception, car key in hand. He pushed open the swing door and she flew ahead of him. Out into the dank evening. He zapped his key and she saw lights flash. Heard the clunk of unlocking. She clambered into the Range Rover while he pulled open the driver's door and jumped into the seat.

"No time for good manners." He selected reverse gear. Backed out and swung the wheel round again.

"It's an awful thing to say but we were right all along."

"You were right. Unfortunately."

"I hope Mr Deacon keeps his head," said Bethan. "Goodness knows what Morgan's state of mind is at the moment."

"Try his phone again. Tell him we're on the way but on no account must he let Morgan know."

"Okay." She busied herself with her mobile.

"What's happening?" Ray kept meticulously to the 30 miles an hour limit as they passed the primary school, and put his foot down the moment they sailed past the derestricted sign on the town outskirts. The sturdy vehicle began devouring the miles.

"It's ringing but he's not answering," said Bethan.

"He could've dropped the darned thing."

"I'll keep on trying."

"It's a blessing we were in Knightly and not t'other place. We should get there in ten minutes," said Ray.

"I could try Mrs Deacon's mobile, I suppose."

"You're in charge but just to reassure you, I very much doubt she'll come to any harm. Morgan needs her as a bargaining tool."

"That's sick."

324

"It is. But it's happening and it seems like you and I are the only ones who know the background."

"What do you propose doing?"

He gave a short bark of laughter. "Playing it by ear, my lovely. I'll park in the lay by and walk up the track. Unless you can tell me how to sneak up unseen."

"If you go into Phil Sartin's field, you should be able to find a gap in the foliage and come out round the side of the house."

"Perfect. The less thinking time we give Morgan, the better," said Ray.

"I'm coming with you."

"Over my dead body."

"So be it."

He glanced across. "You sound like a headmistress. Or one of those tough lady barristers."

"Keep your eyes on the road."

"I rest my case."

She turned her head towards her window so he couldn't see her smile.

"If you come with me, hang back, keep your phone in your hand and if I say the word, call the cops."

"Okay."

They drove on in silence. When Ray changed gear ready for the slope down into the village, Bethan took out her phone and stowed her bag beneath the passenger seat. Ray guided the big vehicle around the bend, past the turning to the track, and brought it to a halt in the lay by.

They got out in silence. He took the key from the ignition but left the vehicle unlocked. She followed his powerful frame as he headed down the track. They climbed over the farm gate, still out of sight of anyone who might be watching from the house. Keeping close to the hedge, he walked several metres before stopping to examine the thick shrubbery at the side of The Sugar House's front garden.

"Someone, some time, has done what we're about to do. Hang on to me and keep your head down."

Bethan hesitated.

"Don't be shy. Hook your fingers into the back of my belt."

She followed him as he plunged into the stunning swathe of foliage he'd inherit if he ever succeeded in buying the house.

"I need to check out Mr Deacon's car. If he's sitting in it, I'll find out if there's something to help us gain access."

"And if he's not?"

"We need to get in. Period. We know Mr D has his keys with him so Morgan must have bolted both doors. Come to think of it, when I inspected the shed this morning, I noticed an extending ladder."

"You're thinking of the balcony?"

"Right. But this kind of breaking and entering needs to be a two-man job. You up for it?"

"Of course." Bethan swallowed hard. "Do you want me to do the talking or do you want me to climb?"

He hesitated. "Our delightful friend's unlikely to have added you to her Christmas card list. If I can get the ladder secured, are you happy to climb it while I keep her talking?"

"I'm not afraid of heights."

"Sure you're sober?"

"I'm sober."

"Adrenalin's a powerful drug. Even if Mr D's still outside, I'd like to keep him out of this."

On impulse she stood on tiptoe and kissed his cheek. "Good luck, Ray."

She heard him suck in his breath. "We'll both need it. Now, walk down the edge of the flowerbed behind me so our footsteps don't give us away."

Again, she followed him. Almost walked into him when he came to an abrupt halt. A hedgehog had ambled across his path, heading for the lawn. He reached behind for her hand and clasped it. She waited while he approached the car and checked it.

"There's no sign of him and we haven't time to speculate. This next bit could be a tad noisy but I'll do my best. Meantime try ringing Morgan's mobile. With any luck it'll distract her. You do have her number?"

"Yes. Eddie gave it to me. What shall I say?"

"She probably won't answer. If she does, make it up as you go along but don't wind her up."

He moved into the shadows. Bethan heard the soft snick of the shed door unlatching. Something she'd noticed before was the Deacons' lack of security precautions but they knew the area and this omission assisted Ray to carry out his plan. Hopefully, the balcony door to the master bedroom would be unlocked as it had been on all the viewings she'd attended.

Within moments Ray had the ladder extended. Bethan had progressed far beyond nervousness in her determination to get the better of the house sitter. Ray walked back to join her and whispered his next instruction. As he retraced his steps, she walked at the same steady pace. Four feet crunching in synchronisation upon gravel sounded like two feet. No one listening from within could know someone was creeping towards the ladder while Ray stood ringing the bell.

Bethan waited in the shadows until she heard the sound of Ray's voice. To her relief, the outside light had come on so she could plainly make out the ladder she knew he'd wedged securely. Waiting for her to make her ascent. She kicked off her shoes. She could hear Ruth's voice now. Mocking. Strident. Accusatory. Ray's response was a rumble by contrast. But he'd silenced Ruth. He had her attention. He commanded attention wherever he went and this skill had arguably never been more important than now.

Bethan climbed the ladder without hesitation but slowly, keeping her eyes fixed on the balcony. She gripped the wrought ironwork as soon as her head was above the level of the top rail. Moved up another step. Grimaced as the iron rung bit her instep. She swung one nylon-clad leg over the balcony rail. Brought the second leg over so she stood within reach of the door. She stretched out her hand. Turned the handle. *Please let it not be bolted.*

Chapter Twenty-Five

Slowly she pushed. The door swung forward. The bedside lamp bathed the room in a soft, rosy glow.

Bethan could smell luxury. Despite the situation she marvelled at the way scent spoke a message. She saw Suzanne Deacon, lying on her side in bed, blonde head facing away from the balcony.

"Mrs Deacon? Please don't be afraid." Bethan kept her voice low. "It's me, Bethan Harley."

No response. Bethan tiptoed over to the door and waited until she heard Ruth's voice. Praying she wasn't locked in, Bethan gently depressed the handle, relief swamping her as the voices from below became audible. The house sitter must have opened the front door, keeping it on the safety chain, to speak to Ray.

She heard Ruth laugh.

"There's an old country saying, Mr Kirby. Mind your beeswax."

"I take your point and I appreciate your loyalty to your friends, Ms Morgan. Or may I call you Ruth?"

Bethan wondered how susceptible Ruth Morgan would prove to be.

"You may call me whatever you like, Mr Kirby. What possible gain could be achieved by my letting you in?"

"We could have a nice, civilised discussion. I enjoyed your company when we walked up the hill together that time. You're an educated woman stuck in a backwater. I told you that, didn't I?"

"You thought I might like to do a bit of office work for you."

"Ouch. I'm sorry if I sounded patronising because it certainly wasn't what I intended. You're obviously a cultured person. I'm amazed you get on so well with the Deacons."

"What do you mean by that?"

"Oh, come on, Ruth. I wouldn't mind betting Mrs Deacon and you are poles apart when it comes to your musical tastes and the books you read."

Ruth didn't answer.

"I caught a glimpse of her CD collection, mostly schmaltzy stuff and songs from the shows," said Ray. "Don't get me wrong. My partner sings a lot of material your friend would enjoy. I imagine your personal CD collection doesn't include Barry Manilow or Tom Jones. No offence to Messrs Manilow and Jones, but tell me if I'm not right."

"I enjoy Chopin. Sibelius. Debussy."

"Just as I thought. I told you I couldn't understand how someone like you could become buried in a place like this."

"A place you seem hell bent on moving into."

"Touché. But it's different for me. I'll still need to spend time in London."

"And, of course you have a partner to share your rural idyll. You have money. Power. Companionship."

Bethan stood at the top of the staircase, holding her breath. This was the critical part of the operation. She held her mobile phone in her hand, ready to ring for help. If – a very big if – Ruth Morgan let Ray into the house and pulled a knife, or worse; a scream from Bethan should distract her enough for Ray to overpower her. They could keep the house sitter company while Suzanne Deacon continued sleeping sweetly in the master bedroom. That's what Ray had envisaged. She prayed that scenario wouldn't happen. Or if it did, that the strategy worked.

Bethan heard Ray begin to explain how he mightn't be moving in as part of a couple after all. Playing the sympathy card. Morgan didn't comment.

"Do you play chess?" Ray asked.

"Of course, but very rarely nowadays."

"Do the Deacons play?"

"No. I did try and teach Suzanne but those two are more into Scrabble."

"So that exquisite, carved jade set in the front room is ornamental rather than recreational? What a shame."

Bethan's shoulders relaxed at the sound of Ruth's chuckle. Was this working? Would the woman invite Ray inside for a game? Confide in him even? The house sitter appeared to be enjoying the conversation. Bethan took a step backwards. The ring tone of her phone chimed.

Downstairs, all was quiet. Bethan felt as though her stockinged feet were stuck in a quagmire. Too late, she switched off her mobile.

Ruth Morgan didn't move. "Very clever, Mrs Harley," she called. "I take it you took the scenic route to gain entry. Why don't you deal with your call and come down and join us?"

"Ruth. I apologise for asking, but are you armed?"

"Not in the way you mean, Mr Kirby."

"Nor am I. No one wants or needs to call the police. Do you know where Mr Deacon is?"

"I have no idea. I suggested he find himself a hotel for the night. He's probably drowning his sorrows in some bar by now."

Bethan collected her wits and crossed the landing to the master bedroom, its door still half open. She closed it behind her and turned the key, looking around wildly for a suitable chair to barricade the two of them in. On the bed, Suzanne Deacon stirred. Flung an arm across the pillow and murmured something incomprehensible.

Bethan called her daughter back. "Poppy, I'm not at home."

"I know, Mum. Dad is, though. He rang to ask if it was okay for him to use his key. He's coming to Callum's to collect me tomorrow morning. How cool is that?"

"It's lovely, darling. I'm going to ring your father now."

"Mum, are you okay? Where are you?"

"I'm fine. I have to ring off now, Poppy. Take care. Speak soon."

Bethan punched in her home number. Heard it ring out. Wondered what was happening downstairs.

Her husband picked up the call. "Hi, Bethan."

"Tim. Listen to me. This is important. I'm with a client and we have a deranged woman in the house."

"What's the address? I'll call the police."

"Please Tim, not yet. My client's trying to talk the woman round but we could use some back up. Can you come to Three Roads? You know the lay by on the left?"

Bethan closed the call as she heard a soft knock on the balcony door. To her relief, it was Ray. She crossed the room and unlocked the door.

"And all because the lady loves *Milk Tray*." He turned the ornate brass key to lock the door again. "Unless you're too young to remember the advert."

"Sorry. That was my daughter telling me her father has turned up. I've asked Tim to get over here in case we need another pair of hands."

Ray shrugged. "Your call, Bethan. Morgan says she's unarmed but I don't want to knock her out or strong-arm her into submission unless it's really necessary."

"Perhaps I should go down and speak to her?"

"And if she tries to strangle you?"

"I don't think she will. She's desperately unhappy and as confused as Mrs Deacon but in a different kind of way. We don't want to light her fuse by crowding her." Bethan glanced at Suzanne. "Mrs D's still asleep. You can hover on the landing and watch what happens."

"All right but take care. She said she wasn't armed but she'll have had time to fetch a knife. Did you see that rack of blades in the kitchen? Sheesh."

"I did, but somehow I don't feel threatened."

"I bloody well hope you're right." He pulled a black shoe from each jacket pocket. "You might need these."

They left the room. Bethan approached the top of the stairs. "Ms Morgan?" She tried again. "Ruth?"

There was no reply. Bethan moved down a step. Then another. Halfway, she called again and still received no response. Could this be a trick? As she stood in the hallway, she heard a knock at the front door and it was much too soon for her husband to have arrived.

"Mr Deacon," she said, reaching for the door chain, pulling back the bolt to allow her client entry into his own home.

A stranger stood on the step. "I'm sorry to intrude," he said. "I know you're not Mrs Deacon but I'm looking for Ruth Morgan."

"She doesn't live here. I mean, of course Mrs Deacon does, but Ms Morgan was here just now." Bethan looked around helplessly. "You'd better come in."

Ray came down the stairs as she secured the door. "How long since you saw Ruth, sir?"

"It's only a matter of days. But I've been ringing her over the last 48 hours and getting no reply. She never goes away because of that pesky cat so I thought I'd drive over and check on her. There are no lights on in her cottage, and she didn't come to the door. It dawned on me she could be round here. I remembered the way because I came to a drinks party here years ago, not long after Ruth became friendly with Mr and Mrs Deacon."

"Good man." Ray strode forward and shook hands. "I'm Ray Kirby, prospective purchaser of this house." He waved towards Bethan. "This is Bethan Harley, my estate agent."

"Huw Blayney. I apologise for interrupting but I'm very concerned about Ruth. She spends far too much time on her own and, between you and me, I think her friends often impose upon her generosity."

Bethan and Ray exchanged glances.

"I'll see if I can find her while you explain to Mr Blayney what's been going on." Bethan took the first few steps towards the kitchen, calling Ruth's name.

She heard the low rumble of Ray's voice explaining the situation to Ruth's friend. She pushed open the kitchen door and felt for the switch. Instantly the overhead lighting came on. No Ruth. Bethan called again, despite her assertion to Ray, unable to resist the urge to swivel her body and check the woman wasn't poised ready to spring.

The light was on in the utility room. Bethan jumped as the dog barked a welcome. She'd temporarily forgotten about Sparkles. She noticed the bolt on the back door was pulled back. Tried the handle and found the door unlocked.

She returned to the hallway, Sparkles padding behind her. Both men looked at her questioningly.

"There's no sign of her. She must be out there somewhere and so is Mr Deacon."

No one said a word. From outside, the sound of crunching gravel sent Bethan flying to open the door. Ray stuck out a brawny arm. "You two stay out of range."

He unlatched the safety chain so he could speak through the gap. "Who's there?"

"It's Tim Harley," said a pleasant male voice. "I believe my wife's here."

Bethan walked forward. "Hello, Tim."

Ray looked at her and released the safety chain. "Would you believe all this if it happened in a movie?"

Bethan saw him observing the stilted greeting she exchanged with her husband. The dutiful kiss. Swiftly she introduced Kirby.

"What can I do to help?" Tim looked straight at Ray.

Ray gave a brief run down on the evening's events. "Time to call the cavalry, I reckon."

Tim nodded. "Meanwhile, we three can start searching the area."

"Oh, I say," said Huw. "Surely that's not necessary? Ruth must have gone home, don't you think? She's very loyal. Very protective." He took off his spectacles and stuck them in his top pocket. "Think how upset and frightened she must have been to have barricaded herself and Mrs Deacon in the house."

"Mr Blayney, with respect, we're dealing with a woman whose actions have been less than rational over the last weeks. Ms Morgan should be approached with care. She left via the kitchen and might have armed herself with a knife."

"I'll call the emergency services." Bethan moved to the hall table.

336

"Police and Ambulance, Bethan. Someone should take a look at Mrs Deacon to make sure she's sleeping off a pill and not something more sinister."

As if someone had punched the air out of him, Huw Blayney sank into a chair beside Bethan, his face crumpled, his hands clasped in front of him.

She shot him a sympathetic glance. "I'll make you a hot drink in a moment."

"I'll be all right."

Ray looked at Tim. "How about you and me head for Rock Cottage wherever that may be?"

"I can show you the way," said Huw.

"I don't want Bethan left here on her own."

Bethan was waiting for the operator to respond but couldn't fail to notice the appraising look her husband sent Ray Kirby.

She put the phone down. "They'll come straight here."

"Ray and I are going to try Rock Cottage, Bethan. Can you direct us?"

"Drive past the lay by and keep going until you see a grassy triangle opposite a derelict church. Ruth's cottage faces on to that grassy strip. Be careful."

"I'll drive if you like," said Tim.

"Keep us posted," said Huw. The dog had settled at his feet. He reached down to stroke her head.

Bethan watched Ray unlock the door. "If she's not there, you could try The Devil's Pool."

"Why would she go there when it's dark?"

337

Bethan shook her head. "A hunch? Anything is possible tonight, but I very much hope I'm wrong."

"Lock yourselves in again. Make a pot of coffee."

"Women's work?"

Ray grinned. "Of major importance."

Tim squeezed her elbow as he slipped past. Reassurance? Or something else?

Bethan locked the door behind the two men. This held all the signs of being a long night. And it hadn't slipped her mind that Eddie Deacon must still be out there somewhere.

Chapter Twenty-Six

Ruth strode along the track and started to climb the hill. She would find Eddie. He hadn't driven off in his car so he must be out here somewhere. She would talk to him. Make him see sense. Tell him how Suzanne had asked her to convince him to change his mind. The Harley woman and Ray Kirby would clear off soon. Suzanne would probably sleep until morning.

Eddie wouldn't thank those two for being in the way if they were still there when he returned but they were arrogant and interfering enough to hang around like a bad smell. She laughed aloud at her own joke.

It was good to imagine walking through the front door with Eddie. This time she'd be in the right and her persecutors in the wrong. Once he confirmed he'd changed his mind about selling up, those two would be sidelined, as they deserved.

Ruth hugged her arms around herself. She'd grabbed one of Suzanne's many jackets from the utility room but the garment didn't offer the warmth of Ruth's choice of weatherproof clothing. Suzanne was a fair-weather walker and Eddie almost as bad.

She climbed on. Up the hill, facing the non-existent traffic and keeping a steady pace. She wondered why Eddie hadn't taken the car. Probably he'd realised he was over the limit. At the top of the hill she turned off the main road and followed the forestry track, fingering the torch jammed into the jacket pocket just as the moon slipped out from behind banked cloud. Convenient. The ground wasn't too slippery though it would be, down at the pool.

She could hear the sound of the waterfall now. She'd reach her destination soon. As to why Eddie Deacon would choose to walk down here and stay after twilight didn't occur to her. She'd made up her mind how the story would end and all she needed was his co-operation.

She saw the inert shape lying on scrubby ground between track and pool. "Eddie?" She hurried forward. Sank to her knees beside him.

"Eddie, can you hear me?" She touched her fingers to his throat and found a pulse. It still beat. He hadn't had a heart attack and quit the world.

She didn't know whether to be relieved or frustrated. She had no way of getting him home. Her mobile phone was in the pocket of her own jacket back at The Sugar House. Stupid man. Why did he have to keep on impeding progress?

Ruth moved Eddie so he lay in the recovery position. On the point of removing her jacket and covering him, she hesitated. Who'd know if she rolled him closer to the edge? Wouldn't that be a fitting end to all this? She thought of the benefits gained. The grieving widow would need company, someone reliable to make sure she ate properly, someone to drive her around. She would need a housekeeper companion. Suzanne would never have the confidence to tackle moving on her own. Ruth had met Penny only once and that was before she married and had her children. The poor, bereft daughter would be so, so relieved when Ruth offered to move into The Sugar House and look after her widowed mother.

Lost in her fantasy world, all she was aware of was the constant rush of the nearby waterfall. Still she hesitated.

"Can you hear me, Eddie? I'm going to move you. If you can wake up, we'll walk back together."

Still he made no response.

"Eddie?" She tugged at his arm. Pinched his cheek.

Ruth looked around. The moon still withstood the gathering clouds. She'd tried to wake him and he hadn't responded. So be it. Who was there to know how precisely Mr Deacon met his end? He'd made this decision for her.

She placed both hands together in some kind of silent prayer before stooping and rolling Eddie's inert form a little closer to the bank. This had to be the kindest way. She wouldn't even need to use the sharp blade grabbed from the kitchen and tucked inside Suzanne's fleecy gilet.

Deliberately wounding him would put her in prison, wouldn't it? A simple fall into the rushing waters would be deemed a tragic accident. At the post mortem, any damage to the body would be pronounced consistent with its bumping against the steep cliff side.

"Stop! Stay where you are, Ruth."

Shocked, she screamed and let go of Eddie. She scrambled to her feet and reached a hand inside the jacket she wore hanging loose.

"Don't even think about it." Ray sprang forward and tackled her while Tim dashed to grab Eddie beneath his armpits and drag him to safety.

Ruth dissolved in Ray's arms like a rag doll left out in the rain. As she'd hoped, he relaxed his iron grip. She jerked an arm free and lashed out at him. Steel flashed in the moonlight.

Ray Kirby cursed as the blade caught the back of his hand. Ruth wriggled from his grasp. Tim Harley lunged at her, snatching the knife, flinging it away. The house sitter flailed and kicked but without success.

"I owe you one, mate," said Ray. "You must be a rugby player."

And all the time, the water went on tumbling into The Devil's Pool.

Ray rested his bandaged hand on the Deacons' kitchen table. Bethan had made coffee and helped herself to bread, butter and cheese. She'd found a jar of homemade beetroot chutney in the fridge. Realised the handwriting on the homemade label matched that of the note to Eddie Deacon which she discovered on the floor in the drawing room when she and Huw Blayney went around drawing curtains and blinds against the fast-looming darkness. She'd shuddered and replaced the jar.

"I still think you should have gone in the ambulance with Eddie." She sat down next to her husband, facing Ray.

"Thanks to Tim, I hardly lost any blood," said Ray. "No lives were lost. I might have a job driving back though."

"You can have a lift with Bethan and me," said Tim. "I guess we'll be here a while longer though. Hugh Blayney's still answering questions."

"I should let the hotel know I'll be too late for dinner." Ray looked up at Bethan.

"I'll ring and make sure they leave something for you. They'll have a night porter on duty." She wondered whether her husband had twigged the dynamics of earlier events but there was too much going on to bother about what Tim might or mightn't be thinking.

"Thanks," said Ray. "I'm relieved they carted Mrs Deacon off to hospital."

"She was still out for the count and she'll be monitored through the night. I'll go down early in the morning and see how both of them are."

"I'll come with you," said Tim.

"No, you're collecting Poppy from her boyfriend's, remember?"

Bethan and Tim stared at one another.

"Those must have been potent sleeping pills," said Ray, breaking the silence.

"Ruth made it clear that was all she gave Mrs Deacon," said Bethan. "She was so calm. Helpful, even."

Ray blew air through his lips. "Poor, tortured woman. Stuck in a cell with goodness knows what to come now."

"Ruth Morgan tried to kill you, Ray."

"She lashed out at me, Bethan."

343

"She took a knife from the kitchen. Eddie Deacon's lucky she didn't use it on him. Thank God you got to her when you did."

"Huw told me he wouldn't desert her," said Tim. He'll keep tabs on her wherever she's sent. Visit her. He sees something in her, doesn't he?"

"She's an intelligent woman." Ray grimaced. "I thought life in mid Wales was pretty tranquil until tonight."

"It usually is." Bethan smiled at him. "Now I can't help wondering whether you've changed your mind about moving here."

"No way," he said. "Try and get rid of me."

Bethan clamped her fist to her mouth. Stifled a sob. Watched her husband's face tighten as he read the expression on Ray Kirby's face.

Huw Blayney walked into the room. Tears trickled down his cheeks.

"I still can't believe this is happening. You couldn't ask for anyone more caring and dutiful than Ruth. Apparently, she was worried about the dog being left alone. Isn't that typical?"

Bethan stared at him. "Actually, I hadn't thought about Sparkles. Will they put her in the police pound or whatever it is?"

"Ruth would hate that to happen," said Huw.

Bethan stared at him in disbelief.

Tim got up and pulled out a chair for the older man. "I'm sure Huw's right. Surely, if we let her out before we leave, she'll be all right in her usual bed?"

"I could sort her out in the morning. I'll need to get a cab to bring me over so I can collect my car," said Ray.

"No!" Huw Blayney almost shouted. "I'll be responsible for the dog. That's what Ruth would want."

Bethan nodded. "That's so kind." She turned to Ray. "I can pick you up from the hotel before I go on to the hospital tomorrow. The Deacons are, after all, my clients and they don't seem to have made many friends in the village, apart from Ruth."

"Thank you," said Ray. "Ironic, isn't it? The one person the Deacons could always rely upon is no longer around to help them."

The End

About the Author

© Hazel Hannant Photography

Jill Barry is a former air hostess, secretary and guesthouse owner who now finds inspiration for her novels in her own quiet corner of Wales. She is the author of various contemporary and historical romance novels, including *Love Thirty*, *Love on the Menu* and *Homefront*. She also writes novellas and short stories. *The House Sitter* is Jill's first venture into the crime genre.

For more information about Jill Barry please visit www.jillbarry.com or find her on Facebook and Twitter.